AINSLEY KEATON

The Beachfront Inn

vinci
BOOKS

By Ainsley Keaton

Sconset Beach

The Beachfront Inn
The Beachfront Surprises
The Beachfront Reunion
The Beachfront Secrets
The Beachfront Girls
The Beachfront Sunsets
The Malibu Girls
The Beachfront Christmas
The Beachfront Retreat

Vinci Books

vinci-books.com

Published by Vinci Books Ltd in 2025

1

Copyright © Ainsley Keaton 2022

The author has asserted their moral right to be identified as the author of this work in accordance with the Copyright, Designs and Patents Act 1988.
This work is a work of fiction. Names, characters, places and incidents are the product of the author's imagination or are used fictitiously. Any resemblance to actual persons, living or dead, places and incidents is entirely coincidental.
All rights reserved. No part of this publication may be copied, reproduced, distributed, stored in any retrieval system, or transmitted in any form or by any means, including photocopying, recording, or other electronic or mechanical methods, nor used as a source for any form of machine learning including AI datasets, without the prior written permission of the publisher.
The publisher and the author have made every effort to obtain permissions for any third party material used in this book and to comply with copyright law. Any queries in this respect should be brought to the attention of the publisher and any omissions will be corrected in future editions.
A CIP catalogue record for this book is available from the British Library.
Paperback ISBN: 9781036703707

MIX
Paper | Supporting responsible forestry
FSC
www.fsc.org FSC® C018072

Printed and bound in Great Britain by Clays Ltd, Elcograf S.p.A.

Chapter One

Ava

December

Smug billionaires were going to be the death of Ava Flynn. She just knew it. She represented them in criminal tax court because she'd been hired to defend their cheating ways, and she'd done just that, very well, thank you, for the last 28 years. But she didn't have to like it.

Men like John Wilson, Ava's current billionaire client, took pride in not paying any tax, ever. Not for them to help pay for infrastructure, military and social programs. No, paying for the upkeep of the country was for the little people. But, occasionally, their stupid accounting tricks failed them, and the Southern District of New York came calling.

That's when Collins and Lahy stepped in. And Ava, like the dutiful soldier she was, did her job spectacularly. She had to.

Her husband, Christopher, left her to go to God-knows-where with God-knows-whom, cleaning out their entire investment account in the process. One million dollars gone, just like that.

And living in New York wasn't cheap. Her Upper West Side apartment had quite the mortgage attached, and she'd spent almost $300,000 on her daughter Charlotte's Cornell education.

When she got the job at Collins and Lahy all those years ago, she had to make big bucks. Her triplets, Charlotte, Samantha and Jackson, had just been born. Her husband, the children's father, Daniel, had been killed in a car accident when she was five months pregnant.

All at once, she was faced with raising three children on her own in one of the most expensive cities in the country. Expenses for private schools, activities and basic necessities for three babies awaited her, and she had to make as much money as possible.

Hence the job at Collins and Lahy, a job she'd always despised.

And now, finally, Ava had reached the end of her rope. It was something about John Wilson's smug face and his obvious hair-plugged forehead that made her burn with white-hot anger. Or maybe it was the fact that the guy was a frequent flier. He was always getting in trouble with the Southern District because he was always determined that he would not pay one single penny in taxes.

Sell your island in the Pacific, jerk-off, and, guess what? You can pay all your taxes. Who needed an entire island?

Apparently, John Wilson did.

"You're going to the hearing?" John said.

She shook her head and looked at the clock, suddenly feeling she couldn't breathe. She stood up and went to the window. Down below, the expanse of Manhattan, and all the lights, twinkled at her.

It was 8 P.M. on a Friday, and, as soon as this meeting was over, she had another four hours of work ahead of her. That was the price of the 82nd floor, she realized - to work in an office this high in the air, with such a view, came at a very steep price. In this case, the price she paid was that this office was virtually the only place she ever saw, at least six days a week.

As she stared out the window, seeing a light blanket of snow on the ground way, way, way down below, she took a deep breath. Her jaw hurt, probably because she was a teeth-grinder in her sleep - yet another sign her life had taken a wrong turn somewhere along the line.

She turned around and saw the smarmy look on John Wilson's face. "Actually, no," she said, unable to stop the words from coming out of her mouth. "I'm not going to go to the hearing."

His face turned from smarmy to stone-cold in a second flat. "What does that mean?"

"I mean I won't be going to the hearing."

"You're assigned to this case. Maxim told me you are. He told you'd be the one guiding this case through the courts from start to finish. My case starts with a hearing on Monday. Now, if you're telling me you aren't going, you'd better have a good reason."

He crossed his arms in front of his chest and glared at Ava. His eyes were cold, lifeless, and steely-light blue. The eye color that looked so cute on Siberian Huskies looked menacing on this guy.

"I'm going out of town. Stan can cover me on this hearing. I'm very sorry. My grandmother has Alzheimer's. She's almost 100 years old, and I don't know how much time I have with her."

He raised an eyebrow. "Out of town where?"

"San Francisco," Ava said, without missing a beat.

"And she's 100?"

"Yes. She'll be 100 on Monday, as a matter of fact. Her nursing facility is holding a big party for her, and I'm going to be there."

The lies were piling up. Her maternal and her paternal grandmothers were dead.

He steepled his hands and stared at her. "I was born at night, but not last night," he said. "I'll be checking up on your story. Since I know you're lying, I'd like to know what the real story is. I pay this firm $1,000 per billable hour, and I deserve some respect."

"What's wrong with Stan covering?"

He leaned forward, his pale blue eyes focused intently on her own. "Nothing is wrong with Stan covering. That's not the point. The point is, you're supposed to be there. My case has been assigned to you. Not to Stan, but you. Now, if you're not going to be there at my first hearing, I want a good reason. That's all."

Ava was backed into a corner. She suddenly realized her career was probably on the line.

Maybe she unconsciously willed this result into motion. Jackson would tell her this. Her son was always into very New Agey books like *The Secret* and stuff like that. Something about believe it, be it, and manifesting your dreams into your real life just by your imagination. Or something like that.

If you could manifest a good reality just with your thoughts, you could certainly manifest a bad one.

Maybe her being fired was actually the good reality, and she didn't yet know it?

The thing to do would be to back down and admit she made a mistake, and she'd be at the hearing, no problem. *Sorry for the confusion. It won't happen again, Mr. Wilson, I promise.*

She'd worked at this firm for the past 28 years, and it all could be over in a flash. This guy had a big influence on Collins and Lahy because of all the money he paid the firm every year, and pissing him off further wasn't a good idea.

She cocked her head and thought about Jackson and what he would have to say about what came out of her mouth next, unbidden and unable to stop. The words were like a rushing river going over silt and rocks, unceasing and violent.

"I do have a good reason," she said. "And the reason is, I don't want to represent you. I think you need to pay your taxes instead of paying us millions a year so you can shirk your responsibility. Did you ever think that everybody else has to pick up the slack because you and guys like you won't pay your taxes? Just who do you think pays for the military, the VA and infrastructure? The tooth fairy?"

She didn't mention the social programs, administrative agencies and regulation enforcement taxes paid for because she was 100% sure this guy didn't give a crap about any of that.

After those words came out, her hand involuntarily went to her mouth.

Did she really say that?

Then, she thought she probably should've gone all out and told him what was *really* on her mind. If she would've been a bit braver, she would've told him that he and his kind were nothing but vampires, sucking the life out of this country and contributing absolutely nothing in return. The guy was a corporate raider. He bought distressed companies for pennies on the dollar and then sold off the parts like a car thief who chopped up cars for money. He was responsible for thousands of people losing their jobs every time he did this, and he never even cared.

After she said her piece, he nodded his head, almost imperceptibly.

"I see," he simply said. And then he got up, gathering up his coat and hat in his arms. "Well, Ms. Flynn, you take care. I'll show myself out."

At that, he left. He didn't slam the door. He shut it quietly behind him.

After he left, Ava was completely alone. More alone than she'd ever been before.

She went back to the window. By that time, the snow was really coming down. She thought about calling an Uber to take her back to her condo, which was a good forty-five minutes in traffic from her office. She knew she had more work to do, more motions to file, more research for an appellate brief she was working on, more memos to write.

Yet, as she stared at her desk, she realized she'd hit a wall. She literally couldn't think about doing anything at all.

She called her best friend, Hallie, to tell her about what had happened. She had to unload on somebody, and she knew Hallie always had her back, no matter what.

After she talked to Hallie for about an hour, she pulled out the hide-a-bed and crawled into it, not even bothering to change out of her pantsuit, an action she'd found herself doing more and more these days. She pulled the covers over her head and turned off all the lights. She breathed in deep and, as the snow turned to sleet, the crisp rat-a-tat-tat on her window was the only sound she heard. That was enough to lull her to sleep. She didn't even set her alarm. The next day was Saturday, so there was no reason to.

Since she "quit" on her work "early," she would have to work all weekend, again.

But, right at that moment, she had her cozy blanket pulled over her head. The sounds on her window assured her there was a world outside of her luxurious office, and she felt more comforted than she had in a long time.

Chapter Two

Hallie

Hallie Gleason had talked to her best friend, Ava, and she felt worried. She knew Ava had always been unhappy in her job. It was a terrible fit for her friend, a job mopping up after billionaires who won't pay taxes, because it had always galled Ava that there were people in the world who didn't want to contribute to society. And it really galled her friend she was the one who was helping them get out of their societal obligations.

So, a part of her was happy Ava finally stuck it to one of them because they deserved what she said and more. But another part of her knew that if Ava was fired, it could be bad. Very bad. After all, Ava's rat-bastard-no-good husband skated off with all the investment money, apparently staying one step ahead of the loan sharks who were going to kill him if he didn't pay his gambling debts. So, Hallie knew Ava was broke.

Hallie had no idea what her friend would do if she lost

her job. Actually, it wasn't really a question of if, but when. You don't tell off a billionaire to his face and keep your job, not if your job depended on your ability to ass-kiss with the best of them.

Come what may, Hallie knew, she would support her friend, as she always had. She and Ava went back to 1985, their freshman year at the University of Missouri-Columbia. They were assigned the same dorm room through the lottery system. The two went through college as roommates all the way through, getting an off-campus apartment together their sophomore year, just the two of them, then getting a different off-campus apartment with two other roommates their junior and senior years.

They were there for each other through all-night cramming sessions, where they attempted to read and absorb a semester's worth of material in one night. When Ava got mono her freshman year and could barely lift her head, let alone attend class, Hallie found fellow students in all of Ava's classes and bought their class notes. She also spoke to Ava's professors about her illness because her friend literally didn't have the energy to do so herself.

When Hallie got a DWI her junior year, Ava bailed her out and helped her find an attorney. At that time, Hallie's parents were going through a rough patch financially, so Hallie didn't have the money to pay court and attorney's fees. Ava footed that bill and refused to let Hallie pay her back.

Hallie still had fond memories of fraternity parties and midnight movies shared with her friend. Drinking games and canoe trips. Spring break at Daytona Beach, where they stayed at the hotel that MTV was filming their spring break concert specials. They were together at the infamous "five down" football game where the national champion

Colorado Buffaloes "beat" the hapless Missouri Tigers on a final play, but it turned out the Buffaloes got five downs, not four, so really the Tigers were the true winners. That game still galled Hallie and Ava.

She and Ava and the rest of their friends would go to the tiny Blue Note dive bar on the weekends to catch up-and-coming acts like REM, The Red Hot Chili Peppers and The Pixies. The Blue Note at that time had a capacity of around 500. Little did Ava and Hallie know these same acts would soon be selling out arenas all over the world.

And little did they know that their freshman year, Brad Pitt was wandering around that same campus. To this day, Hallie imagined she'd seen him at a Sigma Chi party, not that she would know if she actually did, because, at that time, he was just another good-looking fraternity boy with a bad mullet and a popped collar.

Those were the days of tanning beds and girls wearing enormous bows in their teased and permed hair, of wine coolers and all-you-can-drink Friday nights at By George, a bar at the edge of downtown. The Missouri Tigers football team sucked so much that they won one game the girls' freshman year in 1985. The fans got so excited about winning that one game that they stormed the field, tore down the goalpost, and paraded it through town.

After college, they went their separate ways as Hallie came to New York to follow Nate, her husband. She'd met him at MU, and he managed to get a job as a hedge fund manager at Barclays. They married soon after college, and Hallie had her daughter, Morgan, when she was just 23. Scott was making enough money that Hallie could stay home with Morgan, so that was what she chose for herself - to be a stay-at-home mom.

Meanwhile, Ava was attending Harvard Law school.

The Beachfront Inn

Ava, too, ended up in New York after graduating from Harvard and having her triplets, Charlotte, Jackson, and Samantha. Ava's husband was killed in a car accident before the babies were born, so Hallie was there for her after this tragic event. She watched Ava's kids while Ava worked and wouldn't hear of Ava paying her for her services, even though Ava tried to insist. Hallie made sure Ava got an apartment in the same Upper West Side apartment building she lived in, so it wasn't a problem for Ava to drop her kids at Hallie's before going into work.

Hallie sighed and tossed and turned in her bed. She'd been suffering from insomnia lately, and didn't really know why. Her doctor told her that her insomnia was because of menopause. He prescribed hormonal replacement therapy, which did help with the hot flashes and the mood swings she'd been experiencing. But, unfortunately, insomnia seemed to remain.

Nate was sleeping next to her, snoring loudly. Hallie put a pillowcase over her head to block out the sound, but it wasn't effective. Her husband's snores could wake the dead.

She tiptoed into the living room and made herself a bowl of cereal - she'd read somewhere that the tryptophan in milk was supposed to ease insomnia. Hallie was doubtful about that, as nothing seemed to help, but she was willing to try anything.

She called Ava. It was 2 AM, but she knew her friend probably wasn't sleeping, either, considering what went down at the law office.

"Hey," Hallie said. "I didn't wake you, did I?"

Ava started to laugh. "What do you think? As if I could sleep at this point. I doubt that I'll get any sleep at all until the hammer falls on me come Monday. Ironic. I used to not sleep because I had so much work to do. Now I can't sleep because I'll soon have too much time on my hands and no money in the bank." Ava sighed. "How did this happen? How did I get to 53 and still have my life unsettled? This wasn't supposed to happen. I wasn't supposed to get to this point and have such a feeling of being trapped yet staring down the barrel of financial ruin at the same time. God, I've made so many awful choices in my life."

Hallie took a deep breath, thinking about awful choices. Her life choices weren't the best, either.

"I know what you're saying," Hallie said. "I mean, I haven't been able to sleep for weeks now, and it's because of Nate."

Hallie meant that Nate's snoring was keeping her awake, but as she said those words, it dawned on her.

It wasn't Nate's snoring that was keeping her awake.

It was his presence in the bed.

All at once, that epiphany literally brought her to her knees as she fell off her easy chair onto the floor. Why hadn't she figured that out before?

"What do you mean, you can't sleep because of Nate?" Ava asked.

At this point, Hallie was crying.

"Hallie?" Ava said. "Hey. I'm here at my law firm still. I'm sleeping here this weekend, but I'll cab it to you. Something tells me you need somebody to talk to right now. And I sure could use a friend, too."

"Okay," Hallie said. She and Ava were past the point where they politely declined each other's invitations because they didn't want to inconvenience the other person. Hallie knew it would be a huge pain for Ava to cab it from her downtown law office to Hallie's apartment on the Upper West Side, but Hallie would do the same for Ava if the tables were turned, and Ava knew it.

20 minutes later, Ava was at Hallie's apartment. Hallie had already opened up a bottle of wine, and she was feeling tipsy.

"Hey," Hallie said to her. "I know it's 3 in the morning, but I suddenly felt like I couldn't breathe. So, a glass of wine seemed to be the thing to do right now."

"What's going on?" Ava asked.

Hallie poured her a glass of wine and took a sip of her own. "I hate doing this to you. After all, you're about to lose your job. You don't need me and my bullshit to worry about, too."

Ava rolled her eyes. "I cabbed it up here in the middle of the night because you needed me. Now, spill it. Before I spill this wine on you." Then she picked up her wine glass and pretended to be about to pour the wine on Hallie's head.

Hallie sighed and then poured herself another glass. "I sometimes fantasize about my husband dying." Then she nodded her head. "Yes, I said fantasize, not fear. I don't fear him dying. I think about what life would be like if he weren't around, and I want that life. Isn't that awful?"

Ava's eyes got big. "Well. I mean, wouldn't divorce be easier?"

"Yes, yes, of course. I mean, no. God, I sound so selfish. But divorce would be such a nightmare. Months of attorney negotiations and property division, and what would I tell Morgan? And I don't have the guts to go through with it. With telling him I want out. He's done nothing wrong. It's just that..."

"He just isn't right," Ava said.

"Yes." Hallie thought about the fact that she and her

husband rarely spoke anymore and hadn't had sex in years. They never did have much in common to begin with and really only got married because Hallie got pregnant with Morgan, and they both thought the baby should have a two-parent home.

They didn't really speak much to one another simply because they didn't have all that much to say. When they were both home, Nate was in the study, reading or watching television in there or surfing the internet, and Hallie would typically be in the living room or the bedroom, doing her own thing, too - reading, watching Netflix or HBO Max shows or just getting lost in the Wikipedia wormhole.

Except Hallie was usually doing her own thing with a bottle of wine on the nightstand.

She'd even registered for an eHarmony account just to see what was out there. She would never actually answer an inquiry from anybody on that site. Still, she really wanted to see what would be awaiting her if she ever got the guts to walk away from Nate.

It was all pointless, though, because Hallie knew she'd never have the guts to walk away from her husband. It was too scary to even contemplate life without the security Nate provided her.

For all Hallie knew, Nate was having affairs. He certainly could be, for he was working a lot. He could be like the man who was caught cheating on his wife because, on 9/11, the wife called the husband and asked where he was, and he answered "the office."

The only problem was that his office was in one of the twin towers.

The sad thing was, Hallie couldn't care less if Nate was having an affair or not. It simply never factored into her

The Beachfront Inn

day-to-day thinking. If he was having an affair, whatever. If he wasn't, whatever. Six of one, half a dozen of the other…

Ava put her hand on Hallie's. "Hallie, what do you want out of life?" she asked.

"To not get to the end of it and look back and say it was all a waste. That I got stuck in an unhappy marriage and never left it because I just didn't have the guts or the energy to do so. I know, I know, I raised Morgan to be a halfway decent human being. I mean, she's not a serial killer or a drug addict or in prison, so I guess I did something right."

Ava smiled, getting her sense of humor. Ava knew Morgan actually was a decent person. Her daughter lived in San Francisco in a renovated Victorian home with her wife, Emma Claire, and worked as a photographer.

Hallie's daughter was the one thing that made her proud. If she got to the end of her life never having divorced Nate, therefore living unhappily for most of her life, she at least could point to Morgan as something she did right. But Morgan would be the only thing she could point to. She certainly couldn't cite anything personal, she'd be able to show St. Peter as evidence of a life well-lived.

"What else do you want?" Ava asked.

Hallie shrugged and poured herself yet another glass of wine. "To not need four glasses of wine to get through the day. To be able to sleep more than three hours a night. I don't know. What else is there?"

"What else, indeed?" Ava asked.

"It's hard," Hallie said. "My identity all these years was as a mother. That was how I defined myself, as Morgan's mother. I could never define myself by my marriage because, to be honest, Nate has always been a complete stranger to me. And I've never had a real career, as you know. I've had various jobs but no career. That's so pathetic, isn't it? Defining yourself by your kid? What's wrong with this picture?"

"I think you're not alone," Ava said. "I think there are a lot of women in your shoes. Maybe if you could define what you want, you could figure out how to get it."

Hallie shook her head. "I don't know what I want. I raised Morgan. She's doing great. She and Emma Claire are looking to adopt a child from Zimbabwe. Her job takes her all over the world. She's been featured in *National Geographic*, and she's looking into buying a gallery in San Francisco. I mean, she calls me to check on me, and I call her for the same reason, but there's nothing she needs from me. You know?"

Ava chuckled. "I wish I knew what you're talking about, but I don't. All three of my kids are a mess in one way or another. On the one hand, I feel like they do need me. On the other, I'd love to have a turnkey kid like you've got. You've nothing to worry about with Morgan. I can't say the same for Samantha, who's flightier than a hummingbird, or Jackson, who's trying to make it in the cutthroat world of acting in LA, or Charlotte, who's stressed with a newborn. Plus, I get the feeling her husband isn't the most supportive man in the entire world."

"What do you mean, Charlotte's husband isn't supportive?" Hallie asked.

"I don't know. It's a feeling I get from her. She won't talk about him when I ask her how he's doing. She just changes the subject. And Samantha told me Matthew never wanted there to be children. You remember that Charlotte got pregnant while on the pill, right? She told me before they got married that they'd both decided not to have children. I don't know. I just have a bad gut feeling that things might not be okay with Charlotte and Matthew."

The Beachfront Inn

"I hope you're wrong about her," Hallie said. "Poor Charlotte. I pray her marriage isn't wrong like mine always was. You know the age-old question - is it worse to want something you can't have or have something you don't want? I think I know the answer to that question. I think it's much worse to have something you don't want." She shook her head and poured another glass of wine. "God, I'm so exhausted all the time. My hair hurts, I'm so exhausted. I never thought I'd be this tired at 53, yet so not able to sleep."

Ava put her arm around her friend, and Hallie soaked Ava's shoulder with her tears.

"We're quite the pair," Ava said. "Aren't we?"

Hallie nodded. "I'm so sorry. Instead of unloading this stuff onto your plate, I should be listening to you. You're the one who's having a crisis. I'm just the same old me. Lonely, bored and stuck. I've been this way for over 30 years, and I'll probably die this way. But you're having a major thing happening, and here I am, babbling away."

Ava shrugged. "It is what it is, and I said what I said to that jerk, John Wilson. I'll figure it out."

Hallie took another drink of her wine and then poured herself yet another glass. "I envy you."

"You do?"

"Yeah. If you lose your job, you have a resolution for your unhappiness. You hate your job as much as I hate my marriage, but you have that resolved if you lose your job. I just don't see how I'll ever have my thing resolved."

"I'll have it resolved, but I'll be broke," Ava said. "I don't know what's worse, really. Waking up and working a job I hate with every fiber of my being or waking up and realizing I'm out of a job without a good plan B."

"Trust me, you'll be better off if you get fired, even if

you're going to be broke. A whole world can open up to you because you dared to tell a billionaire to go to hell. Man, I wish I had the guts to do the same to Nate. I mean, not tell him to go to hell because he doesn't deserve that. But tell him I want out. That's what I need to say, but I don't have the courage."

Ava took a deep breath. "How did we get here? Our mothers weren't a mess at this age, were they? I know mine wasn't." Ava's mother was a respected federal judge and always had her act together. Ava's father had died when Ava was just six years old, so Ava's mother raised her and her sister Sarah essentially on her own.

"No. Mine wasn't either," Hallie said. Her mother was apparently still in love with her father. They had the kind of relationship that Hallie dreamed of having. They still teased each other, still kissed in the kitchen and still ate off each other's dinner plates when they went out to eat.

"Here I am," Ava said. "53, about to be unemployed, and I haven't seen my sister for 20 years. My mother hates me, she's always hated me, and I hardly ever see my kids, even though one of them lives in town."

As for Ava's sister, Sarah…Ava and Sarah were at odds and had been for quite some time. Hallie knew Ava and Sarah's issues were deep-rooted, even if the proximate cause of them not speaking was a fairly superficial argument. But that argument was really the catalyst that ruptured Ava's relationship with Sarah, not the actual cause.

"So, here we are," Hallie said. "Our lives are a mess. Thank God Quinn seems to be doing fine. Otherwise, our Sunday brunches would be totally depressing."

Quinn Barlowe was their other best friend. Hallie and Ava met her at a Pilates class about 15 years before and, after just a few brunches and girls' nights together, all three women knew they were going to be a tight threesome. Quinn was beautiful and fit and was a country girl through and through, having grown up in the tiny Georgia town called Helen.

Unlike Hallie and Ava, Quinn seemed to be living her best life. She was a sought-after interior designer with an enviable list of wealthy clients. And, even though she was a head-turner and extremely witty and friendly, she never dated. She had no use for men. Even though there were many successful men who'd asked her out, she turned them all down flat.

"No desire to put up with pissy moods," Quinn would say. "And say what you want, anybody who says that women are the ones with mood swings don't know any man because every man I've ever known has more PMS moods than any woman I've ever known, and that's the truth."

Hallie envied Quinn, too, for living life on her own terms. From the outside looking in, Hallie would seem to have The Life. Her husband was a handsome and successful hedge fund manager who made a half-million a year. Her kid was accomplished and happy. She lived in the Upper West Side in a beautiful condo.

Those same people would look at Quinn as not as successful just because she didn't have a relationship or children. But Hallie knew the truth.

If she could switch places with Quinn, she would.

In a heartbeat.

Chapter Three

Ava

On Monday, Ava knew she would have to face the music. Other than her sleep on Friday night in her office, she barely got another three hours of rest over the weekend. And, aside from her middle-of-the-night talk with Hallie, she'd spent the entire weekend in her office.

She knew the Sword of Damocles would fall on her head as soon as Monday morning came, so, when her assistant informed her that the senior partners had scheduled an emergency meeting and she would have to attend - she rarely attended partnership meetings, as she wasn't a partner - she took a deep breath and tried to steel her nerves.

So, they fire me. So what? She could just find another job. Maybe.

She looked in her full-length mirror and saw herself reflected. Could she find another job at her age? When she would be competing with all those winsome twenty-some-things who take the abuse and say nothing but "thank you, sir, may I have another," like Kevin Bacon being paddled in *Animal House*? Yes, she was 53, but she'd taken care of herself over the years. Peloton bike workouts, Pilates and Yoga had kept the pounds at bay, for the most part.

She tried to throw herself into her work, but she couldn't focus. Perhaps for the first time in all the years she'd given this firm, she couldn't focus on much of anything.

What was she going to do if she got fired? No matter how in-shape she was, and no matter how youthful she looked - and, she had to admit, she looked decent for her age - she was still 53.

Her naturally red hair was still as red as it ever was, with only a few flecks of grey, and her face was, for the most part, unlined. She got in the sun too much, which brought out her freckles and an occasional sunburn. But she was lucky in the wrinkles hadn't begun in earnest just yet.

But she was 53. Nobody would want to hire her, let alone pay her a salary close to what she was making with Collins and Lahy. The questions were going to be thrown at her like so many darts. Almost 30 years with the same firm, and no partnership, eh? What's your problem? And what's this I hear about your insulting a billionaire to his face? Those would be the spoken questions, albeit asked more politely than Ava thought in her head.

The unspoken question would be much more devastating, though - "At the age of 53, why should we hire you over somebody who we can get fresh out of law school, who isn't burned out? Who hasn't burned bridges? Who isn't 12 years away from retirement age?"

She had no answers for any of it.

Hallie called. "It happened yet?" she asked.

"No. 3 o'clock."

"If it happens, it's a good thing. You hate your job, and you should get out."

"I do hate my job," Ava told Hallie. "But it's my identity. Being a lawyer is all I've known. I mean, I'm a mother, but I don't think I was a good one. Otherwise, my kids would come home for Christmas once in a while. I was a wife, but, again, I seemed to have failed at that. Otherwise, I would still be married."

"At any rate," Hallie said, "come what may, we'll deal with it. You want me to call Quinn, too?"

"Yes," Ava said, nodding her head. "I mean, if I get fired, yes, call her. If not, well, I'll be burning the midnight oil, getting ready for some hearings I have set for tomorrow, so, unless you guys want to come here to my office, I'll have to beg off for tonight."

"Text me," Hallie said. "Listen, I gotta go. Love you."

"Love you."

---

3 PM was finally here. Ava got a phone call from Paul Levine's assistant, telling her to come to the conference room. Paul was one of the senior partners, and he was apparently the one who had called this meeting to order.

As Ava marched to the conference room, she bowed her head. Why did she feel like dead woman walking? She imagined Sean Penn in that movie, walking to his execution. Too bad she wasn't going to see the saintly face of a nun in the window before the hammer fell.

She got to the conference room - the walk from her office to this room seemed endless - and took a deep breath before she turned the door handle and stepped into the space. Every senior partner was there already, around the table, and, when she walked in, they all turned around to look at her.

She felt like an insect, insignificant and about to get smashed.

Paul nodded at her. "Ava, hello. Have a seat."

She found the only open seat and sat down. She said nothing but just looked at the faces of the men who were openly staring at her.

Looking around the table, she just now noticed the partners were all men. There wasn't a woman among them. She didn't know why she never noticed that before - probably she didn't notice before because she'd never seen them all in one room like this.

There had been the occasional woman partner before. She knew this. They never seemed to last, though. Ava realized most of the women got off the partnership track when they had their families. They just couldn't work 70-80 hours a week and have any semblance of a family life, so they were never even considered for partnership by this firm.

She felt oddly comforted by the lack of diversity, as she realized that perhaps the reason why she was never made partner had nothing to do with her being a big loser, but rather, had everything to do with her gender. She, too, had gotten off the partnership track years before when she was raising her kids. She'd hoped she got back on when the kids were grown and no longer were dependent on her, enabling her to put in the requisite hours. Yet, a partnership never happened for her.

She should have been furious by her sudden epiphany about the fact that all the partners were guys, and she would be later. But, right at that moment, she simply felt a kinship for all the other women who had been passed over by this firm.

Paul cleared his throat.

"Uh, before you say anything, I know why you're calling this meeting," Ava said. "I'll apologize to Mr. Wilson. I don't know what got into me. It was like I was possessed by a body snatcher or something. I literally couldn't stop myself. I've been putting in 70 hour weeks, just like I'm supposed to. My work is beyond reproach. Don't forget, we've won three appeals this year, just on the strength of my briefs. If that's not evidence of my abilities, I don't know what is."

She was, once again, spilling out words, unbidden, and she didn't quite know when they were going to stop. She only knew she had to try to save her job. She felt like if she didn't, she would somehow just disappear.

She already felt invisible to the outside world, but she wasn't invisible on the 82nd floor. She was the author of legendary appellate briefs, well-researched and well-reasoned and written with flair. She was the confident defense attorney, arguing for her clients in trial after trial, gaining the respect of judges and prosecutors alike.

She was somebody, dammit, and if this job were snatched away from her, she would be nobody.

That was really the problem. Because, no matter how much she hated her own clients, she gave them her best defense, and she was really good at what she did. She commanded respect in her field, whereas she didn't in the other parts of her life.

"Ava," Paul began. "All of that is true. You are, without a doubt, a rock star brief writer. You've won your share of difficult cases. You definitely put in the hours. But John Wilson is our biggest client. He's made it clear that if we don't let you go, he'll pull his business and go elsewhere. I'm sorry, but we have no choice. We have to let you go."

Ava swallowed hard. She somehow had convinced

herself that maybe this meeting was for something different, that maybe she had a chance to not get fired.

She would plead for her job. Ask them for a second chance. Tell them she'd kiss John Wilson's ass as much as they asked her to.

She would do all those things.

Instead, she suffered yet another devastating incident of diarrhea of the mouth.

"Listen, John Wilson might be our biggest client, but that's only because he just won't pay his taxes, so he has to hire us to get him out of all the government audits and prosecutions. And, quite frankly, I find that guy immoral and maddening. He has a yacht on the Mediterranean, mansions all over the world. I've been to his home in the Hamptons. It's one of the biggest ones in Bridge. 30,000 square feet, with original Picassos hanging on the walls. He has his own island. Yet he won't pay his taxes? Why doesn't he just sell that island in the South Pacific and get right with Uncle Sam, and he won't need us anymore?"

She realized she was standing up. Her hair was coming loose from its tight chignon as she spoke. She self-consciously touched the back of her head and attempted to tighten up the chignon again, but it was no use. Half of it tumbled out and down her back, while the other half remained bound to her head, which was much worse than if the entire thing came tumbling down.

She knew she looked a mess, which was fitting, as that was exactly how she felt.

"Ava, I know what you're saying. But you're working for a white-collar defense firm. Our clients are all wealthy individuals who-"

"Feel they're above the law or above paying taxes or both," Ava said. "I know. I signed up for it. Also true.

But..." She was about to say she'd had it. John Wilson was the final straw. But wouldn't that mean Hallie was right, and her getting fired really was a cause for celebration?

Deep down, she knew this was the case. Her getting canned was the best thing that could've happened to her. If she thought her clients were such jerks, and she did, then what was she doing enabling them to keep acting like the East River scum they were?

How could she ever live her best life if she didn't believe in what she was doing?

Yet, she was terrified at the same time. It wasn't her dream job, but it was *a* job.

Paul came over to her and put his hand on her shoulder. "Ava, I think you'll be happier without us. You don't believe in what you're doing. That's fine. Not many of us actually do. You're clearly conflicted, to say the very least. Regardless, we have to let you go. Now, this partnership meeting is over. I just need you to sign your termination papers in full view of all the partners so that we can be witnesses. Then I need you to meet with Rebecca from HR. She'll go over your severance package with you."

So, for the next humiliating two hours, she reviewed termination papers and went over her severance package with Rebecca from HR.

By 6, she was on the subway - she didn't want to spring for an Uber or a cab because God knew when she'd find another job, and her severance, although generous, wouldn't get her through two years in New York City - heading home. She had a bottle of Chardonnay, which she picked up at a liquor store on her way to the subway, as well as two pints of Talenti ice cream in black raspberry chocolate chip. She hung miserably onto the strap while the car lurched along.

It had been a while since she'd been on the subway, but it wasn't long before the smells and sights brought her back to the days when her riding the subway was a twice-daily affair. The scent of pot mingled with that of urine, body odor, liquor breath and some kind of sickly-sweet Febreze smell that was coming from a woman about her age, who had a bottle of the stuff and was futilely spraying her seat with it.

She was reminded of the crazy murderer she read about who put Christmas tree air fresheners on the bodies of his victims, apparently in a futile effort to cover up the smell of the rotting corpses. This lady with the Febreze had the same chance as that killer in covering up the smells of this subway.

Ava finally arrived at her condo, where Quinn and Hallie were waiting for her. They both had a key to her place. They were sitting at her kitchen island, having already cracked open one bottle of Pinot Grigio, while a second bottle was on the counter, waiting in the wings.

Ava took one look at the two girls and burst into the tears that had been threatening ever since she opened her big mouth and insulted her firm's biggest client.

"What am I going to do now?" she asked as Quinn and Hallie held her.

"We're going to figure it out, girl," Hallie said. "Together."

Chapter Four

Ava

Two hours in, Ava, Hallie and Quinn were having a good time. Ava was on her third glass of chardonnay, while Hallie and Quinn had polished off the first bottle of pinot and had started on the second one.

Quinn was munching on some cheese and crackers and gulping down the remainder of her glass. She was almost six feet tall, blonde and gorgeous, with huge green eyes, a strong Roman nose and a bow-shaped mouth. She was effortlessly slim, which made Ava green with envy as Ava was always trying to keep her own weight under control.

Hallie was doing the same as Quinn, munching on snacks while drinking wine. Hallie wasn't quite as tall as Quinn. She was around 5'6", and she was quite cute, as opposed to being stunning, as Quinn was. With dark hair, hazel eyes and a button nose, she resembled a younger Sally Field.

The three women were listening to the music of their

youth, as tunes ranging from The Police to ABC to Howard Jones filled the air. The women all agreed that 80s New Wave was the best music unless you count 90s grunge. Not the music of today, though.

"But isn't that what every generation says?" Quinn pointed out. "The music of their youth is the best, and the new stuff is crap."

"True," Ava said. "But I can't get into rap, no matter how hard I try. We're still listening to *The Safety Dance* 40 years later. Will we still be hearing Megan Thee Stallion or Ariana Grande in 2060? I doubt it."

Hallie and Quinn both agreed with that, although Quinn pointed out she was surprised that *The Safety Dance, Come on Eileen* and *Don't Dream It's Over,* amongst other 80s classics, had the staying power they proved to have.

"Happy they're still played everywhere we go, but who knew back then they would be?" Quinn wondered.

"Kill, marry, screw *Sixteen Candles,*" Hallie said, pointing to Ava. That was a game the ladies sometimes liked to play when they were drinking.

"Okay, I'll bite," Ava said. "Marry Jake Ryan, screw Jake Ryan and kill the oily goombah who was marrying Samantha's sister."

"Good ones," Quinn said. "But you gotta marry and screw two different people. You're cheating," she teased.

"Oh, come on," Ava said. "Who else is in that movie besides Jake Ryan? The Geek? And, besides, he was so hot, he deserves both the marry and the screw."

"True," Hallie said. "I'll give you that. Almost 40 years later, and I'm still searching for my Jake Ryan."

"Aren't we all," Ava said. "Aren't we all."

"Don't forget, John Cusack was in that movie," Quinn

said, referencing one of Ava's favorite actors. "Maybe he's one you can marry or screw."

Ava started to laugh. "Yeah, but John Cusack played a dork, too, but I get your point. I'm sticking with Jake Ryan."

While the music played, Ava drank one glass of wine after another. She was trying to ease the panic rising in her chest as she contemplated her future. She was filled with worry about being unemployed with a severance that would last only about two years.

When she discovered Christopher had drained their investment account, she wasn't as panicked as she should've been. She was making a yearly salary of $250,000 at a firm that had employed her for over 28 years. She'd replenish her investment account in no time.

Now what?

Ava could feel herself tipping over from a happy drunk to a sad one. That was the problem with drowning your sorrows. Once the effect of the alcohol started to wear off, you were not only left with your original problem, but you also had to deal with a hangover.

And, with Ava, the chickens came home to roost that evening even before the hangover began.

"What am I going to do?" Ava asked, trying hard to tamp down the tears that were threatening.

Quinn came over to her and put her arm around Ava's shoulders as Ava leaned on the kitchen island, her head hanging down.

"Darlin', you're going to be fine," Quinn assured her. "Better than fine. That place was crushing you. Grinding you down to dust. What did you think would happen - you were going to meet your maker 30 years down the line, knowing that you spent your whole life cleaning up rich guys' messes? Could you imagine yourself on your deathbed, having all those regrets that you spent so much time in a job you despised? There's a reason why you gave that jackass John Wilson what-for, and that's that he had it coming to him."

"Yeah," Hallie said. "And, besides, your firm obviously doesn't respect women. Didn't you tell me that there wasn't a single woman partner there?"

Ava nodded her head. "I didn't even think about that, or realize it, until today, when I saw them all lined up together in the conference room. But, yes, that's true. No female partners."

"Sounds like an old boy's network," Quinn said dismissively. "No women need apply. You don't need them."

"That's true," Ava said. "But I need something. I don't know how I'm going to go forward. Nobody will hire me at my current salary, not when I'm 12 years away from retirement age. And even if I found a firm that would hire me at my current salary, they're going to demand that I get back to 70-80 hours a week, and I can't stay on that hamster wheel forever."

"That's rough, sugar," Quinn said, pouring herself another drink. "But we got your back. If you need to sell this place and move in with me, I've got room. You can even have Kona sleep with you at night. She's such a snuggly little girl. She'll cheer anybody up."

Kona was Quinn's rescue mutt. She was some kind of pug-shepherd mix and was always full of kisses and tail wags for anybody and everybody who visited Quinn in her condo.

"You'd do that for me?" Ava asked.

"Sure. I know that the rat-bastard hubby of yours cleaned out your investment account, so you might need to downsize if you're going to stay in this high-dollar city. If you lived with me, you'd be able to take a lower-salary job practicing in a firm that can make you proud. Like Legal Aid."

Ava laughed. "You know, I was worried that nobody would hire me once word got around about what I said to John Wilson. But you know what? Legal Aid not only would hire me, they'd throw me a ticker-tape parade for telling that jerk off."

Quinn nodded. "So, you'll sell this place and move in with me?"

Ava just shook her head. "As much as that sounds appealing, I'm so sorry, Quinn, I don't think that it could work out. I mean, there's a reason why I'm not in touch with any of my former roommates, except for Hallie, of course, and that's because living with friends tends to end the friendship. We'd just get on each other's nerves."

Ava noticed the fleeting expression of relief on Quinn's face and knew that her best friend felt the same way about the situation. Quinn's place wasn't all that large and, while she did have an extra room, she was using that extra room as an office, so there would be no way Ava could move in with Quinn without inconveniencing her.

And if there was one thing Ava despised, it was inconveniencing people.

But Ava loved Quinn for offering all the same.

"I would offer the same thing as Quinn," Hallie said. "Seriously, we both would love to see you working at a law firm that doesn't pay you the big bucks but makes you happy. And we know how much you're struggling right now. Your severance won't last that long with your mortgage and expenses."

"Oh, you don't need to remind me," Ava said. "Damn. You know, I sometimes wish that I had Sarah's situation, as ashamed as I am to admit that. Man, does she have the life out in California. She'd never have to worry about being broke and out of options."

Quinn came over and put her arm around Ava. "Sugar, you've been thinking a lot about your sister lately, haven't you?"

"Is it that obvious?" Ava asked.

"Well, you've brought her up a lot lately. Maybe you should try to contact her again."

Ava shook her head. "I've texted her and called her and sent her smoke signals. I don't know. I've been dead to her for the past 20 years, and I still don't really know why.

Sarah's disappearance from Ava's life was the one thing that truly broke Ava's heart. Losing her job was bad, just because she didn't know what to do next with her life. Her daughter Charlotte's cold attitude towards her rankled her. Still, while she and Charlotte had gone through short periods where they didn't speak, they always made up in the end, even if Charlotte didn't come to visit her during the holidays like Ava wanted. But her often-strained relationship with Charlotte was small potatoes compared to the rift with her sister.

Before they stopped seeing each other, the two sisters were extremely close. Ava always believed that Sarah loved her, and Ava always adored her younger sister, which was why it was so damned difficult to come to terms with their rift.

Ava had to admit she was angry with Sarah. Not just hurt, but furious with her. She would've loved to have Sarah's support during this difficult time, but she couldn't have that because Sarah had chosen to cut Ava out of her life. But, underneath it all, of course, Ava still loved her sister very much, which made her all the more furious.

Whoever said that love was more killing than hate knew what he was talking about.

And it didn't help that her mother, a federal district judge, always held Ava at arm's length. That didn't change, even after Ava's first husband was killed in a car accident - Colleen never showed Ava much sympathy after that happened. But Colleen really should have. After all, her own husband, Ava's father, died when Ava was very young, and Colleen never remarried.

But her mother never wanted to hear about bad things in Ava's life because she had no way of comforting her. So, Ava clammed up, constantly internalizing issues in her life. Her therapist would tell her she handled things with denial, pretending that they didn't happen. But Ava knew better. She never pretended that bad things didn't happen. She suffered many, many sleepless nights over her multitude of failures.

"Come on," Ava said. "This is getting depressing. Why don't we sit on the couch and find something on Netflix? I'm in the mood for a good Cary Grant comedy like *Bringing Up Baby* or *Arsenic and Old Lace*. Or any kind of black and white comedy will do." Cary Grant was Ava's favorite actor, and she'd seen everything he'd ever been in at least twice.

"Sounds good," the ladies said in unison.

Unfortunately, there wasn't a Cary Grant movie on Netflix, but they found an old Audrey Hepburn film, which was second-best in Ava's book. The movie, *Roman Holiday*, took Ava's mind off of her various dilemmas. She knew she would have to face reality at some point. But, for that moment, with her two best friends and Audrey Hepburn in Rome on a scooter, reality seemed far away.

And that was how Ava preferred it.

Chapter Five

Ava

September

For nine months after Ava lost her job, life went just how she feared. She went to headhunters and interviews but never got any jobs. Her experience and abilities apparently meant nothing in the legal world. The only thing that mattered was that Ava was too expensive, too old, too not willing to put in 80 hours a week. She was beginning to panic, as she knew that things would soon be dire.

One day, after a particularly humiliating interview where the managing partner who interrogated her told her, in no uncertain terms, she was just not what he was looking for, she sat in her condo, looking around. She loved her place. It was exactly how she wanted it. Hardwood floors, crown molding, a modern kitchen with granite countertops and a stone backsplash. She even had a small balcony, where she grew tomatoes and flowers.

She knew she would have to give this place up. The mortgage was just too high. If she didn't get a job soon - not just any job, but a job with a salary commensurate with what she was making before - she was simply going to have to move. Maybe even move to a cheaper part of New York. As in Albany or up-state. She'd miss the city, but it had become unaffordable.

Then again, she could always move back to her hometown of Kansas City. She had cousins there, aunts and uncles, too. The cost of living there was much, much lower than in Manhattan. But that would also mean she'd have to pass yet another bar exam, and she knew she didn't want to face that nightmare again.

One 16-hour exam over two days was enough for any lifetime.

She was cooking herself an egg and a slab of bacon, even though her stomach was feeling queasy, when she got the phone call.

"Hello, can I please speak to Ava Flynn," a voice asked. She didn't recognize the number on her caller ID, but it was a local number, which was the only reason why she picked up.

"This is," she said.

"My name is Scott Wadlow. I'm the administrator of the estate of James Bloch."

"Okay." James Bloch was one of the few clients of Collins and Lahy that Ava had been able to stomach. He was a wealthy older gentleman who had a tax evasion case, but Ava felt sympathy for him because it wasn't his fault. His accountant had screwed up, big time, which meant that

James owed $20 million more in taxes than he paid that year.

Ava went to bat for him because he'd lost his trial and was on the hook for millions in penalties and interest. She filed his appeal, argued it in the district court, and won. He still had to pay the extra $20 million, but he didn't have to pay the extra $7 million in penalties and interest that he would've had to pay if she didn't win his case.

After that, he called her often, and she found him easy to talk to. She had lunch with him at least once a month. And, because he was essentially a stranger, not somebody close to her, she found herself telling him all about her feelings about Christopher leaving, about how cold her mother and sister were to her, how lonely she felt and how she felt she'd failed her children.

She hadn't spoken to him for at least the last six months. She'd called him many times but always got his voice mail.

Now, with this disembodied voice over the phone telling her that he represented James' estate, Ava knew that he was dead. The kindly older gentleman who treated her to latkes and matzo ball soup at Frankel's Deli was gone.

She felt her insides crash to the floor.

"I'd like to meet with you as soon as possible," Scott said.

"Why? What is this about?"

"James left you a bequest in his will."

Chapter Six

Ava

Two hours later, she found herself in Scott's office. To say she was stunned would be understating the matter. She was grieving, too, because James was such a good guy, a solid mensch, and, during the hours she spent talking to him, she imagined him much like the father she never really had. She never imagined that he'd leave her anything in his will, though. He had four children, and, as far as she knew, none of them were estranged from him.

"Have a seat," Scott said, motioning to the chair in his office that was right in front of his desk.

Ava obliged, clutching her purse in front of her. She said nothing, waiting for Scott to speak.

"Mr. Bloch left you a bequest in his will," Scott said. "As I was saying over the phone."

"Yes," Ava said, now feeling intensely curious. "And what was this bequest?"

"He left you a house," Scott said. "On "Sconset Beach on Nantucket. Do you know where that is?"

Of course, she knew where that was. It was a place where a lot of her billionaire clients had second and third homes.

"A house," she repeated stupidly.

"Yes." He gave her a file with pictures of the house she'd inherited from James. "It's right on the beach. Have you ever been out there?"

"No," Ava said. "I can't say I have." She didn't know, but she had the impression that the island was a playground for the very wealthy. She wasn't quite sure how she would fit in there. However, if there was a house for her out there, she would...do something with it.

"I've inspected the property," Scott went on. "It's very nice, to say the least. Eight bedrooms, all with a connected bathroom. Fireplaces in all the bedrooms. Newer carpet, crown molding. A swimming pool and rooftop deck. Some of the bedrooms have terraces that face the beach. Others have terraces that face the street. It has an eight-car garage and its own little parking lot next to the house. It's really a beautiful space."

Ava tried to process this information. It occurred to her she had her money situation resolved unless this property was mortgaged to the hilt. However, knowing James, she doubted that this was the case. "I can sell this home, right?"

The wheels were turning in her head. She could sell the home, which would give her enough of a windfall that she could afford to live in her condo indefinitely.

Scott went on. "The property is valued at just under $7 million," he said. "However, there's a clause in his will. You cannot sell it for at least five years. Nor can you take out a mortgage against it. If you take a mortgage against it, you forfeit the property immediately."

"Oh." Ava was disappointed. She knew what property tax was like on Nantucket. On a property worth $7 million, she'd be paying about $20,000 a year in property taxes, which wasn't that big of a deal.

Was it?

Yes, yes, it was. That would mean she'd have an extra $20,000 a year in expenses to worry about on top of her current New York expenses. She could maybe rent the place out, but that would be a headache, too, as she'd have to find renters who she could trust not to trash the place.

"How much will the estate tax be?" Ava asked.

"About a half-million," Scott said. "But the will allows the Commonwealth of Massachusetts to attach a lien on the property if you can't pay that."

Ava shook her head. "No, I can't pay that," she said. "So I guess the Commonwealth of Massachusetts will just have to take out a lien."

She opened her mouth, but Scott answered the question she was going to pose next. "Another stipulation in the will is that you can't rent it out to anybody for the first five years. The good news is, after five years is up, you can do what you want with the place."

Ava furrowed her brow as she stared at the pictures of the property. It certainly was lovely, and, although it was a Cape Cod with wood shingles, as homes generally were on Nantucket, it had a beachy feel.

"What, so, this means that I-"

"Have to live in it, yes. Unless you want to leave that property vacated for the next five years, but that would mean that you'd be paying a pretty penny every year to maintain a home that you don't live in. I'm not sure what your financial situation is, but I'd imagine that this house would be an expense that you're not going to want."

It wouldn't just be an expense she wasn't going to want. It would be an expense she simply couldn't swing.

"Why would he leave this house for me?" Ava asked.

"According to the note that accompanied his will, he wanted to leave it to you because you saved him $7 million in penalties and interest when you argued his case. He wanted to leave you a piece of property that equaled what you saved him."

"I see." Ava wasn't entirely convinced she deserved the property, even on that basis, but she didn't want to question it. She always tended to question good things in her life, and she was determined not to question this.

Ava smiled for the first time since she was able to process the news that she'd soon be the proud owner of a beach home.

James was really a lovely man. Perhaps in all her years working for Collins and Lahy, he was one of the few clients she actually liked.

"Can I rent this place out, I mean, you said that I can't, but can I do something else with it? Like an Airbnb?"

"Yes, actually. Several years ago, James got a business license for the place. He was going to have one of his granddaughters run it as an inn. However, his granddaughter, Jessica, lived there but never did run it as a bed and breakfast. But the license is still in effect, as James renewed it every year. You're lucky that you'll be able to run it as a B&B because those licenses are difficult to come by on the island. James had the right connections to make sure that happened."

Scott gave Ava some keys and some paperwork, along

with the file that had the house pictures in it, and Ava was sent on her way.

She would have to break the news to Quinn and Hallie.

That would be hard. Those two ladies were her lifeline. And now she would face life without them.

Well, not exactly. She'd stay in touch. But it wouldn't be the same.

Unless she could talk them into coming with her.

Chapter Seven

Ava

That night, the ladies had another alcohol-fueled pow-wow, this one taking place on the rooftop of Ava's condo. It was a beautiful early September evening, unseasonably warm. The night sky was aglow in brilliant red as the sun set behind the buildings.

Any resident could use the rooftop terrace, so Ava knew she had to get up there early to claim it for herself and her friends. There were three sofas up there, along with a hot tub and a fire ring. Lights were strung up ahead, and, on a clear night, she could see for miles around the city.

As the three women shared a bottle of wine, she explained the plan she had come up with.

"I looked into it," Ava said. "And this particular spot is a hot one because it's right on the beach. All oceanfront houses are occupied year-round, and they command a pretty penny. Since it'll be a beach bed and breakfast, I can command a minimum of $400 a night per room during the peak season and $300 a night during the off-season. Quinn can use her interior design skills to spruce the place up. It'll be a lot of fun to have parties there, too. And, since it will be on Sconset Beach, I have the perfect name for it - the 'Sconset Inn'."

Surprisingly, this name wasn't yet taken.

Ava knew she was throwing a Hail Mary, but the more she thought of it, the more she thought that it'd be a good idea to have her best friends in on the deal with her. Quinn was constantly complaining about the city and had threatened to move, more than once, to a less crowded place. She also talked about moving to a place where she could actually own a car and drive it and not have to rely on cabs and Ubers to get everywhere.

"I grew up in a town with less than 1,000 people," she'd say before complaining about the constant hassle of trying to hail a cab or get an Uber. On the rare day she'd take the subway, she'd talk about the loudness, the smells and the constant encroachment on her space.

It didn't help that Quinn was such a head-turner. Because she was such a stunner, she regularly got felt up on the subway. She also had difficulty walking down the street without getting cat-called. All of that was wearing on her.

Yet she stayed in the city.

Now she had a reason to leave, and she was getting into it.

"Oh, lordy," she said. "Count me in. I've always wanted to live on a beach, and I sure can't afford a house in the Hamptons."

"Really?" Ava said. "You really want to take this leap with me?"

"Sure, why not? I got a pretty good clientele here, but I'm tired of the grind. You know I've been fixing to leave for years now, but I just needed a good excuse. This sounds like as good of an excuse as any. And there are plenty of fat cats on that island who'll need my services."

Ava hugged her. "I'll hire you first thing to redesign the place. I've seen the pictures, and the bones are good, but the look is dated. I'll have to find an investor, but I can make it work."

Hallie took a deep breath. "God, I can't believe you guys are leaving," she said. "I don't know how I'm going to get along without our weekly pow-wows."

Ava nodded her head. "I wish I weren't leaving, but I don't really have a choice."

"And you know how unhappy I've been in the city for a long time," Quinn said. "I've been here for over thirty years, and I'm exhausted. I didn't want to tell you ladies that I was eyeing going back to Georgia and finding my own little cottage on the beach. I wasn't going to say anything until I was good and ready to leave. So, yeah, the thought of living on a beach sings to me."

Hallie lightly fingered the stem of her wine glass. She seemed to be lost in thought. "I'd love to come, but I just can't do that to Nate. I'm...not ready."

Ava knew how much Hallie struggled to spark something in her marriage. After Ava and Hallie had their middle-of-the-night talk about her unhappiness, Hallie had thrown herself into the possibility that she and Nate might make things work. They started intense marriage counseling and, although Hallie told Ava that it wasn't doing much good, she stuck it out.

Ava was asking her to rip the band-aid off her marriage.

Hallie just wasn't ready for that and Ava wasn't going to push her into it.

Ava nodded her head. "Hey, it's not a problem. I didn't really think that either of you ladies would uproot your lives for this. It's a thrill that Quinn is coming out, though. And, Hallie, you know that you'll always have a place to stay when you come to Nantucket."

"Uh-huh," Hallie said, staring into her wine glass. "Although it does sound tempting, living on the beach like that. God, I wish I could go. I really can't imagine life without you two ladies."

"And we can't imagine life without you," Ava said, putting her arm around her friend.

Hallie stared at the wall, her face perfectly blank. "I'd like to come out for at least a little while, though. I haven't been anywhere for so long. I'll talk to Nate and see what he thinks. If he lets me, I'll come and help you settle in."

"That would be great," Ava said. "Whatever you can manage. And we'll still be best friends. I won't be that far away."

"Oh, but who am I going to call in the middle of the night the next time I have a panic attack about my marriage?" Hallie asked.

"Still me," Ava said.

"Or me, sugar," Quinn said. "We're always going to be there, even if we can't just jump in an Uber and hang out with you in person. But we're always gonna be there by phone or FaceTime or Zoom. Believe that."

As Ava looked at Hallie's face, she knew that Hallie was devastated by her news. Her heart went out to her. She wished she could stay in the city, because she so hated to hurt her friend.

But she couldn't stay in the city. She had to jump on this opportunity.

She prayed that Hallie would be able to bounce back, but she feared that her friend wouldn't be able to.

And that was the one dark cloud hanging over this whole thing.

Chapter Eight

Hallie

The next evening, Nate was home early from work, and Hallie had a roasted chicken with all the trimmings waiting for him. A bottle of wine was opened, and Hallie had downed two glasses before Nate got home.

She would talk to him about going with Ava to help her open her new B&B, and she was nervous. What if he said no? He controlled the purse strings, so it would be difficult for her to go if he refused.

She was grieving the potential loss of her only lifelines. Hallie contemplated ending it all when Ava told her she was moving to Nantucket. After she and Ava had their middle-of-the-night talk, Hallie knew she had to change her life. So, she saw a doctor who prescribed Zoloft for her depression and Ambien for her insomnia.

She briefly contemplated taking all of the Ambien and Zoloft at once and never waking up.

Then she pictured Morgan in her mind's eye, not to

mention Quinn and Ava, and knew she couldn't do that to the people she loved. But it was something she fantasized about.

She'd despaired. Ava and Quinn were literally her only sources of happiness in her world. Now, they were going to be an hour's flight away.

They might as well be living on the moon, Hallie thought.

Still, if she could just stay with Ava for a month or so, that would give her a break from her life and maybe give her the strength to find something that could make her happy without her best friends at her beck and call.

"Hey," Nate said, looking at Hallie's chicken. "Looks good. What's the occasion?"

"Occasion?" Hallie asked. "Does there have to be an occasion for me to fix roasted chicken?"

"Yeah," he grunted. "There does."

And that was true, Hallie thought. She used to cook all the time. She had a ton of cookbooks and loved to try out different recipes. But lately, she didn't have the energy to shop for food, let alone prepare it, so Nate usually ordered out, and Hallie usually drank her dinner.

Hallie got out some plates. "Well, there is something I wanted to talk to you about."

Nate raised an eyebrow. "I knew it. I knew you had to want something from me." He shook his head. "You never do anything nice unless you want to butter me up."

Hallie closed her eyes. Their marriage therapist would tell her to let that dig go. But Hallie couldn't help but think that Nate wasn't listening to a word their therapist said. If he was, he wouldn't have made that dig in the first place.

"Sit down," Hallie said lightly. "I already have the

chicken cut up, and I even made buttered artichoke hearts. Your favorite."

Nate narrowed his eyes at Hallie but sat down. He put his napkin on his lap, and Hallie dished out some chicken, artichoke hearts and a baked potato on each of their plates.

Hallie poured the wine for the two of them.

"None for me," Nate said after Hallie poured him a glass. "You drink mine. I know you want to, anyhow."

Hallie laughed lightly. "I do like my wine," she said as she took Nate's glass and put it on her side of the table. She downed her glass and then started on Nate's.

"Yes, you do," Nate said pointedly. "A little too much."

Hallie took a deep breath and bit her tongue. She was tempted to tell him she drank too much because she was so unhappy, and the reason she was so unhappy was because she was married to him.

She closed her eyes, willing her heart rate to decrease. She had to get through this without attacking Nate, even though he was clearly trying to bait her.

"Okay," she finally said. "How's the chicken?"

"How do you think it is? It's dry as shoe leather. You really shouldn't try to cook."

"And the artichoke hearts?"

"Too sour. You put too much lemon in there like you usually do. I think you're trying to kill me. You know how much lemon bothers my acid reflux."

Hallie took a gulp of wine, finished off Nate's glass and poured another. "If you would just take your Omeprazole, you wouldn't have a problem with the acid reflux, now would you?"

"I don't take that junk," he said. "You know that."

"I do know that. I also know that you can't eat anything without your acid reflux acting up, and you do zero about it except complain. Ava takes Omeprazole. She used to get really awful acid reflux, but that stuff cured her completely. She used to stay awake at night because her acid was bothering her so much."

"Good for Ava," Nate said. "Now, what did you want to talk to me about?"

Another deep breath. "Ava is moving. To Nantucket. So is Quinn."

"And? What does that have to do with me?"

"I'd like to go with her," Hallie said. And then she quickly added, "just for a little while. She inherited a house that needs renovation, and I'd like to help out."

"How will you help out? You've got zero skills. You know nothing about renovating houses. You know nothing about anything, for that matter, except for how to make my life a living hell. And how to smother our daughter out in San Francisco."

Hallie cocked her head. She didn't think she smothered Morgan. "What do you mean, smother?" she asked him.

He rolled his eyes. "Morgan lived here in New York City. She's a photographer. If she wants to make it in that business, she should be right here in this city. But she's not. She's across the country. Why do you think that is?" he asked.

"Her wife–"

"Don't call Emma Claire that," he said. "Two women can't be married. Marriage is between a man and woman, period."

"Tell that to the United States Supreme Court," Hallie said. "But I'm not going to go into that particular argument with you again. Her wife wanted to live in San Francisco. Emma Claire grew up there."

"And what is Emma Claire doing?" he asked. "That she couldn't be doing right here?"

"She's the one who's dealing with the adoption plans," Hallie said. "And she's going to stay home with their new child when she comes over here from Africa."

"And? She couldn't do that in New York City?" he asked.

"I don't know," Hallie said.

"Right. Well, I think that Morgan moved 3,000 miles away because she wanted to get away from you. That's what I think. And I don't blame her."

"Why was she trying to get away from me?" Hallie asked.

"Because you were smothering her, that's why. You have no life, so you tried to take over Morgan's life."

"What's that supposed to mean?" Hallie asked.

"Exactly what I'm saying. You have no life whatsoever. You were trying to use Morgan to get a life, and she wasn't having it. So, she moved away. And I don't blame her."

Hallie downed the rest of her glass of wine and poured another. She started to feel sick. Maybe her sudden sickness was because she'd downed four glasses of wine in less than 15 minutes, which was a lot, even for her. Or maybe it was because of the cruel words Nate was saying to her.

Or maybe it was because Nate was right - she *was* trying to use Morgan as a vessel to have a life, any kind of life at all.

But what did she really do wrong? When Morgan graduated from NYU with a BFA in Photography, she worked for a downtown gallery as a curator. Hallie was excited for her daughter, so she managed to get a volunteer position as a docent at that same gallery. She did her own research on photography and famous photographers because she wanted to help Morgan with curation. She suggested curating photographs from some of the photographers she'd studied and was disappointed when Morgan didn't take her suggestions.

And, several times, she did show up at the bar where Morgan met her girlfriends on Tuesday nights. She wanted to get to know Morgan's friends. Be a part of her life. She missed Morgan so much because, even when her daughter lived in town, she didn't see Hallie very often.

So, Hallie volunteered at Morgan's photography gallery, and she showed up to have drinks with Morgan and her friends several times.

Was any of that a crime?

And, yes, she made a fool of herself whenever Morgan got a B in anything in high school. She usually marched over to the teachers to try to talk them into changing the grade. She even did that for Morgan in college. She didn't want her daughter to struggle with her grades because she wanted Morgan to have the very best chance in life. She was never successful in getting the grades changed, but she had to try.

She also guilted Morgan into visiting her at least once a week. That wasn't asking for anything, really. She just wanted Morgan to have dinner with her once a week, that was all. She would order Chinese food from the restaurant down the street and she and Morgan would watch movies together and eat Egg Foo Young or Orange Chicken. On the weeks that Morgan couldn't make it because her work was too demanding, Hallie would cry on the phone. On several occasions, she showed up at Morgan's gallery, unannounced, with Chinese food.

Morgan's boss finally told her she couldn't come to the gallery anymore. She lost her volunteer job at that gallery, and she couldn't bring food to Morgan there anymore, either. That might've been because she'd gone to Morgan's boss several times, insisting that he buy some photographs from local photographers she'd studied on her own. She saw talent in those photographers and, even though Morgan's boss told Hallie that the photographs weren't right for the gallery, Hallie kept insisting that Morgan's boss give these photographers a chance. Just a chance.

She was only trying to help. She was desperate for that gallery to succeed because she was desperate for Morgan to succeed. But apparently, Morgan's boss didn't want her help.

Turns out, Morgan didn't want her help, either.

So, Morgan moved across the country. To get away from her.

She started to cry.

The second the tears started to flow, Nate threw down his napkin and walked into his office. The chicken was half-eaten, and so were his artichoke hearts.

She called Ava. "I have to talk to you. And Quinn. Let's meet at our place, huh?"

"You got it," Ava said.

Chapter Nine

Hallie

Fifteen minutes later, Ava, Quinn, and Hallie met at a sushi restaurant that served amazing saki bombs. The ladies decided that this was their special place to meet, just because they loved the sushi at this restaurant, and the saki bombs were the best in town.

Hallie ordered a plate of sashimi and a seaweed salad and, of course, a saki bomb, which was saki dropped into a glass of Japanese beer. Ava and Quinn ordered the same, and the women split a tempura appetizer.

"So, what's going on?" Ava asked as the waiter brought around the saki and beer. The ladies were sitting on the floor in a private room because this was how this restaurant was constructed. It had five tiny private rooms with tables and cushions on the floor, and the women preferred to enjoy their sushi and saki in these little rooms.

"I'm coming with you guys," Hallie said. "For at least a month or so."

Quinn put her hand up, and Hallie slapped it in a high five. "You mean the old ball and chain's going to let you go?" she asked.

Hallie took a deep breath. "Not exactly." The seaweed salad arrived, and Hallie picked up a set of chopsticks and dug into the dish. "But I have a little money in a separate account. Nate doesn't know about it."

Hallie's parents had given her money over the years for necessities. Nate was the breadwinner, so he put the money he made into a separate account. His investment accounts were also only in his name. Hallie told her parents about this, and they started sending her money, unbeknownst to Nate.

It was more than humiliating that she was 53 and still getting money from her parents, but it was what it was. It was enough money to go out to eat and buy all the wine she needed to get through her life. Unfortunately, the amount of wine she needed was getting out of hand, and she knew it. She usually bought Two Buck Chuck at Trader Joe's, but, even so, she was still spending at least $100 a month on the stuff.

"So, you have some money, which means that you don't have to beg Nate for the money for the trip, is that it?" Ava asked. "Hallie, you don't have to spend your money on this. You'll have a place to stay, with me, and-"

"No," Hallie said, shaking her head. "I'll pay my way. We'll be buying groceries and alcohol and going out to eat. I can't have you paying my way. I have enough to get by for a month or so."

"Okay," Ava said. "But what will Nate do when he finds you're gone?"

"I don't know. Throw a party, I guess." Then she grinned. "Hey, maybe I'll be gone a month and, when I get back, he'll have some new woman living with him." She smiled big at the thought as she dug into her seaweed salad and drank her saki bomb. She raised her glass. "To Nate finding somebody new while I'm gone."

Ava and Quinn didn't raise their glasses to that, so Hallie lowered hers and finished her drink.

Quinn shook her head. "Sugar, you shouldn't wish for something like that to happen. Should you?"

"Yes," Hallie said. "I pray that something like that would happen. All I want is to get out of the marriage without feeling like the bad guy, and if Nate just found somebody else, my problems are solved."

Quinn looked at Ava and then back at Hallie. "I was wondering," she said. "And it's not my business, so tell me to butt out if you want. But how come you don't try to find a job?"

Hallie took a deep breath. "Well, Nate wanted me to stay home with Morgan, so I did. And, by the time Morgan was a teenager and didn't need me to be around all the time, I just didn't have any skills. My degree at MU was in Speech Communication, which was a useless degree to begin with. Add in 14 years of not working, and I was pretty much unemployable."

"Hallie did work," Ava said to Quinn. "She waited tables at Applebee's in Times Square. And you also worked in a factory, right?" Ava said.

Hallie nodded her head. "I was pathetic. I got fired from three different waitressing jobs because I couldn't handle them. Waiting tables is harder than it looks, let me tell you. I spilled stuff on customers, didn't get their food to them on time, so the food was cold when it got to them, I forgot drink orders all the time, and I couldn't make change properly. I got fired from the factory for being too slow. I don't know. I pretty much failed at every job I tried."

She'd even worked at a Wal-Mart in New Jersey as a cashier. She got fired from that job because her drawer was always short. She wasn't stealing, but her bosses suspected she was because her drawer was sometimes short $200 or more. She just wasn't good at making change.

Quinn put her hand on Hallie's shoulder. "Sugar, you just haven't found your niche. You've been trying to fit a square peg into a round hole, and it just isn't fitting right. But you're brilliant and talented. You'll find what you're supposed to do."

Hallie sighed. "I'm 53. Don't you think I'm a little bit old to be finding myself? I mean, I think I've given up on the idea that I'm going to have a life. You remember that I was even fired from a volunteer position. At the gallery Morgan worked at. I was a volunteer docent for the gallery, and they fired me and banned me from coming into that gallery. How pathetic is that?"

Ava put her hand on Hallie's right shoulder. Quinn was still gripping Hallie's left shoulder. "Hallie, you know why you lost your volunteer position."

"Yes," Hallie said. "I was a pathetic loser who tried to control the curating process because I wanted to help Morgan succeed. And Nate thinks that Morgan lives in San Francisco because she couldn't stand being in the same city as me, and he's right, you know. Nate can't stand me, Morgan feels that I smother her, and now you guys are leaving."

Hallie didn't want to tell her best friends about her fantasy of taking all of her Ambien and Zoloft and just going to sleep and never waking up again. If she admitted she'd thought about this on more than one occasion, they would insist she go into a mental hospital, and that was one thing she didn't want to do.

That would be hitting rock bottom.

No, if she decided to overdose, she'd do it without telling a soul she was ever considering such a drastic step.

"Hallie, you aren't a loser," Ava said. "Stop thinking like that."

"I feel like one," Hallie said. "I'm no use in this world."

"We love you, sugar," Quinn said. "Don't you ever forget that."

Hallie smiled a tight smile because she was trying hard to hold back tears. Yes, Quinn and Ava loved her. But they were going to be gone. Then what would she have?

"I'm still hungry," Hallie said. "I think that I'll get a Dragon Roll. You guys want to order any more food?"

Ava and Quinn glanced at each other. "No, I'm good," Ava said. "But go ahead, get something else. We got all night."

Hallie ordered a Dragon Roll and another saki bomb. The ladies sat and drank and talked for the next few hours, and Hallie was feeling better.

She had something to look forward to - the trip to Nantucket. After she got back to her real life with Nate, though, she would have to face up to her issues.

She might make it through. She might not.

Either way, she was good. Live, die. It was all the same with her.

Chapter Ten

Ava

October

The day was finally here! Ava had already packed her things up and sent them to the new beach house, and all her furniture would be waiting for her when she arrived. Quinn was already planning to get into that home and realize Ava's vision for the place.

Quinn, for her part, was bouncing off the walls, even more than Ava was. "I can't wait to get to the beach," Quinn said. "Even if it's freezing, I'm going to get in that water."

"Better you than me," Ava said.

"The only thing is, I'm gonna miss my little Kona," Quinn said.

Kona would be coming out to Nantucket, but not until Quinn was settled in her own home with a yard. For the

The Beachfront Inn

time being, Kona would stay with her next-door neighbor, Jacqueline.

Ava had spoken with Jackson out in L.A. He worked as an extra on a significant Apple Plus series but could get a few weeks off to help Ava settle into her home. Ava was grateful that Jackson would be so accommodating, and she was more than excited to see her son. She had also called Charlotte, who lived in Boston, right down the street from her mother. She hoped that Charlotte could visit her out on Nantucket, but, of course, her daughter was non-committal about that.

"I have too much going on here with Siobhan," Charlotte had said. "And Matthew is having problems at work. I don't think I can get away."

Ava was disappointed, but at least Jackson could make it out. That was something to celebrate, in Ava's estimation.

Ava and Quinn called an Uber to take them to the airport, where Hallie would be meeting them. Quinn had already sold her interior design business and had applied for a new business license on Nantucket. She had a new website up and running and had already gotten some contacts out of some New York business groups.

A couple of hours later, the three ladies were in the air. Hallie and Quinn were excitedly drinking champagne and eating a sandwich in the first-class seats that Ava had booked for all of them. They were sitting together, and Ava was seated right behind them, flipping through a magazine. She had her usual glass of wine that she sipped while munching on some Wasabi almonds, which were her favorite nuts.

"Jackson's going to meet us at the Nantucket Airport, right?" Quinn asked, turning around.

"Right."

"Is he going to have all his big celebrity friends there too?" Hallie asked with a teasing smile.

"Sure," Ava said. "Reese and Jennifer are going to be our first celebrity guests."

Jackson had previously been coy about what show he was working on, but Ava had recently found out that he was an extra on *The Morning Show* and had, in fact, met both Jennifer Aniston and Reese Witherspoon. Granted, he only worked on that set for two weeks and was, once again, looking for steadier work, but he told Ava that he thought that the contacts he made on that set might lead to bigger and better things.

"You're the next Ryan Gosling. I can just feel it," Ava had said to him, trying to be as hopeful as possible.

"Right. Well, I'll see you when you get here."

"*The Secret*," Ava reminded him. "Manifest your own reality. I did."

"Yeah, you manifested your reality by shitting all over a billionaire, mom. Then you absolutely got lucky. Like you found out that you got your own fairy god-dude in that old rich guy. Sorry, mom, but I'm not going to use your example as guidance for my own life. But nice try."

The plane landed in Boston, and the ladies got on the commuter airplane that would take them to Nantucket.

45 minutes later, the island came into view.

The plane touched down at the Nantucket Memorial Airport, and the ladies immediately went to the baggage claim and waited for the carousel to spit out all their multitude of bags. Then Ava wheeled her bags to the curb and waited for Jackson to drive around in his rental SUV and pick them up. Before they knew it, Jackson appeared by the curb.

"Hey, mom," Jackson said, coming over and loading her

The Beachfront Inn

bags into the back of the vehicle, along with Hallie and Quinn's bags. He kissed her on the cheek. "You're looking good, lady."

She sighed as she got into the car, buckled up and looked over at her youngest child by five minutes. Jackson was her blindingly handsome son, 6'3", lean and muscular, with a chiseled chin, a defined Roman nose, a cleft chin and wide-set green eyes. His dark hair was cut closely cropped on the sides, higher and choppy on top, and his teeth were perfect.

Ava never really knew where Jackson got his looks. Daniel wasn't tall, only 5'9", and she, herself, was only 5'4". Jackson got her green eyes and Daniel's dark hair, but Daniel, while attractive, wasn't a stunner. She certainly wasn't, either. At best, she was cute, with her curly red hair, freckles and an average shape. But Jackson was male-model material. In fact, he'd done modeling in L.A. and was commanding a pretty high price these days. That enabled him to rent this beautiful brand-new SUV that she and her two friends were sitting in.

"You're looking good yourself," she said, looking back at her friends in the backseat. "Quinn, Hallie, you remember my son."

"Of course," Quinn said. "As if I'm going to forget a handsome devil like that. How you doing?"

"Great," Jackson said with a grin. "You're looking good, too, Quinn. And Hallie, how the hell are you?"

"Fine, fine," Hallie said.

Although Hallie said she was fine, she looked anything but, Ava thought. She was concerned about her friend. She knew that Hallie was severely depressed, and she just didn't know how to help her. She prayed that this trip would be a balm for her best friend, but she knew the truth. Once

Hallie went back to New York, she would sink into an even deeper depression than ever because she would lose her lifelines.

Ava worried about that scenario night and day.

"Okay, mom, now where are we going? I don't know this island."

"'Sconset Beach," Ava told him.

"Oh, yeah. I think that's a really ritzy area."

"As are all the areas on this island," Ava said. "I don't know how well I'll fit in here, but I'm here, nonetheless. Yay, me."

Ava gave Jackson the address to the place, and he punched it into his Google Maps.

"And away we go," Jackson said.

As they drove along, Ava thought that this island looked like time had forgotten about it. Everywhere she looked were houses that probably were built during the 1700s, many of which had decks on their roofs.

"Those decks are called roof walks," Quinn said as she saw Ava pointing them out. "The story is they were built on top of the houses for women who watched for their husbands to come home from the sea. Now they're just used for people who want to sit and watch the waves roll in. I also heard they were built for fire prevention. If there was a chimney fire, you could just go up on one of those roof walks and pour sand on the fire to put it out."

Quinn apparently had done her research on this place, for she knew quite a lot about the island's history. "This place started out as a whaling town and a place for the richies from Boston and New York to get away from the city," she told Ava. "Most of these wood-shingled homes were whaling homes, owned by ship captains. The ginormous brick homes were mainly owned by the rich people from Boston and New York as summer homes."

"What else did you find out about this place?" Ava asked.

"Well, this island is probably a place that is after your own progressive heart," Quinn said. "Early on, Nantucket was a place for suffragettes and abolitionists and people who were into progressive causes of the day. Because Quakers settled it, there was a religious bent to the founders, but it was a religion based on equality, community and taking care of the earth." Quinn nodded her head. "The DNA of those founders still runs through this island, so the Nantucket natives have the same values we all have."

"What else did you find out?" Hallie asked Quinn.

"This place attracted people like Henry David Thoreau, Ralph Waldo Emerson and Frederick Douglass to come and attend lectures, and all kinds of liberal theologians. And John James Audubon, the Audubon Society founder," Quinn said. "Also, Lucretia Mott, who was a women's rights activist and abolitionist in the 1800s, she came and lectured too."

"Wait, didn't that Audubon guy own slaves and thought that black and indigenous people were inferior to whites?" Hallie asked.

"Yeah, that's right," Quinn said with a shake of her head. "The guy loved birds and nature, but his fellow man, not so much. But it was appropriate for him to visit Nantucket because one of the other things to know about this place is that half of it is undeveloped nature." Quinn took a breath. "I don't know. The whole vibe of this place is peaceful and a place where everybody is equal to everyone else. Even if it's also a playground for the rich and the super-rich."

Ava looked around at all the buildings, seeing that every one of them was apparently built pre-twentieth century. The overall architecture was Salt Box, with the natural cedar shakes, pitched roofs and two stories in the front of the house and only one in the back; Federal Style, which were symmetrical red brick buildings with classical columns; and Greek Revival, which were grand houses designed in the style of ancient Greece, with the white stone, friezes and Doric columns.

"So, are there any modern buildings on this island at all?" Ava asked Quinn.

"Sure," Quinn said. "People build new houses all the time, but they must resemble the older architecture. I read that the rules demand that any new house must have a pitched roof and natural shingles that can't be painted. I don't know. I kind of like those rules because the entire island looks like it hasn't been updated since the 18th century. It gives Nantucket a very quaint feel, and there aren't any ugly mid-century buildings to make the place look cheap. No rundown strip malls, either. For that matter, you can't have a neon sign on the island."

If there was one thing about Quinn, Ava thought, it was that she could be counted on to give a good lecture about architecture and local history. Being an interior decorator gave Quinn a good eye for structures and decors of different styles of homes, and she was also a bit of a history buff.

"Yeah, mom, and I heard that most of the people on this island aren't here year-round," Jackson added. "Just about every house sells for $3 million and up, so it's safe to say that this island is a playground for the rich. Can you imagine? Having a summer home worth millions?"

Ava just smiled. "Yes, I can imagine. Quite a few of my former clients at Collins and Lahy have homes out here and in the Hamptons." *Out of the frying pan, into the fire.* It seemed Ava just couldn't get away from billionaires, no matter how hard she tried.

Cobblestone streets and quaint shops of just about every type passed for a downtown Nantucket. Most of the shops were housed in two-story brick structures and natural-shingled Cape Cods, with old-fashioned street lamps and trees lining the streets. It being the off-season, the downtown area was quiet, and many of the shops and restaurants were closed for the season.

Ava smiled, thinking about downtown New York compared to this downtown. The people who lived here during the whaling days could've entered a time capsule to come to the modern day and not be disoriented. They probably would've marveled about how little had changed.

But that same time traveler in New York City? Hoo, boy, would that person be confused!

"Look at the windows on these old buildings," Quinn said, pointing to one of the historical structures that housed a jeweler. "Do you see how they look wavy?"

Ava nodded as she looked closely at the building's windows. "Yeah, come to think of it," she said.

"Well, that means that the windows were installed before the 20th century, probably before the 19th century. Back in the day, glass blowers used to create windows by putting the glass close to a furnace and blowing it and spinning it. Modern windows are made by machines, so they don't have the wavy appearance."

"I never even noticed older buildings having wavy windows," Ava said. "How interesting."

"And did you know that the entire island is considered to be a National Historic Landmark?" Quinn asked. "By the way, the house that you inherited, it's not a historic house, is it? If it is, you might have problems getting a permit to do major interior renovations."

"Actually, no," Ava said. "The house was built in 1988, so I don't think that it's going to be a problem getting the permits to gut it, if that's what needs to happen."

Ava looked out the window and noticed something. "There aren't any traffic lights on this island, are there?"

"Nope," Quinn said. "Only stop signs and roundabouts. And a ton of courtesy. It's going to be tough for us to adjust to this island, but I'm here for it. It's going to be great to actually see courteous drivers for a change."

"I heard that this island was known for its cranberry bogs," Hallie said. "And they even have a cranberry festival every year about this time."

"That's true," Quinn said. "And we just missed the cranberry festival. But I read the bogs out here are amazing. You ever been in a cranberry bog?"

"Can't say I have," Ava said. "I always thought that cranberries grow on trees."

"Nope," Quinn said. "They grow in water, billions of them in one place. Guys in waders harvest the cranberries, and little kids in rain boots get in these bogs and scoop them up in a bucket."

The quartet headed down a road called Milestone that was marked by a tunnel of trees, their leaves colored bright red and yellow, and then entered the village of 'Sconset. As they drove along the quiet street, Ava marveled at the multitude of cottages that were completely covered in vines.

"Are those vines ivy?" Ava asked Quinn, knowing that her friend would have the answer. She always seemed to have the answer when it came to things like this.

"Nope," Quinn said. "Roses. Can you imagine? In the springtime, these cottages will be covered in blooms. I've seen pictures online, and these cottages look really spectacular in the spring."

Hallie shook her head. "I used to try to grow roses, and I never could. I didn't have the knack. I know that you're supposed to do a ton of things to keep the blooms going, pruning and fertilizing and things like that. I couldn't imagine what it would take to maintain the roses that grow on these houses."

"Well, I think that these roses have been around for so long, they don't have to be maintained," Quinn said. "But what do I know? It's not like we could grow roses in our apartments back home. I can't wait until it's springtime here. Not only will these cottages be covered in gorgeous roses, but apparently the street that we just drove down to get here will be covered in daffodils, which are my favorite flower because of I love the color yellow. And I guess that hydrangeas are really common out here, too."

Ava smiled and nodded, eagerly anticipating seeing the riotous color that would cover her new village in just a few months. For now, though, she was struck by how desolate 'Sconset village seemed. Nobody was walking around the Main Street, and there wasn't a light on in any of the houses, even though dusk had fallen. A beautiful brick and mortar Gothic revival chapel, which seemed to be the focal point for the village, was deserted. The parking lot was covered in a blanket of fallen leaves, with not a single car in sight.

"This chapel doesn't look like much right now," Quinn said, "but when the throngs of people come to town after Memorial Day, it's going to be the place to be in this little town. They hold lectures there, concerts and all sorts of games."

"Sounds like a very family-friendly place," Ava said,

taking a deep breath. Her senses were being jarred by the discombobulation of being in this beautiful ghost town after having been in a concrete jungle for so very long. It was safe to say that there would be no car honking, no bird-flipping, no yelling out car windows to get the f 'out of the road, you moron!' There would be no more subway rides, no more crowded sidewalks, no more elevators and no more sirens screaming through the night.

Ava wrapped her arms around her, wondering what she got into. This island was beautiful, even in autumn, because it was clean, historically preserved, and gorgeously maintained. At the same time, Ava wondered if she would feel a bit lonely and isolated. After so many years of living in a 200-unit condo complex in a city that never sleeps, it would be an adjustment to move to this hamlet that seemed like it was never going to wake up.

It was more than strange to imagine that this little chapel would be the hub of activity for the tiny village. It was like the scene in the movie *Butch Cassidy and the Sundance Kid* where Butch and Sundance go to Bolivia and end up in a deserted railroad station surrounded by cows. A disgusted Sundance muses whether that railroad station might be the center of the Bolivian action.

"You doing okay, Sugar?" Quinn asked Ava. "You look like you're having a sad."

"Having a sad," Ava said. "Yeah, I guess I am. I guess I'm going to miss my old neighborhood. The bodega where the owner knows me and asks about my kids, the coffee shop where I used to hang out whenever Chris and I had a fight. I loved that shop because I could be anonymous, yet I felt comforted by being out around a crowd of people. The Chinese restaurant where I ordered take-out at least three nights a week. I would eat my cold noodles in front of a good Netflix show. That was my go-to ritual after having a hard day. I'm going to miss going to the ballet, the theater and the opera and having so many world-class museums and art galleries right at my fingertips."

Hallie put her arm around her friend from behind and squeezed her. "Oh, but Ava, think about the trade-off. You're not going to be able to get Chinese food when you can't sleep at 2 in the morning, but you're also not going to be cleaning up sleazy billionaires' messes. You're not going to be barked at by managing partners who clearly never appreciated you, and you're not going to be yelled at by cranky judges who woke up on the wrong side of the bed and are taking it out on everybody in the courtroom. You're going to be managing a bed-and-breakfast that's all yours. All the hard work and long hours that you'll be putting into renovating your house and running your inn will be all for you, not for a bunch of men who never knew what a fantastic talent they had right under their noses."

Ava just nodded her head, wondering if the trade-off would be worth it when the newest hot musical hit Broadway, or when she was in the mood for some gourmet food prepared by a world-class chef, or when a new exhibit comes to the Met, or maybe when she runs out of cold medicine and no stores are open to sell her NyQuil.

No matter, she was committed to this new venture. This new house was hers, she had no Plan B, and she was just going to have to make it work. No matter what, failure was not an option because, at this point, failure meant a very uncertain future and maybe poverty.

They arrived at Ava's new home, and Ava immediately felt awed. "Oh my Lord," she said, looking at the enormous Cape Cod home. "If I would've seen this place from the street, I would've thought it was a condo complex."

"It's cute," Hallie said, stepping out of the vehicle and going around to the back of the SUV to get her bag. However, Jackson, ever the gentleman, waved her away.

"I'll get everybody's bags," he said, "you guys just go on in. I'll catch up."

"I couldn't let you -" Hallie began, but Ava just shook her head.

"Let him get the bags," she said to Hallie. "He loves it."

At that, Jackson grinned at his mother. "You know me pretty well after all."

"Cute, nothing," Quinn said. "This place is a mansion. Of course, after living in the cracker boxes we've been living in for all these years, I guess anyplace is a mansion."

Ava had to agree with Quinn. From the outside, she certainly did feel she was looking at a mansion. The house was an enormous Cape Cod with natural wood shingles and a sunny wrap-around porch that faced the narrow tree-lined street. It was two stories tall, with the second story bounded by a beach-facing terrace that spanned its length. The house was incredibly deep. Several pitched roofed segments reached towards the property's back, which faced the beach.

There was a parking lot that could easily house ten cars next to the house, and there were also several garages for even more cars. While one side of the house faced the beach, the other half had a swimming pool. A lookout point was at the end of the parking lot, with two benches dedicated to lost loved ones.

Ava wondered if the house would be in a state of disrepair. On the outside, it seemed that this wasn't the case. But she did know that, once they got inside, there probably was lots of work to be done.

She turned her key in the lock and opened the door. Hallie, Quinn and Jackson followed her through the house. The electricity worked, which was evidenced when Quinn flipped on the lights in one of the bedrooms.

The house had a musty smell because it had been unoccupied for a spell. A distinct pungent and salty odor grew stronger as the group got closer to the terrace that overlooked the beach. They stepped outside and went over to the glass wall that bounded the terrace, which was large enough for several pieces of furniture, a hot tub, a fire ring and several tables and chairs, and looked down at the beach, where the ocean raged. Seagulls leaped along, looking for crabs or food scraps to eat. However, other than that, the beach appeared to be deserted.

The wind whipped up, and Ava felt a huge raindrop land on her nose. "Come on, guys," she said. "Let's get inside and figure out what needs to be done. Then I propose we build a fire and find a restaurant that might be open and get some chow." Ava noticed on the way in that many of the eateries were closed for the off-season, so the prospect of finding a decent meal wasn't great.

But Ava was determined to have a positive attitude about this abrupt change. She was a survivor, come what may.

She would make this thing work, no matter what. She literally had no choice.

Chapter Eleven

Ava

The same night Ava moved in, she got the unpleasant news that her sister was on the road from California, with the intent to visit her. Everybody else had gone to bed already, snoring in their sleeping bags in various parts of the house. Then, she saw she had a text - a text! from her mother. *Ava, your sister is taking a road trip your way.* And that was it. Short and sweet. No ETA. No spelling out the reason why her sister was coming to her. None of that.

And Ava wasn't happy, not in the least.

She tossed and turned in her sleeping bag, trying to get some sleep, but she couldn't. So, she went out to the terrace and listened to the waves come in and smell the briny air. It was a cool early October night, so she had a blanket covering her, and she was huddling up underneath it.

Why was Sarah coming out here to steal her joy? Was it really necessary to have a sister who hated her descending upon her home like a locust?

The Beachfront Inn

After all, Sarah had made it perfectly clear she had nothing in common with Ava and she was too good for her. Which really got Ava's goat because Sarah and Ava were always close when they were young.

There was only one year between the two of them, well, actually only 10 months. Sarah was always more popular than Ava in school, so even though she was the younger of the sisters, she was Ava's protector of sorts in junior high and high school. Sarah was the one who was the head cheerleader, the homecoming queen, the trendsetter queen bee. She was definitely one of the Golden People.

When Sarah started wearing T-shirt dresses with high heels to school, scores of other young girls were suddenly doing the same. When Sarah discovered a new dance and debuted those moves at the homecoming dance where she was crowned Queen, that dance became the latest rage. It was like The Hustle, the popular dance Ava learned when she was in sixth grade. One time, Sarah had to wear a single white glove to school because she was covering up a bad case of Eczema. Before Ava knew it, every other girl in school was showing up in a single white glove.

Yet, Sarah protected Ava from the bullies. Ava never quite fit in. She was more studious than outgoing, more awkward than effortless. She was never invited to a single party in high school, never went to a dance. While Sarah was always around 125 pounds, at 5'7", Ava topped out at 175 pounds, even though she was only 5'3". Sarah was beautiful - long blonde hair, perfect peaches and cream skin, big blue eyes. She had guys flocking all over her all the time. Ava never had a guy even look at her. Sarah was always the first one picked in gym class. Ava was always the last, even the day when guys had to pick girls as their square dance partner.

Worst of all, Ava didn't know how to talk to her peers. She would always say the wrong thing at the wrong time, which led her fellow students to believe she was stupid, when she was anything but. Ava hated being a social pariah, especially when her sister ruled the school. It was humiliating hearing Sarah talk about this party she was invited to and that one, this boy was sending her love notes in school, and that boy was jealous. Ava never had anything to report on these matters. While Sarah was going to parties on Friday nights, Ava was home studying and watching the *Dukes of Hazzard* and *Dallas*.

And Ava was bullied. She was never pushed inside a locker, but people made fun of her hair, weight, and her pre-Invisalign crooked teeth. Whenever Sarah was in the hall and somebody was harassing Ava, she would stick up for her big sis.

Sarah got into a hair-pulling fight with one girl who was relentlessly calling Ava "Blubber," apparently after reading the Judy Blume book by the same name. She pushed another girl into a locker because the girl was calling Ava "Pippi Longstocking," which was always Ava's nickname, even though she despised it. Sarah always ate with Ava in the cafeteria, so even though Ava was never part of the popular crowd, she could eat at the same table as them.

No doubt about it, Ava adored Sarah, and Sarah adored Ava. Which was why it was so hurtful when the two girls quit seeing each other some 20 years ago after they had a huge falling out.

Ava still didn't know quite what the argument was about. All she knew was she went out to California for a visit, a much-needed vacation she had been looking forward to for months. She had three small children at home - the triplets were only 4 years old, and they were a handful. Of course, Ava had a nanny, but not a live-in one, so whenever she was home, she was dealing with various kid-related disasters. She was working 50 hours a week - she hadn't yet started her 70-hour workweek because her kids were small, and her firm gave her a bit of a pass.

She got out to Sarah's home and was stunned by what she saw. Sarah lived in a mansion. Not a McMansion, but a full-on mansion like a celebrity would live in. It was one of those modern glass and steel homes that was right on the beach, and Ava was amazed by Sarah's view of the Pacific Ocean. She didn't know what to expect, but after Sarah told her that her boyfriend was a math professor at Cal State, Ava thought Sarah's home would be modest.

The reality was that the home was anything but modest.

Sarah was excited to give Ava the grand tour of the home, which had everything. A movie room, a game room, 10 bedrooms, an indoor pool and an outdoor one, a gym and a day spa, complete with a full-time masseuse and acupuncturist. A steam room and sauna. A gorgeous terrace that was large enough for a group of 100 people to mill about, with three hot tubs large enough for 20 people apiece. An army of help kept that place going - maids, butlers, cooks and personal trainers. The ceilings in this place were impossibly high, probably a good 30 feet.

Sarah bubbled on about their 50-foot yacht, called the *Monterey Siren*. "Just wait until we take you out on that thing, Ava. I know you get seasick, but I'll give you some Dramamine. We'll take the boat to Catalina Island. That place is so beautiful. So much untamed nature. We can go hiking, parasailing and zip-lining, do some scuba diving and then go to Avalon and have some dinner and do some casino gambling."

Ava just nodded her head, unable to speak. She

suddenly felt incredibly frumpy in her mom jeans, knitted sweater and flat shoes. Her hair was untamed and in a ponytail, and she really needed a cut. Sarah was impossibly slim, as usual, and she was dressed in designer jeans, a silk top and Chanel stilettos. She looked chic and put together, with her blonde bob and a full face of makeup. Her big blue eyes were bright, her full lips outlined in a ruby red that suited her well. She looked like Charlize Theron, both in the face and body.

"Uh, that sounds like fun," Ava said, when she actually thought she wanted a much more low-key vacation. She was exhausted and wanted nothing more than to hang out with her sister and watch movies, play board games and have dinners on the gorgeous terrace. Parasailing and scuba diving sounded like absolute hell to her.

"Does it?" Sarah asked with a wide smile.

"Sure, sure," Ava said. She had her bags in the foyer, and she eyed them.

"Oh, where is my head? Let me take your bags and show you to your room."

The two ladies went up the stairs, and Ava was shown to a bedroom that was as large as the living room of her condo. It was homey, though, with hardwood floors, cathedral ceilings and a wood-burning fireplace. The attached bathroom was appointed with a large jacuzzi tub and a marble shower for two.

"Are all the bedrooms like this?" Ava asked.

"Oh, you don't like it?" Sarah asked. "We have larger ones, but this one is close to ours. I can show you some of the others."

"The others are larger than this?" Ava asked, looking around.

"Well, yes." Sarah cocked her head. "Do you like it?"

"Of course. I just thought that maybe you were putting me in the nicest bedroom and I was going to tell you that I didn't need all this space. My living room could literally fit in this bedroom."

Sarah just laughed. "No, this is one of the smaller rooms."

Ava spent the week there, seeing the way that Sarah lived. They went to Catalina, and Ava surprised herself when she got into hiking, parasailing, scuba diving, and all the things she dreaded doing.

She also met Sarah's friends, who were all as gorgeous and in-shape as Sarah was.

And why shouldn't they be? They all had regular facials and massages, and they all had personal trainers and personal chefs. They all had all the time in the world to get plenty of rest.

None of them worked 50 hours a week, after which they had to get home to 3 kids under the age of 5 who demanded all their free time. None of them were struck down by a fate that not only took away their husband, but also subjected them to having three babies at once, when they were only prepared to have one. None of them knew what it was like to barely have time to pee, let alone take a long bath once in a while. Ava couldn't remember the last time she took a long bubble bath because, every time she tried, she had at least one kid pounding on the door and crying about somebody else being mean.

Ava found herself resenting these women. Every one of

them. Especially Sarah. She felt betrayed by her sister, an architect by training who now was nothing but a lazy dilettante who sponged off her boyfriend. And dilettante wasn't even a good word for her because a dilettante at least *pretended* to know something. Sarah seemed to have nothing in her head anymore except knowledge about reality television, soap operas and celebrity gossip.

Ava finally had enough. Of all of it.

It happened on the second-to-last day of the vacation, and Ava was about to go back to her real life of hell. She was sitting at yet another brunch with the bubble-headed nitwits that Sarah counted as friends, and Ava felt like screaming. Around the table were Ava, Sarah and Sarah's friends Lauren, Rina and Elizabeth.

"I'm going to get a couple's massage with Larry today," Lauren said. Lauren was a brunette with a fake rack and even faker lips. She couldn't make any facial expressions because her features were frozen with Botox.

Larry was her personal trainer and boyfriend. Lauren had two children and a husband, billionaire William Blake, who was pretty clueless about what was going on under his nose.

Ava put Sarah's friends into two categories - those who were having an affair behind their husband's back for no good reason and those who were having an affair because their husband was also having affairs. Ava found the slippery morality of these women nauseating.

To her knowledge, though, her sister didn't fall into either of those categories. Ava didn't think that Sarah was being unfaithful to Nolan.

Lauren was in the first category, which Ava found the more noxious. She could almost understand the ones who had affairs because their husbands also were. Good for the goose, good for the gander and all that. She didn't agree with such logic, of course - if your husband's having affairs, get out of the marriage, and don't subject your children to your moral emptiness. Yet, if the husband was the one who cheated first, Ava supposed that having affairs was understandable, if not excusable.

But the ones who were sneaking around just because...

"Lauren, you have a couple of little kiddos around your house, don't you?" Ava blurted out. "Do you think for one second they don't know what's going on between you and your personal trainer? I know they're only 5 and 7, but, trust me, kids know more than you think. You're just setting them up by giving them a role model that sees nothing wrong with stepping out on -"

Lauren batted her eyes and looked over at Sarah. Sarah's face turned eight shades of red. She knew what Ava thought about her friends, but she apparently didn't think Ava would be quite so open about it.

"Ava's joking," Sarah said to Lauren, putting her hand on Lauren's arm. "She doesn't really care about what you do with your private life. Ava isn't that judgmental, are you, Ava?"

Ava got quiet, and the ladies started talking again.

"Did you hear?" Rina asked the ladies. Rina was a tall and thin redhead with long straight hair and an even straighter body. She was younger than the others, as she was around 22, when Sarah and the others were nearing their mid-thirties. "A promoter of this hot club in L.A. just recruited me to show up tonight. What do you ladies say? We could fly on Vincent's private jet, make an appearance and maybe get lucky tonight."

Rina was also in the first category - she was running around on her husband, Vincent, a 60-year-old CEO of a large pharmaceutical company. To Ava's knowledge, Vincent was not also pursuing extracurricular activities.

"That sounds like fun," Sarah said, touching Ava's elbow. "What do you say, Ava? That would be a really awesome way to end your vacation out here."

Going to a loud and crowded club and having people spill vodka tonics on her while she fought her way to the bar to get a drink sounded like the very opposite of "fun" or "awesome" to Ava's ears. And Sarah knew this about her.

Why would Sarah want to spend their last evening together doing something Ava absolutely despised doing?

"You ladies go," Ava said. "I have a long flight tomorrow, and then it's back to the salt mines the next day. I really should get to bed early."

"Oh, come on, Ava," Sarah said. "You've never been on a private jet. How many chances will you get to fly on one?"

"Believe it or not, Sarah, flying on a private jet has never made my bucket list. And," she said, addressing Rina directly. "What exactly do you mean by recruited to come to this club?"

Rina just shrugged. "Club promoters pay beautiful women to show up. And celebrities, too, but I just get recruited for my beauty."

Ava was perplexed. "And you get paid for showing up?"

"Yes," Rina said, nodding her head. "I sometimes get $5,000 if the club is really hot and the promoter wants a lot of gorgeous women around."

"And when you go to a club, you meet men?"

"Of course," Rina said. "Duh."

"And this is your only source of income, aside from Vincent?"

"Yes," Rina said. "It's fun money."

"Fun money," Ava said. $5,000 just for going to a club

for the evening? And this was literally this woman's only profession.

"Yes, fun money," Rina said.

"Come on, Ava," Sarah said. "It's your last night here."

"Right, and I was hoping that you would know me well enough to understand that going to a sweaty, crowded club would be the very last way that I would want to spend my last night here."

Sarah stuck out her lower lip and then apologized to the ladies. "I'm sorry. My stick-in-the-mud sister here is going to chain me to the house tonight, I guess."

"Sarah, go ahead with your friends," Ava said. "I have a television show with my name on it. Go, have fun."

"No, I better stay home with you," Sarah said. "What kind of hostess would I be if I left you alone on your last night?"

"Go," Ava said. "Please."

"No," Sarah said, looking around the table. "There will be other trips to L.A. Rina gets recruited quite a lot to show up at different clubs."

Of course, Sarah only pretended to be okay with not going on the private jet to the L.A. club, and she was also apparently still stewing about Ava's remark to Lauren about her fooling around on her husband while she had two small kids at home.

And Sarah let Ava have it.

"I knew I shouldn't have invited you," Sarah said as she drove her brand-new Jaguar back to her home. Ava was cranking up the air in the passenger's seat because it was a muggy August day.

"What, to brunch?"

"No, out here to visit me. I forgot how judgmental you are."

"What are you talking about?"

"You know what I'm talking about. Your voice was practically dripping with contempt when you were talking to Rina about her job."

"What job?" Ava asked, exasperated. "The woman is paid to show up at clubs. That's literally her profession. But I guess that's more of a profession than the rest of your friends have, so I guess I have to give Rina some credit."

"There. That's the tone of voice you had when talking to Rina about going to the club. Don't think that I didn't notice your imperiousness."

"Imperiousness. Good word. Ask any one of your friends what that word means, and I can guarantee you they won't know."

Sarah rolled her eyes. "Really? Really."

"Yes, really. I'm sorry, but your friends are so insipid, amoral, shallow and plastic. They all make me sick. Doesn't it disturb you just a little that Lauren is sleeping with her personal trainer when she has kids at home? And that Rina picks up men whenever she goes out, when her husband is working his rear-end off to pay for that private jet she's taking to L.A.? Doesn't any of this faze you at all?"

"Of course," Sarah said. "But it's not my place to say anything to them."

"But you're hanging out with them. And Lauren's a no-account-"

"And that's her life," Sarah said. "You don't know anything about her."

"I know she's showing her kids that having a boyfriend on the side is acceptable. Not to mention showing the kids that laying about and sponging off of somebody else is perfectly fine. Lauren, Rina and Elizabeth have all set the women's movement back about 100 years."

Sarah gripped the steering wheel so hard that her knuckles turned white. "Don't you mean to include me in that assessment, sis?" Sarah asked Ava with gritted teeth. "Go ahead. Tell me about it. Tell me about how I'm also a lazy bitch who doesn't meet your exacting standards on what a woman should be. Go ahead. Tell me about how I'm just as bad as those three women you just blasted."

Ava shook her head. "Yes. You are as bad. Yes. You're also setting back the women's movement 100 years. Maybe you're not as immoral as your friends are, but you're just as insipid and lazy."

"Insipid and lazy? Really. Really. At least I'm not some fat unhappy hausfrau raising three brats and driving herself crazy."

Fat. *Oh, so it's come to this.* Ava wasn't heavy at that time. She was overweight in high school, but she had worked hard to lose it, and, at the moment, she had an extra ten pounds or so.

"You only think I'm fat because you're hanging out with women who would give Karen Carpenter a run for her money. And, yes, that includes you."

"You're jealous."

"Oh, yes, I'm sooo jealous. I know what your friends do to stay rail-thin, and I want no part of it. Rina and Elizabeth eat about 500 calories a day because they're always talking about it and obsessing over every little calorie they put into their mouths. And you know that Lauren only stays slim because she gets lipo all the time. She has her plastic surgeon on speed dial. Did you know that? True story. She called him while you were in the bathroom, and he's apparently number one on her phone. Her kids are numbers two and three, and her husband probably isn't on her speed dial at all."

"That's because she's sleeping with her plastic surgeon and has been for the past year."

Ava nodded her head. "That tracks."

"What does that mean?"

"I mean, it's on-brand for her. I know I don't have to spell it out for you."

Ava knew that Sarah didn't have to eat like a bird or get lipo because she was just naturally thin and always had been. Which was another reason why Ava resented her sister. Sarah could eat anything she wanted, and if Ava looked at a cookie, she gained weight. What justice was that?

"You-"

"What happened to you?" Ava blurted out, not letting Sarah make one more dumb comment because, if Sarah did, Ava would scream. "Really? You were an architect and a very talented one at that. You graduated *Summa Cum Laude* from K.U., top of your class. You got your Master's at UC Berkeley. You were going to set the world on fire. What happened to you?"

"I met Nolan, that's what."

Ava shook her head. "Oh, that's all, then? You gave up your life for what? Sarah, you're better than this. You're better than this. I never thought that you would be this lazy. I never thought you would keep company with women like Rina and Lauren. And I never thought that you would give up your entire life for a man."

"Sorry, Ava, but just because your life is in the toilet doesn't mean that you have to take it out on me."

"What do you mean, my life is in the toilet?"

"I mean that I wouldn't want to trade places with you for all the tea in China. You're heading for a nervous breakdown between your job and raising three kids."

Ava bit her lower lip. "Talk about something that you never have to worry about - having a nervous breakdown. Unless, of course, you crack up because your manicurist is out of town, and you can't get your nails done in time for your silent auction. Then again, I can see how something like that could send you over the edge."

Sarah shook her head. "I won't sit here and let you talk to me like this. You better call yourself a cab and stay in a hotel tonight. I'd suggest the Monterey Plaza Hotel and Spa."

Ava narrowed her eyes. "Fine. You want me to stay in a hotel tonight? You got it."

By that time, the two women had arrived back at Sarah's palatial home. Ava got out of the car, slamming the door. And then she furiously went into her room and threw her clothes into her rolling suitcase and, with shaking hands, she called herself a cab. Then she left without a word.

Since that trip, the sisters had talked on the phone a few times here and there, but the strain was too much, and they were no longer close. Ava perfunctorily invited Sarah out to New York for the holidays several times, and Sarah politely came up with excuses on why she couldn't make it out. Usually, her excuse was she was going skiing in Switzerland or going to Prague or heading down to Jamaica or something similar. Which would remind Ava about why she was angry with Sarah in the first place.

What she wouldn't give to live Sarah's life just for a little while. Must be nice to be spending December in Jamaica instead of freezing her rear end off while valiantly trying to hail a cab. Must be fantastic to actually get more than 4 or 5 hours of sleep a night.

It had to be amazing not to worry about getting a stress ulcer before the age of 35.

Chapter Twelve

Sarah

As she stared out the window of her boyfriend's 20,000 square foot beach house overlooking the Pacific Ocean, Sarah Flynn was on her third glass of wine. She would soon be hitting the harder stuff. Specifically, a dirty martini.

She went into her spacious kitchen and got out the olive juice and gin and poured it into a martini glass and started to sip. She loved the bitterness of the olive juice, which somehow smoothed out the bite of the gin. She enjoyed top-of-the-top shelf gin - her boyfriend, Nolan Shea, habitually bought Nolet's Reserve Gin at $600 a bottle. The gin she was drinking right at that moment, Cambridge Distillery Watenshi, cost $3,000 a bottle and was considered the rarest gin in the world.

Of course, this brand of gin, along with all the other luxuries she had enjoyed these past 23 years, would soon be a thing of the past. She smiled ruefully as she sipped on her glass while she observed her mother packing delicate figurines from around the globe into boxes. Boxes that represented all she owned in the entire world.

Her rescue mutt, Bella, a beautiful pit bull mix, was standing by her side as she looked out the floor-to-ceiling wall of windows and thought about what her next move would be. Bella was a smart pup, that was for sure, and very in tune with Sarah's emotions.

She could see that the ocean was raging at that moment. It seemed to be high tide. The sky was grey, and the wind was whipping - she could see the umbrellas on the beach swaying savagely. California was in a perpetual drought, it seemed, but today, it looked like the sky would finally open up.

Her luck. It never rained, but, on this day, the day she would have to get in her car and leave, it apparently would storm.

Then again, it raining made it a fitting coda to her life with Nolan, who was a trust-fund baby. It was storming the night she met him in a bar 23 years ago - that was why she was in that bar in the first place. She was walking home to her apartment from her job - her car was in the shop, and her job was only a mile away from her place - and the sky had opened up out of nowhere. She needed to get out of the rain.

The Irish dive bar with the wooden floors, dart boards, fireplace, scuffed tables with graffiti scrawled on the surfaces and loud music that usually favored the Drop Kick Murphys or Flogging Molly was where she ended up to get out of the weather.

He bought her a beer and gave her a ride home that night. The rest was history.

Sarah walked over to her mother and, once again, started to pitch in with the packing.

There was the simple plate she picked up in a café in Paris. She loved the plates in that café so much she offered to buy them. They weren't for sale, but the café owner gave her one for free.

"Just make sure you come back again," the owner had asked her, and she agreed. She and Nolan went to that café every day for the month they stayed there.

Then there was the dolphin carving she picked up amongst the Mayan ruins in Belize. She was transported back to the bamboo hut that housed the carvings and other treasures as her mother wrapped up the ornately carved piece of stone.

The fan from China, red and black, had come in handy when she and Nolan stayed in a Beijing hotel where the air conditioner was on the fritz. Sarah's idea was to rough it on that trip, to live amongst the people and not the hoi-polloi. Which they did and had the best time ever that month, aside from that weekend without the cool air blowing through their hotel room.

The snow globe from Prague. The Maori basket from the Australian bush. The wine glasses from Venice. The amethyst carving of a flamingo from Brazil.

So many souvenirs and treasures, so many memories...

Although she and her mother worked in silence, she knew what was going through her mother's head. The same thing that was going through her own.

"I know, I know, I know," Sarah said. "Don't say it."

The older woman shook her head again. "I told you. I told you. Make sure that man puts a ring on your finger because if something ever happens to him, you're roadkill. And here you are - roadkill."

Her mother was a respected judge in the United States

First Circuit Court in Boston, but she somehow had the vocabulary of a trucker.

Sarah took a deep breath. "Roadkill. That's such a lovely way of putting it, mother." She took another sip of her martini.

"Well, what would you say about it? Here you are. You've given this man 23 years of your life, and now you're out on the street. With nothing. No job, no home. Nothing but your dog."

Sarah took a deep breath. "I know what you're really thinking, mother. You think that I should've been more like my sister, Ava. She would never have gotten herself in this situation, right? After all, she's this hot-shot lawyer in New York City, making all the money for herself. She would never have to worry about being put out of the house because her boyfriend died."

"She *was* a hot-shot lawyer, and you're right about what I'm thinking," her mother said, nodding her head. "Not to mention the fact that you don't have the brains that God gave a gnat. You could've at least gotten him to make a will. You knew that he was dying a year ago. You could've pressed him then."

Sarah slapped on a tight smile and closed her eyes. "He didn't want to make a will," Sarah said.

Truth be told, him not making a will was a bone of contention between her and Nolan. Nolan had been diagnosed with ALS exactly one year ago. He'd been feeling stiff in the morning and thought it was a problem with the mattress. He always did yoga with Sarah, one of the few men she knew who practiced sun salutations and vinyasa. It kept him limber and supple, so it was frustrating when he couldn't perform the yoga poses that he'd never before had a problem with.

He bought a new mattress but soon found that he was so stiff that he couldn't keep up with Sarah on the yoga mat at all. He also started to slur his words.

Then he hosted a barbecue one day. He brought out the plates to the gorgeous terrace that overlooked the ocean, and he dropped them. They shattered into a million pieces when they crashed into the Spanish tile.

A trip to the doctor for what he assumed would be a routine checkup - he didn't think anything of his sudden clumsiness or stiffness or slurred words - brought him the devastating diagnosis of ALS.

The death sentence had been handed down, and, just like that, a vital and healthy man who was hale and hearty enough to hike The Alps and zipline through the Amazon rainforest was struck down.

Sarah was by his side when he lost his ability to speak, move his muscles, or chew his food. She made smoothies with mangoes, figs and avocados she picked from the trees growing on their spacious property. She changed his adult diapers when his around-the-clock nurse couldn't because she was busy with something else. She waited on him hand and foot. She took him to all of his doctors' appointments, and then, when all hope was gone, she took him to experimental treatments that were being offered in Switzerland.

She spent all her waking hours on the internet, looking for anything promising. She read so many articles from medical journals around the world she felt she could find the cure for ALS if somebody had given her a grant to do so. She'd learned how to read studies, which wasn't easy to do, and, by the time Nolan had died, she could interpret scientific data as well as any expert.

It was all for naught, of course. Sarah knew this even if Nolan never wanted to admit to it.

"And didn't it tell you something that he didn't make a will?" her mother said as she wrapped up a ceramic pelican that Sarah got on a trip to Greece. She had spent the day in bed with food poisoning, and Nolan had bought that figurine to cheer her up. "A man not only won't commit to you, but he won't even make a will to make sure that you're cared for if he prematurely buys the farm."

Sarah shrugged. "I asked him, but he kept putting it off." Sarah knew why Nolan didn't make a will, and it had nothing to do with her. It had to do with denial. Nolan never wanted to admit that he was dying, even when he was struck with a disease that had an almost 100% fatality rate. A disease with a mean life expectancy of about 3 years after diagnosis.

He told her that he would beat the disease, no matter the odds. After all, he had access to the best doctors in the world. He was a young man, only 55 years old. Just one year before, he was sky-diving and climbing mountains. There was no way that he would accept that he didn't have long to live.

If he made a will, he would be admitting defeat in his mind. He would be telling the world that he was dying if he did something like that, and he didn't want to face it.

Of course, his making a will meant nothing of the sort. It was simply pragmatic. God knew that a man as wealthy as Nolan should have a will, period. To not have one was simply irresponsible. But Nolan would not be talked into making one.

Sarah should've been angry about that. After all, she'd given up her entire life for him. Her career was in shambles because of him. Her present situation, that of being out on the street without a dime, was because of what he did to her. The least he could've done was make a will to include

The Beachfront Inn

her and ensure she'd be taken care of. But he didn't, and now, here she was.

The irony of the situation was that Nolan's wife, Olivia, would get all of his billions. He'd never divorced her, which was most of the reason why he and Sarah had never married. As with the will situation, finalizing a divorce from Olivia was admitting defeat to him. Never mind that the woman had long since moved in with another man and was currently living in the South of France, in a home Nolan bought for her on the Mediterranean.

Now, Olivia was the owner of 100% of Nolan's considerable estate. The woman hadn't seen him in 30 years, didn't bother to see him before he died, even though she knew about his diagnosis, and she was the one who was a billionaire, not Sarah. Sarah, the woman who gave Nolan her entire life for the past 23 years, was left with nothing.

Her mother gave Sarah one of her patented disgusted looks. "And why didn't you tell him that he either make a will or you'd walk out that door? You gave up your career for that man. You changed his diapers for the love of God. That had to count for something."

It was true enough that Sarah had given up a career for Nolan. Nolan was a professor at Cal State, who had summer and winter breaks, and he had wanted to spend those breaks traveling. And, since he was also a wealthy trust-fund baby, he had the money to go wherever he wanted to go.

When they met, Sarah was a 30-year-old architect, having graduated *Summa Cum Laude* from the University of Kansas with a degree in commercial architecture and getting her master's at UC-Berkeley, the #2 architectural school in the country. She was working for a large firm in downtown Los Angeles. A large firm that wasn't willing to give her three months during the summer and a month during the winter to travel. And, really, no job would give her that much time off. Not at her age and lack of experience, anyhow.

But Nolan demanded the whole summer and winter, 16 weeks in all. So, Sarah had to quit. She quit with the agreement that Nolan would take care of her. Which he did, very well, for a long time. She had to admit that.

Along the way, he did something unforgivable to her, but Sarah had to put that incident out of her mind. She had been in denial about his unpardonable actions for the past twenty years because if she ever allowed herself to really examine her feelings about him and what he did, she would've killed him.

And no jury would ever convict her.

And now, well, going back to being an architect wasn't an option for her, partly because of what he had done to her and partly because of what her "friend" Lauren had done to her. Her mother knew about what had happened, and, to her mother's credit, she wasn't going to harass Sarah into trying to get back into designing buildings.

Now what?

"Well, you know what you have to do," her mother said. "After we get a truck for your things."

"That won't be necessary," Sarah said. "All my things are just figurines and plates and souvenirs and wine glasses. They can all fit in the SUV, with room to spare."

That made her feel sad, for some reason. Here she was, 53 years old, and her worldly possessions could literally fit into the trunk of an SUV.

At least she had her Bella. It was really true - wet noses and wagging tails were some of the best things in life.

The Beachfront Inn

"What am I supposed to do?" Sarah asked. "Enlighten me, mom."

"You're going to Nantucket. Your sister is heading that way, and it's high time you guys made up. Ava inherited a house out there, and she's going to make it into a B&B. I can't think of a better use of your time right now than to make up with your sister."

Suddenly, Sarah got a pit in her stomach. "Ava's on Nantucket Island?" Sarah asked. "I'm not going out there. I don't want to deal with her."

"The whole point of you going out there is that you're going to have to deal with her. I don't know what happened between you two, but, whatever it is, it's going to end now. And, if you don't want to go out there and face her, tell me what your Plan B is."

"I'm sure Ava doesn't want me out there."

Her mother sighed. "Would you please stop worrying? It will work out. Besides, maybe you can offer your services to her as a sommelier."

"I'm not a sommelier," Sarah protested. "I'm not anything. I have no skills. I have nothing to offer anyone."

"Come down off that cross because somebody needs the wood. Yes, you've been a layabout these past 23 years, a wastrel, a loafer. But now you need to get off your tuchus and make your life count for something."

Sarah shook her head. Ava. The last person she wanted to see. Ava would make her feel 2 inches tall. At the moment, she only felt 3 inches tall, and Ava would cut her down another inch because that was what her sister did.

Sarah tried to think about what the whole quarrel was about, but she really couldn't. All she knew was that the sister she had adored all her life was a stranger to her and had been for the last twenty years.

No, she knew what it was about, really. It was about Ava's impression that Sarah had The Life. Ava was working all the time while trying to raise three kids, and her life was messy. Meanwhile, Sarah was going all over the world and living in a mansion that overlooked the Pacific Ocean. Sarah enjoyed weekends visiting wineries in Napa, afternoons lounging by the pool, and Tuesday morning Bloody Mary brunches with her uber-wealthy friends.

And she was bored out of her skull. Nolan was a math professor, which meant she and he had very little to talk about, and entertaining his egg-head friends was an exercise in absolute tedium for her.

Most days, she wanted to scream she wasn't living the life she had set out for herself. She was supposed to be somebody, somebody other than a jet-setter's girlfriend.

Yet, she stayed. Why? She knew why. She was afraid. She loved him for the first few years, thoroughly and totally, and she literally would follow him to the ends of the earth. After that? Well, he was taking care of her, and, after what had happened to her, she couldn't go back to being an architect. She was barred from seeking a license.

So, it was crippling fear that kept her with him for all those years. She literally had no options but to stay.

And now, he was gone. Yet, she couldn't muster up any feelings for his passing, any more than Andy Dufresne, the hero in her favorite movie *The Shawshank Redemption*, would feel for the passing of one of Shawshank's prison guards. Because that was what Nolan had been for the past twenty years, really - Sarah's prison guard.

And she hated to think that his dying was a relief for her. But that's what it was. A relief.

A relief yet panic-inducing all at once.

"Listen, you told me that you were taking all those wine

classes," her mother reminded her. "Going to Napa all those weekends, finding out about different kinds of wine and varietals and how to make them. Right?"

"Yes," Sarah said, nodding her head. It was a hobby she had decided to pursue. She and Nolan had been to many wineries in Italy, France, Greece, Spain, Portugal, Australia, New Zealand, Brazil, South Africa, and, when they were home, in Napa, Sonoma and Temecula. She became fascinated and learned all she could about wine. "So what?"

"Well, I suggested to you that Ava might need a sommelier. Does that ring a bell?"

Sarah shook her head. "Ava hates me. She won't hire me."

"Bull. She thinks that *you* hate *her*. She thinks that you look down on her. And listen, it's hard for her. She has a serious case of comparisonitis. Always has."

"Comparsonitis? How does she pale in comparison to me? Is that what she thinks?"

"Of course, that's what she thinks. She was always so jealous that you laid around and had everything handed to you while she worked her butt off around the clock."

Sarah sighed. "And I was always jealous she actually made something of herself. She was independent and whip-smart and wrote briefs for the Supreme Court. People respected her. Nobody ever respected me."

To tell the truth, Sarah always felt Ava looked down on *her*, so she was more than surprised to think Ava felt the same way.

Then there was the matter that Ava had those gorgeous kids. Sarah could never have kids, and she would've given anything in the world to have been able to experience motherhood. Ava had everything that Sarah ever wanted - a respected career and a family. Also, unlike herself, Ava wasn't dumb enough to throw away her entire life for a man.

"Ava's on her ass now, too," her mother said. "But, there's a new beginning around the corner for both of you girls. Now, let's get these boxes put into your Range Rover, and let's skedaddle. I have to be on the bench a week from Monday, so time's a-wasting."

Her mother got behind the wheel and buckled up. Her mother would have to drive the first leg because Sarah had been drinking, but Sarah would take over in a few hours.

Sarah waved at her lavish beach house, the place that looked so beautiful on the outside, but looks were deceiving. Somehow, she would drive across the country. With her mother. In the pouring rain.

Oh, joy.

She was heading out to Nantucket Island, and she had no idea, no clue, how she would be received. Considering the fact she had barely spoken to her sister in twenty years, she imagined that her reception would be a cold one.

A cold one, indeed.

Chapter Thirteen

Sarah

"Are you sure Ava doesn't mind my coming out?" Sarah asked her mother as they sat in an Amarillo diner eating their supper. Sarah took the southern route through the Arizona and New Mexico desert. The two women stopped at a motel in Phoenix, Arizona the first day and Amarillo, Texas the second.

The ladies had been on the road for 10 hours each day, and Sarah was exhausted. However, her mother was fresh as a daisy, as she slept much of the way when she wasn't reading books in the passenger seat. Poor Bella, however, was beyond antsy. She didn't like traveling very much.

The trip was already 20 hours old, and Sarah had another 30 hours of driving in front of her. The very thought of driving three more 10-hour days made her want to scoop out her eyeballs with a dull knife, but she was just going to have to suck it up and keep going. She literally had no other choice.

Sarah was footing the bill, as her mother, true to form, didn't offer to pay for anything. Not that Sarah could fault her logic, as her mother informed her that, yes, Sarah made her bed and she had to lie in it - her mother said that phrase several times just in the past day or so - which meant that Sarah needed to pay for the trip out east. In full.

Sarah had a very small savings account she'd opened up before she met Nolan. It had $1,500 in it back in the late '90s when she and Nolan got together and had accumulated a modest amount of interest since then. Which meant she had around $2,000 that had to somehow pay for gas, food and motels. Plus, she would have to foot the bill for the car ferry once she got to Hyannis, which was another $400. Thank God her mother was able to pull strings to get her car on that ferry, and it was the off-season. Otherwise, there was no way she would've been able to take her car to the island.

Sarah did the trip calculator before starting her drive. It came to a little under a thousand dollars, not including food or the ferry fee. Which meant she had no margin for error.

Hence, the diner. That was all that Sarah could afford. They were going to eat breakfast the next day at the small breakfast bar in the Holiday Inn where the ladies were staying. Sarah wasn't looking forward to another breakfast of rubber waffles, gelatinous eggs, greasy sausage and soggy pancakes, but it was free, and that was important.

Sarah had a sense of humor about it all, though. She had to laugh that morning when she ate at the previous breakfast bar at the Comfort Inn where they stayed the previous night.

"This made-to-order omelet is the height of luxury these days," she'd said as she dug into her mushroom, pepper and onion omelet that was made by a young guy in

The Beachfront Inn

a chef's hat, as customers lined up to put various veggies and cheeses on their plates to be added to their own omelets. "I guess my days of eating a personal-chef-prepared breakfast of lox imported from Denmark served with a freshly-baked bagel and a Dom Perignon mimosa are well and truly over."

Her mother looked uncomfortable when Sarah asked her about Ava welcoming her. "She knows you're coming," her mother said.

"That doesn't answer my question, Colleen," Sarah said. She always called her mother by her given name when she was annoyed, as she definitely was at that moment. "The question was whether or not she minded my coming."

"I heard the question," her mother said.

"And?"

Her mother shrugged. "I don't really know. I texted her that you were coming out, and she didn't text back, so I assume she's fine."

Sarah sat back, her dinner of chicken-fried steak, green beans and mashed potatoes and gravy suddenly seeming not so appetizing. "You mean, I might get out there, and she might tell me to turn right around."

"No. Listen, I know that you two girls had an argument years and years ago. But Ava isn't one to hold a grudge."

"What do you mean? She's held a grudge all these years, thank you very much. She's given me no indication she's ready to let bygones be bygones."

"And what have you done to make amends?" her mother asked her.

"She called me vapid and annoying," Sarah said.

"As I recall, you told me she called you insipid and lazy," her mother corrected her.

"Six of one," Sarah said. "And she never apologized for it, either."

"Did you apologize to her for calling her a fat hausfrau with three brats?" her mother asked.

"Well, no, but calling her a fat hausfrau wasn't as bad as her calling me insipid and lazy. And implying I was no better than my friends."

Her mother leaned forward and pointed her fork at Sarah. "And *were* you better than that bimbo squad?" she asked her.

"Of course. I wasn't sleeping around, for one thing."

"And? How else did you distinguish yourself from that illustrious group?" her mother asked, the word "illustrious" being used as ironically as possible.

Sarah thought about it. "I. I. I…Well, I guess I really wasn't better than they were. I just thought I was because I wasn't shtupping every guy in sight."

"Uh-huh." Her mother raised an eyebrow, and Sarah knew that look anywhere.

"And Ava accused me of setting back the women's movement 100 years," Sarah said. "That wasn't a fair thing to say."

"Sarah, you were doing nothing worthwhile with your life. You weren't raising kids. You weren't working. You weren't even doing the charity work that other rich women do. As far as Ava was concerned, you were nothing but a cipher. Nothing but a sponge." Her mother nodded her head. "But Ava was wrong about one thing. Women a hundred years ago were contributing to society because they were raising families. So you weren't setting back the woman's movement so much as you were just a dreg."

"A dreg. You're calling me worthless."

"Right," her mother said, taking a bite of her chicken pesto pasta. "Worthless. You were worthless."

"I resent that."

"You resemble that." Her mother smiled. "But you're going to get your sea legs. Better late than never, but you're going to get a second chance to fulfill your potential. What that idiot Nolan did will turn out to be the best thing that has ever happened to you. Mark my words."

Sarah opened her mouth to defend herself but shut it again as she realized that her mother had a point. She *had* been living the past 23 years as a worthless sponge who was contributing exactly zero to the world around her. She'd never been unfaithful to Nolan, not even once, but that didn't make her a good person.

She hated to admit, even to herself, that Ava also had a point all those years ago. But Ava had held up a mirror to her face when she secretly felt she was an absolute loser, and that caused her to lash out. Nothing made losers more defensive than somebody poking at their vulnerabilities. She suddenly realized that.

"Anyhow," Sarah said, wanting to change the subject. "How is Ava going to receive me?"

"Why don't you call her and ask her yourself?" her mother asked.

"Because I don't want to."

"Bull. You're afraid to. Admit it. You're afraid of your own sister."

"I'm not," Sarah said unconvincingly. Truth be told, she actually *was* afraid of her sister. Deathly afraid of her. Afraid Ava would turn her away. Afraid Ava would make her feel horrible about herself, even more horrible than she already felt. Afraid Ava would hold up that same fun-house mirror she held up the last time the sisters had been in the same room and she would run away and hide.

But the reality was that Ava would have to take her in. Otherwise, she would live in her car. Granted, her car was a Range Rover. If she would have to live in a car, she could certainly do worse. But she didn't know what she would do with Bella if it came to her being homeless. And she couldn't lose Bella. That dog was the only thing that had been keeping her sane.

"You're scared," her mother pointed out. "Don't even try to snow me."

"How's your pasta?" Sarah asked, not wanting to talk about Ava anymore. Every time she thought about facing her sister after all these years, she got a cold pit in her stomach.

Her mother shrugged. "It's diner pasta. It's not going to set the world on fire, but it tastes pretty good. What about your dinner?"

"It's actually delicious," Sarah said. "I can't think of the last time I ate a steak that wasn't grass-fed, but I have to say, I've missed out. And I'm sure that these mashed potatoes started out as flakes in a box as opposed to actual potatoes, but they're really good, too." She picked up a sad, limp green bean. "Now the green beans are another story. A whole other story."

"Two out of three ain't bad," her mother said.

"True."

"Listen," her mother said after the two women spent a few minutes in perfect silence. "I'll call Ava and see how she's holding up and how much she wants to see you. Then we can go from there."

"Thank you," Sarah said. "I would appreciate that."

That night, as Sarah sat on the bed, flipping through the channels while absently petting Bella, who was snoring on the bed beside her, her mother called Ava.

The conversation didn't seem to go well. To say the very least.

Her mother started the conversation pleasantly enough. "Ava, I wanted to talk about that text I sent you about your sister," she said.

And then her mother sat on the phone, apparently listening to Ava go into a diatribe for at least five minutes. Sarah closed her eyes as her mother was sitting on the phone silently.

"I know how you feel about your sister, but she needs help," her mother said.

A few more minutes ticked by while her mother listened to Ava some more.

"You just have to keep an open mind," her mother said. "Because she's going to be staying with you for the time being."

At that, Ava's voice was loud enough that Sarah could hear it through her mother's phone. Sarah couldn't make out the words her sister was yelling, only that she *was* yelling.

"It's either you take her in, or it's her living in her car," her mother said. "Are you going to make your sister live in her car?"

And so it went. Her mother stayed on the phone for about fifteen minutes before she hung up and looked at Sarah.

"Well?" Sarah asked.

Her mother shrugged. "She'll come around. What are you watching?"

"Something," Sarah said. "Looks like a *Terminator* movie, but I have no clue which one."

"Is Arnold bad or good?"

"I think he's good."

"And there's some little punk on a motorcycle stealing from an ATM using some kind of high-tech shenanigans?"

"Yeah, I think that happened," Sarah said. "I don't know, mom. I haven't been really paying that much attention to this movie. What did Ava say?"

"She said that you were going to stay with her over her dead body, and I told her that that would be arranged if she continued with her stubborn ways."

"Great. Just great."

Suddenly, her trip seemed even more daunting than ever.

Chapter Fourteen

Ava

Before Sarah arrived, Jackson got a call from his agent. "Mom, I have to get back to L.A.," he said. "Sorry I can't stay, but I have an audition for a speaking part in a huge Netflix series," he told Ava.

Ava was bouncing off the walls when she heard the news. Of course, she was sad to see him go, but she wanted more than anything for Jackson to get his big break after so many years of trying to get his dream. "Go get 'em," she said to him. "Knock that audition out of the park."

"I will," he said, kissing her on the cheek. "I'll call you and let you know how it goes."

In the meantime, Ava and Quinn had gone through the house, and Quinn had given Ava a blueprint on the renovations she had planned for the home. Ava loved the designs that Quinn brought to her. However, the more Ava and Quinn went over all the plans for the house, the more Ava knew she would need an investor.

The blueprints called for knocking down walls to open up the space and replacing all the carpet with distressed hardwood floors. Every bathtub would be replaced with jacuzzi tubs. The kitchen had to be expanded into an industrial kitchen, and every appliance had to be replaced. Every countertop surface in the kitchen and the bathroom would be replaced with granite. Every room would get a new coat of paint. The deck, Ava's favorite part of the house, would be outfitted with a new 10-person hot tub and fire rings. All the bedrooms would be furnished with new California king beds with luxury mattresses and high-thread-count sheets.

The renovation estimates were zooming up quicker than she could keep up, and that was before she factored in the staff she wanted to hire. She envisioned a full menu to serve her guests, not just for breakfast but lunch and dinner as well.

Ava took a deep breath as she sat on the deck, breathing in the smell of burning wood from the house next door. It was early in the morning, and, thus far, nobody was on the beach below. It was quite chilly, so she got out a blanket and wrapped it around her shoulders.

She tried not to think of anything, but it was difficult. Her life was spinning, it seemed, and not necessarily in a good way. When she thought about what needed to be done to renovate the house, and how much it would cost, she got a pit in her stomach.

She *needed* this bed-and-breakfast to be a rousing success. Not just because that was how she was - she never did anything half-assed or even quarter-assed - but also because she didn't have a Plan B. If this venture failed, she wouldn't be able to swing much of anything in her life. She couldn't sell the house, and the upkeep would be beyond her means.

She could get a job as an attorney on the island somewhere. But that would mean her taking the Bar again. She had no desire to do that. And, at this point, she had no desire to practice law ever again. She wasn't happy in that profession. It wasn't just she was defending sleazy billionaires who wanted to skate on taxes. It was that she hated every minute of every day while she was practicing law. The endless research and writing. The conflict with other attorneys. The moody judges who sometimes wanted to bite her head off and sometimes wanted to give her a big hug. The pressure on her from all sides - demanding clients, screeching superiors, calculating opposing attorneys and sometimes irrational judges.

She didn't want to do it anymore. She was tired of the endless fighting. Even if she got a job with a slower-paced firm that represented clients she believed in, she still didn't want to do it. When she closed her eyes and imagined herself screaming on the phone with a belligerent opposing counsel, she wanted to vomit.

She never wanted to set foot in another courtroom, ever again.

So, if she didn't want to practice law, she *had* to make her new business a success. But she'd never owned a business, never put herself on a limb to where whether she sank or swam was entirely up to her. Now, she was on that limb, and it was scary as hell.

But how was she going to swing the renovations?

She knew how she would do it, and she dreaded it. She would have to get an investor, and there was only one person who she could turn to for that.

Her mother.

And the very thought of approaching the cold woman who'd never given Ava an ounce of care or warmth filled her with a cold fear.

Chapter Fifteen

Sarah

Sarah was absolutely exhausted by day four of the grueling 50-hour road trip. Her back was killing her from sitting in one position for so many hours in one go, and she was feeling nauseated from all the truly awful food she'd consumed on the road. She was a woman who was used to having healthy organic meals prepared by a personal chef - generally wild-caught salmon, grass-fed beef, free-range chicken, and eggs served with organic veggies on the side. It was all extremely healthy and tasty because chefs have a way of making healthy food taste good.

In addition to her healthy food, Sarah also engaged in regular yoga, acupuncture, massages, chiropractic adjustments, and spin classes. Her body was treated like a temple all these years. Her gut flora was always optimal because she made sure she ate right and got plenty of probiotics and fiber.

But, on this road trip, it was fried chicken, pork rinds,

and Slim Jims all the way, washed down with bottles of Sprite. Why she decided to go all junk-food-junkie, she didn't know, except that maybe she was rebelling against her old life.

After all, Nolan created the menu for the couple - he gave the personal chef the list of dishes he wanted to have that week, and the chef made it all perfectly. Nolan insisted that Sarah have a daily yoga class, complete with an instructor who came to her house every day. Likewise, with the acupuncture, massage, and spin classes - that was all Nolan.

She was rebelling against all that, and she was paying the price. Her stomach had never felt so awful. Her body had never felt so stiff. She desperately needed to do some yoga, as she understood, perhaps for the first time, just how beneficial those daily classes were. Maybe Nolan was right all along about the two of them being health nuts.

Still, as Sarah sat in yet another motel room watching another 1980s era movie - *St. Elmo's Fire*, which she had loved when she was younger - she felt resentful of her late boyfriend.

She felt guilty for being so angry with him - after all, he was the one whose life was cut short by around 30 years - but she couldn't help how she felt. Her life was destroyed because of his actions, yet he was so stubborn that he wouldn't make a will that ensured she wouldn't be on the streets after his death. He must not have cared about her at all. He knew she'd never be an architect again, and he knew he played a pivotal part in this fate.

Her mother was sitting up on the other queen bed next to her, reading a book, something her mother always seemed to be doing. From time to time, she glanced at her daughter.

"What's wrong with you now?" her mother asked her.

"Why?"

"Why what?"

"Why do you think something's wrong?"

"Because you're sitting there with your arms crossed and a pissed-off look on your face, that's why. I know that scowl anywhere. You're thinking about something that's upsetting you."

Sarah just shook her head. "Nolan was really a jerk."

"I could've told you that."

"Why didn't you?"

"I did. I told you he was demanding, you totally give up your life and you were going to regret it."

"You told me that?" Sarah asked, still not looking at her mother. "When did you tell me that?"

"When you quit your job, dingleberry," her mother said. "You called me after you quit to tell me you needed the freedom to traipse around the world, and you were excited, but I knew what would happen. You lost yourself along the way. In fact, you lost yourself the day you walked away from that architecture firm and started living in that mansion by the sea."

Sarah didn't remember her mother warning her not to quit her career, but she supposed it happened. Her mother didn't lie. In fact, her mother was often too honest.

"I don't remember that conversation," Sarah said.

"Just because you don't remember it doesn't mean it didn't happen. I think you just tuned me out, which you've always done when I'm telling truths you don't want to hear."

Sarah took a deep breath. "That's probably true." Conceding that point to her mother pained her, but there was no getting around it. She probably did tune her mother

The Beachfront Inn

out when she was trying to tell her not to walk away from her architectural career. And she now regretted that move.

Her mother waved her hand dismissively. "Well, there's nothing you can do now unless you know somebody who has a time machine. I know you. You're stewing over there about how you messed up your life. Trust me, regrets do no good unless they teach you to become a better person."

Sarah *did* plan on becoming a better person, but she didn't want to say that out loud to her mother, just in case she screwed up again. She never liked to verbalize anything to anybody unless she was sure she could follow through. And, at the moment, Sarah wasn't certain about that. Starting over seemed so overwhelming, she wasn't sure she could do it.

"By the way, does Ava know Nolan died?" her mother asked her. "I mean, she probably does because I'm sure you posted the news on your Facebook page, right?"

"No, actually, I never posted the news on Facebook or Instagram or Twitter. Anyhow, Ava never friended me on Facebook or followed me on Instagram or Twitter, so she wouldn't have gotten the news that way. And I never called her to tell her, either."

Colleen shook her head. "Really. You never told your Facebook pals about Nolan's dying?"

"No. I only wanted my page to be about happy things in my life." Sarah had an image she wanted to maintain on social media. She was determined not to post anything that would contradict that image - that of a carefree, wealthy woman who had it all.

"Well, you're what's wrong with social media, you know. You just want the world to know about what's going great and not tell about the bad parts. No wonder people get depressed when they read social media posts. Everybody thinks everybody else is making out like a bandit and have it made, just because everybody needs to maintain some kind of ridiculous image. I didn't think you were like that, too, but apparently, you are."

"Guilty as charged," Sarah said. "Who wants to hear about depressing things?"

"That's not the point. The point is, you and everyone like you are so damned determined you're going to make everybody jealous of your life that you don't want to show the reality. I don't know why you think you need to maintain a façade to people who don't even really know you, but I guess it's your life."

That night, as she tossed and turned, unable to sleep, Sarah thought about the movie, *St. Elmo's Fire*, again. The scene where Jules had Alec come to get her in the middle of the night because she was too coked-up to drive hit home with Sarah and made her sick. She couldn't sleep that night because she ruminated on that scene, over and over again.

It brought back unpleasant memories for Sarah, that movie, and that scene. And, just like that, Sarah was angry again at her life and at fate.

She had to get on with things. But how?

Chapter Sixteen

Sarah

Finally, after 50 hours of driving over 5 grueling days, Sarah arrived in Boston, where she said her goodbyes to her mother, who had to be back on the bench.

"Thanks, mom," Sarah said, giving her mother a hug. "For coming out and helping me pack and drive here."

"Oh, it wasn't a problem," her mother said. "Now, you don't have cross words with your sister when you see her. You don't get cross with her, and she won't get cross with you. Remember that."

Sarah nodded her head, but she doubted what her mother said was true about her sister. After all, Ava was the aggressor in her visit. She was the one who insulted Sarah's friends and then proceeded to insult Sarah herself. Sarah was merely reacting to Ava's meanness when she called her a fat hausfrau. Anyway, Ava wasn't fat at that time. She was overweight in high school, but she was looking pretty decent by the time she'd arrived in Monterey to see her.

Sarah only called her fat because she knew that that was the one thing Ava was sensitive about, and Sarah wanted to dig the knife in right where it hurt the most. Again, however, she only did that because Ava poked her right where it hurt *her* the most. Ava calling her insipid and lazy hit her where she was most tender and raw, and those words stung like crazy. Sarah wanted to strike back in kind.

After dropping her mother off at her home, Sarah drove to Hyannis and found the Steamship Authority car ferry. Her car was secured on the ferry an hour later, and Sarah had her own seat.

In 2 1/2 hours she would be on the island, and, shortly after that, she would be arriving at Ava's home. She took some Tums out of her bag because she felt incredibly sick. It was the combination of the garbage food she'd been eating, the motion of the ferry on the choppy waters and the prospect of seeing Ava that was making her feel so crappy.

Her head was swimming. She went to the railing and looked out on the open water. She thought about the last time she was on a boat, which was when she and Nolan had taken his yacht out to a resort in Ensenada, Mexico. At that time, she saw several gray whales in the water and many schools of dolphins that leaped along next to the boat. On that trip, she and Nolan ate their weight in stone crabs, went hiking every day and visited 20 different wineries. They paraglided off of cliffs and went surfing every day. They rode ATVs through the mountains and made love under waterfalls.

Now, she was alone, save for Bella, who was such a trouper. At that moment, the pooch was asleep at Sarah's feet.

"Bella, at this moment in time, you're all I have," Sarah

said sadly. As she stood at the railing, she really felt the heaviness of her grief over her lost life. She'd never been alone for any period of time - she had always had a boyfriend, from the age of 15 until the current day. She was the ultimate in serial monogamist because she literally went from one guy to another. Of course, Nolan was her longest relationship, but he certainly wasn't the first.

And now, for the first time, she would be completely alone. Her bed wasn't going to have another person in it. There would be nobody there to tell her she was special. She wondered if she was ordinary after all. She never felt she was - she was the queen bee in high school. When she was with Nolan, she ran with the wealthy women who were married to CEOs, athletes and actors. She kept a rarefied company, and she, too, felt rarefied.

Now, who was she? An almost-homeless super-thin blonde woman who still turned heads wherever she went? She was such a mess of contradictions. She was almost a bag lady, she was flat broke, and she would rely on the kindness of a sister who she hadn't really spoken to in 20 years. Yet, she knew that the men on this ferry were checking her out. Men always had.

But so what? She was still told she was beautiful. Ageless. Of course she was ageless. She'd been getting thrice-weekly facials for the past 23 years and had been pampered all this time. She never lost sleep. She ate well. She lathered on sunscreen every moment of every day. Her life was as stress-free as any could possibly be. She had amazing genetics. All this meant that, at 53, she could pass for a woman in her 30s. But what did that mean, in the grand scheme of things?

What did her looks mean when she literally had $100 in the bank and had no idea how she could make money?

How would being beautiful help her find her own identity out in this world when she had no idea who she really was?

She was getting cold, so she hugged herself, pulling her coat around her tighter. As she got closer to the island, the fog started to roll in and, before she knew it, she couldn't see her hand in front of her face.

When the boat docked, she got off and got her car and drove to Ava's house in the heavy fog. The weather felt oppressive, and she thought about the sunny beach she had left behind in Monterey. Her heart was in her throat, and her hands were shaking as she drove along the road, terrified she would get to Ava's door and be turned away.

At that time, she had never felt more depressed in her life.

Chapter Seventeen

Ava

"Sugar, when is your sister going to be getting here?" Quinn asked Ava. They were sitting around a fire on Ava's deck, listening to the surf and watching the fog roll in like a heavy veil. Hallie was also there, and it was their wine night, which was a Wednesday night tradition with the ladies.

"I have no clue," Ava said. "My mother called me a couple of days ago when they were in Amarillo, Texas. She told me they were still a good three days away. So, I guess Sarah will be here any minute now."

"And what are you going to do with her?" Hallie asked. "Your mother said she would live in her car."

"I'm quite sure that Sarah won't be living in her car," Ava said. "Trust me, that girl has skills, beauty and charm. She'll be living with one of the millionaires on this island before the week is out." Ava rolled her eyes and sipped her wine. "God knows, finagling a rich guy to support her is what she does best. It's the only thing she knows. And she has the looks to get the job done, too."

"How do you know she still looks good?" Quinn asked. "For all you know, she might've aged just like the rest of us did. Crow's feet, laugh lines, extra junk in the trunk."

"Says the woman who can give Nicole Kidman a run for her money," Ava said.

Quinn laughed long and loud at that remark. "Oh, please, Nicole Kidman, my ass. Literally. You see that woman in her bra and panties in *Big Little Lies*? I look like that in my dreams. In my dreams. You just think I look like that because you ain't seen me in a bikini, but you'd never compare me to her again if you did. We're talking cellulite city. My thighs have bigger dimples than Jennifer Garner's cheeks. So does my ass, while we're on the subject of cheeks. And the last time I had an eight-pack was when I got drunk with my cousin from the bayou last summer."

Hallie had to laugh along with Quinn as she described her bodily imperfections. "Why are we so hard on ourselves?" she asked. "I'll bet even Nicole Kidman looks in the mirror and criticizes herself. Meanwhile, men can have beer guts and bird legs and think they're the cock of the walk."

Ava laughed at what the two ladies were saying. "Ain't that the truth," she said. "We ladies are so hard on ourselves. But to answer your earlier question, Quinn, Sarah is still as stunningly beautiful as ever."

"How do you know?" Hallie asked.

"Because I've been stalking her Facebook page for the past 17 years, ever since Facebook started, really. I never friended her, though. Her page is open to the public. Anybody can see her posts. She posted a picture of her and

The Beachfront Inn

her ex-boyfriend, Nolan, just last week. She looks 25. I also stalk her on Instagram, and she posts pictures there, too."

Quinn nodded her head. "This is the sister you hate?" she asked.

"Yes," Ava said. "Well, hate is a strong word, but I definitely don't like her."

"Yet, you've kept up on her all these years," Quinn said. "I think you care about your sister more than you want to admit to."

Ava sipped her wine and didn't say anything. Truth be told, she loved her sister very much. That was why she was so hurt by their estrangement. She was ashamed that much of the reason she was so hateful to her sister when she visited her was because she was so jealous she couldn't see straight.

She didn't like that part of herself very much, the petty inner child who still resented her sister because everything always came so very easy to her. Ava never knew Sarah to work at anything at all. She was effortlessly popular in school. She was the trendsetter and the leader of the popular girl clique, and she never lifted a finger to get to the top. And, once she was there at the top, everybody in the school seemed to be there to serve her somehow. From the trail of football-playing boys carrying her books around the school halls to the crowds of fawning females girl-crushing on her and following her around, Sarah just seemed to glide through life. Her feet never seemed to touch the ground.

Sarah just carried this entitlement into her adult life. Ava resented her for this. Sarah should have had the same trials and problems that everyone else did, but she didn't. She was handed everything when the sisters were growing up and handed everything when she was an adult.

"I guess," Ava finally said to Quinn. "I guess I care

about her. She is my sister, after all. But that doesn't mean I'll welcome her with open arms. I mean, I'll let her stay for a couple of days, just long enough for her to snag her next victim and go and live with him. I feel sorry for her future victim, though I really do. The only thing she knows how to do for a man is spend his money."

Quinn shook her head. "Sugar, you don't know about her life. You don't know about her relationship. They broke up, doesn't that tell you something?"

"Yes, it tells me her boyfriend finally had enough of her layabout and profligate ways and went and found a woman who might pull her weight," Ava said.

Hallie put her hand on Ava's arm. "You're too close to this," she said. "You're too blinded by your resentment of your sister to realize she has her own side of the story. And I think you should listen to it when she gets here. Listen without prejudice, just like the title of the George Michael album all those years ago."

"Okay," Ava said. "I'll try."

Just then, she heard the doorbell ring.

Sarah? Surely not. Surely, Sarah would at least text her before showing up.

Ava's heart suddenly was in her throat. Why was she so nervous?

"Sugar, I'll go and answer the door," Quinn said.

"Okay," Ava said, feeling her stomach plummet into her shoes. It had been 20 years since she'd seen her sister. How should she react? "But tell her to come back tomorrow. We're having such a nice time right now, I just don't want her spoiling it."

Quinn rolled her eyes. "Sugar, I won't tell her that," she said. "You might as well rip off that band-aid right now. If I tell her to go away, you'll be thinking about her the whole time we're up here having a good time."

"Please," Ava said. "Tell her to come back tomorrow."

Quinn raised her eyebrows and shook her head and muttered something unintelligible under her breath. "Okay," she finally said. "But you're making a big mistake."

"Noted," Ava said.

Chapter Eighteen

Ava

As Ava and Hallie sat in their lounge chairs, Ava heard Quinn greeting Sarah at the door. Hallie raised an eyebrow, sipped her wine, and said nothing. Which spoke volumes, really, as did the look on Hallie's face. It was obvious that Hallie, like Quinn, did not approve of Ava's blowing Sarah off.

About five minutes later, Quinn reappeared on the deck.

"Sugar," Quinn said in an exasperated tone. Ava sat up and took notice because Quinn never sounded annoyed. Hallie often did, but Quinn? Never. "Go down there and greet your sister. If you want her to find a hotel tonight, you have to go down there and tell her that. I answered the door, but there was no way I would be the one to give her the bad news."

"It's not bad news," Ava said. "I'm not ready for her. If she wanted me to greet her with open arms, then she should've texted me with an ETA."

"Regardless, she's your sister, and you haven't seen her in over 20 years. What I wouldn't give to see my brother again, just one more time," Quinn said. She had small tears in her eyes that she wiped away.

And, all at once, Ava understood why Quinn was so adamant in trying to get Ava to make up with her sister. She sometimes forgot that Quinn's Irish twin, James, died of brain cancer some years back. James and Quinn were only 11 months apart, born in the same year, which was what made them Irish twins. Quinn told Ava they were as close as two siblings could be. His death had devastated her.

"I'm sorry," Ava said. "I'm being so insensitive. I have a sister, and I need to appreciate that."

"Yes, you do," Quinn said. "Now, let's go downstairs and greet your sister properly."

Ava realized that when she got out of her lounger, her heart was pounding out of her chest. *Breathe, Ava, breathe.*

She was as nervous as a woman meeting a blind date. And she had no idea why.

Chapter Nineteen

Sarah

Sarah waited at the threshold of Ava's house, feeling terrified. Why was her heart pounding out of her chest? Why were her hands shaking like a leaf? This was her sister, dammit, the woman she once adored and who was now a complete stranger. Ava didn't even have a Facebook or Instagram page that Sarah could read every day to keep up with her sister's whereabouts and goings-on. So, Sarah had no clue what Ava was even like these days. Their mother said Ava had lost her job, but that was literally the only thing Sarah knew about her once-beloved sister.

And that was pathetic, Sarah thought, and, what's more, it was all her own fault. Why did she blow Ava off for so many years? If she had to do it all again, she would've left Nolan years ago and made up with her sister. If she would've taken that path, she knew she would've been much happier in her life.

But, she didn't, and here she was. On Ava's doorstep, hat in hand, hoping and praying her sister didn't hate her.

She saw a tall blonde lady coming down the stairs and her heart sunk. Where was Ava?

"Hey there," the woman said when she opened the door and enveloped Sarah in a warm hug. "I'm Quinn, one of Ava's friends. She asked me to come down here and greet you."

Sarah hugged Quinn back and plastered a smile on her face. Was Ava going to turn her away? If so, she didn't know what she would do. She literally spent her last dime ferrying her car here. Which, of course, begged the question of what she would do for money until she found her way. She figured she could sign up to be an Uber driver as soon as she licensed her car and got a new driver's license. Or maybe find a job as a hostess or a waitress.

But, right at that moment, she was flat broke. She couldn't afford another hotel room.

She knew she should've texted Ava to tell her she was coming, but she was afraid Ava would've texted her back to tell her to go away. Better to ask for forgiveness than permission, Sarah thought. If she showed up unannounced, then she could maybe sweet-talk her way into Ava's home. But if she showed up after Ava texted her not to, that was another level.

Sarah nodded her head. "I guess Ava didn't want to see me so soon. I don't blame her. I should've texted her or called her about my coming tonight." She swallowed hard. "I hope she wants to see me, in general, though. Maybe not tonight, but I hope she'll see me sometime soon."

"Just a sec," Quinn said, putting her finger up. "I'll be right back."

A few minutes later, Ava came down the stairs with Quinn and with Hallie, Ava's best friend from college.

Sarah stood there in front of her sister and didn't quite know how to react. Should she go over and hug her? Shake her hand? Just stand there and figure out what she would do?

Because she felt apprehensive, she decided simply to stand there awkwardly. This was the sister she hadn't seen in over 20 years, and she just stood there.

Ava smiled, which made Sarah relax just a little. "Hi," Sarah finally said. "You look good."

Ava nodded her head. "As do you. Of course. You know Hallie from way back, and you just met Quinn," she said, gesturing to the two women. "We were enjoying a bottle of wine on the deck. The fog has just lifted, and it's really a beautiful evening. Maybe you'd like to join us? You and your beautiful mutt there?" At that, Ava kneeled down and let Bella cover her face with kisses. "Sweet girl, what kind is she?"

"She was a rescue," Sarah said. "Probably just a Heinz."

"Well, she's a sweet Heinz," Ava said. "Looks like a Pit mix."

"I think that's what she is."

Ava nodded and continued to scratch Bella's ears. "So, what about my invite?"

Sarah hesitated, suddenly feeling like she was forcing a situation that maybe she shouldn't have. Like she was an intruder, an interloper. She hated feeling that way. "I'd like to join you tonight. But if you would prefer I find a hotel room tonight, I understand."

Ava shook her head. "No, no. Don't be silly. Come on

up on the deck. There's a bottle of wine with your name on it."

Quinn smiled. "Is there a bag I can bring in from your car?" she asked.

"Well, there is," Sarah said, but she didn't want to be presumptuous and just assume she was welcome to stay. "But we can deal with that later. Thanks, though, for the offer."

Ava put her hand on Quinn's shoulder. "Go ahead and get Sarah's bag," she said. "And take it upstairs to the first bedroom on the left. And thank you." Then she addressed Sarah. "I'm afraid there are not many accommodations just yet, but there's a sleeping bag in every bedroom and a pillow. Obviously, I haven't had the chance to get this place furnished and everything."

Sarah felt a sense of relief she and Bella weren't going to have to spend the night in her Range Rover. "I can sleep on the hard floor if need be," Sarah said. "I'm really sorry for barging in on you like this."

Ava waved a hand dismissively. "Not a problem, really. I just know you're used to a certain amount of luxury, and I'm sorry you're going to be roughing it here."

Sarah smiled, perhaps for the first time in a long time. "It'll be just like when we were kids and going camping. Remember that six-mile hike we took in the Smoky Mountains? I can still hear the creek rushing by next to our tent."

Ava nodded her head. "And the black bear got into the camp next to us and ate all their food."

"Who knew that ready-to-eat meals could be so tasty?" That was what the girls ate on that trip - dehydrated meals that, when you added water, tasted like Chicken á la King. After hiking all that way up a mountain, the girls were starving, and anything would taste amazing.

Sarah thought those dehydrated meals were more memorable to her than all the Michelin-starred dinners she'd eaten since then.

"And what about all those trips out to Charleston and Myrtle Beach?" Ava asked. "We usually camped out by the beach then."

"I can still smell the charcoal coming from the camp next door," Sarah said. "And we were so dumb. Remember how we got so excited about catching those tiny clams because we were convinced they would make pearls for us? We thought we would get rich for sure."

"Our Uncle Nick had to be the one to tell us those clams weren't going to make pearls. We were so disappointed," Ava said.

The girls' Uncle Nick was their mother's brother and didn't have any kids of his own, so he was more than happy to take the girls on vacation every summer. They went to Charleston, South Carolina many times, the Smoky Mountains several times, the Rocky Mountains several times and, once, ended up visiting the Grand Tetons in Wyoming. They also went to Yellowstone Park and saw Old Faithful.

"For some reason, you decided you weren't going to let the seagulls land on the beach. Every time they tried, you chased after them," Sarah said.

"Remember how badly I wanted to find a sand dollar? I spent the entire vacation looking for one, but I never did," Ava remembered.

"Yes! I joined you in looking, but we could never find one for some reason. And remember those awful sand flies that stung and kept on stinging?" Sarah said.

"Oh, yes. And you got so sunburned that one time you fell asleep in the sun that you couldn't walk for several days. I still have pictures of your lobster legs," Ava said.

"I still have a dermatologist check my entire body every year because I'm surprised I don't have skin cancer from all those sunburns I got back in the day. But those were the days when we didn't put sunblock on but slathered our skin in baby oil and then laid out on a reflective blanket. With our fair skin, it probably wasn't the wisest choice in the world."

Ava smiled slightly, but Sarah could tell she still wasn't warming up. "I'm quite sure those memories probably don't mean much to you anymore, after all the experiences you've had around the world," Ava said.

You'd be surprised if you knew how much those memories mean to me, Sarah thought.

Chapter Twenty

Ava

When Ava went down the stairs to meet her sister, she was a little apprehensive. Of course, Sarah hadn't aged a day. She was still tall, fit and stunningly beautiful. Her enormous blue eyes were as bright and clear as they ever were. Her cheekbones could still cut glass. Her light blonde hair was cut short and chic. She wasn't wearing makeup, and she didn't need to. She didn't have a single line on her face, and her skin was as supple and smooth as a baby's. She was wearing fitted jeans and a tank top, with a jean jacket over it. Sarah took off her jean jacket when she got in the door, and her arms were toned and strong.

As usual, Ava felt frumpy next to her supermodel-looking sister. *Would she ever stop feeling inferior to Sarah?*

The sisters reminisced some in the foyer about past camping trips they took, and Ava almost forgot about the last time they had seen one another. At that time, Sarah was a woman she didn't know. She was vapid and shallow. Ava didn't think they had anything in common anymore.

Now, with the memories that bonded them as kids brought up again, Ava remembered how much she really did love her sister.

But she still was guarded. She didn't really know why, but she wasn't willing to let Sarah in so easily.

Sarah and Bella followed her, Quinn and Hallie up to the deck. Ava looked behind her and saw that both Quinn and Hallie were eagerly talking to Sarah, and it seemed like those three were bonding already.

The women got to the deck, and Sarah looked around.

"This terrace isn't as nice as yours," Ava said. "But I like it."

Sarah shook her head. "Stop, please. Just stop. The terrace you were on in the house where I lived wasn't my terrace. It was Nolan's terrace. It was always Nolan's terrace. That mansion wasn't mine, either. None of it was mine, only Nolan's. And my memories of our vacations when we were children are precious to me. You don't know how much. So, please stop minimizing things, Ava. Stop trying to apologize for things that you have no business apologizing for. The terrace is gorgeous."

Ava felt embarrassed as she realized she *was* apologizing for things. She assumed that Sarah was secretly looking at her new home and thinking that it was all inferior. How could she not when she had lived in a home that a movie star would be happy in?

"Well, sit down," Ava said. "Tell me about your trip out here."

The ladies all sat down, and Quinn poured Sarah a glass of wine. Ava had to bite her tongue because she wanted to apologize for their choice of wine that evening.

They were drinking out of a bottle of Luzón cabernet that cost less than $30. She was sure that Sarah was used to drinking wines that cost much more than that and probably were as smooth as silk. This wine had a slightly bitter bite, although Ava had tasted worse.

Sarah took a sip of the wine and smiled. "I like this," she said. "It's full-bodied and dry with just a hint of oak, black cherry and citrus."

Ava nodded her head. She didn't know much about wine. She just knew what she liked, but she couldn't possibly tell someone exactly *why* she liked this wine or that.

"I agree," Ava said. "With what you said."

Quinn grinned. "I don't go into all that with wine. If it's tasty and don't give me much of a hangover, I'm good."

Sarah swiveled slightly in her lounger. "Oh, but there's so much more to know about wine," she said. "Tannins and acidity, varietals and regions. Flavors and taste, which are two different things. What wines pair with what foods. I mean -"Sarah stopped. "I'm sorry, wine is a bit of a passion of mine."

Ava cocked her head. She was surprised that Sarah even had a passion all these years, aside from her passion for spending her boyfriend's money.

"I guess you've tasted wines around the world, literally," Ava said. "Most people can drink a glass of wine from Brazil. It's easy enough to find Brazilian wines. But you've actually drunk wine *in* Brazil. And Chile. And Hungary. And -"

"Right," Sarah said. "That *was* my life. Was is the operative word. And now, well, I'm just a middle-aged woman who's starting over and has no idea exactly where to begin. Anyhow, you were asking about how the trip was. It was hell, driving for so many hours for so many days in a row.

The Beachfront Inn

But mom was with me the whole way, so I had a road partner, which made it not as bad as it could've been."

Ava bit her tongue. It hurt that their mother went out of her way to help Sarah move. Their mother would never do something like that for her. Their mother wouldn't lift a finger for her. Yet,Colleen spent 50 hours on the road with Sarah and helped her pack and load up her SUV.

Yet another reason to resent Sarah - she got the maternal attention Ava always hungered for but never got. That was another thing that always came easy for Sarah and never for Ava.

"How did you convince our mother to do that for you?"

"What? Helping me get out of that house?" Sarah shrugged. "I just called her and told her what was going on, and she came out to help." She cocked her head and studied Ava. "I know what you're thinking."

"You do? What am I thinking?" Ava asked.

"You think that our mother would never do something like that for you. Helping you move, sitting in a car for 50 hours. Eating greasy food in greasy spoons and hanging out in Comfort Inns for five days."

"Right. She would never do something like that for me."

Sarah sighed. "That was always an insecurity you've had, isn't it? And you really don't know why I've always been closer to our mother than you, do you?"

"No, but it would certainly be helpful to know because I'm supposed to see her this coming Monday. I have to talk to her about investing in this place."

"I think it has something to do with the fact that our mother always knew that you could stand on your own. She's always seen me as a mess-up who needs her guidance. I think she's just guilty of giving special attention to the daughter who needs it more."

Ava looked at Sarah, thinking that Sarah had grown another head. "What are you talking about? You needed her, and I didn't? Is that what you think?"

"Yes, that's what I think. See, you think I had such an amazing life out in California. I didn't. And mom knew this."

Ava rolled her eyes. "Come on, Sarah, you didn't need to quit your job and follow that man around."

"Yes, you're right. That was a choice I made, and it was the wrong one. And you might think that I can just pick up my life where I left it 24 years ago, but it's not that easy. I can't even get an architectural license anymore, quite literally, but I don't want to go into that. So, I don't really know what-"

All at once, Sarah was crying.

Quinn was the one who was physically closest to Sarah, so she was the one who put her arm around Sarah's shoulder and drew her in. Ava came over on the other side of Sarah and put her hand on Sarah's shoulder.

"Sarah, what is it?" Ava asked her.

"My life just spiraled 20 years ago," she said. There was a box of Kleenex next to her lounger, and she took one of the tissues and blew her nose.

"What happened 20 years ago?" Ava asked her.

"Never mind," she said. "I can't even talk about this right now. But I wanted to get out of my relationship a long time ago. I knew my life was becoming more and more inconsequential, even though for the first four years or so I told myself I was living the life I'd always dreamed of. I always thought I would travel the world when I was a little girl. I was always getting books out of the library about places around the globe. When Nolan asked me to be his globe-trotting partner, I felt like

The Beachfront Inn

Cinderella. So, for a few years, it was fun. I was living the dream."

Ava nodded her head. She *did* remember that about Sarah. When the girls were in elementary school, their mother would take them to the public library. Ava would usually find various mystery novels - Nancy Drew, The Hardy Boys, that kind of thing - but Sarah would find books about places. Sarah would check out books about Sri Lanka, Ireland, and Russia on one library trip. She would get books out about Argentina, Nigeria, and Honduras on the next trip. And so it went. She was always curious about other lands, other people, other cultures, other food.

"What happened after a few years?" Hallie asked. She was sitting with the other ladies and hadn't yet said much. Still, she was clearly interested, because she'd been listening the entire time.

Sarah shook her head. "I wanted my life back. I wanted to throw away the fantasy and go back to what I was supposed to do - design buildings. But I couldn't."

"Why?" Quinn asked. "What prevented you from going back to architecture?"

Sarah looked at the waves that were coming in and sipped her wine. "I can't talk about it right now. It's still too painful all these years later. Too raw. But let's just say my profession was closed to me, and I didn't know what else to do. So, I stayed with Nolan."

Ava crossed her arms in front of her. "Sarah, you're just going to have to suck it up and get back into it. There are architectural firms around here, I'm sure, although I think most of the architects on this island are probably solo practitioners. So, you probably don't belong on Nantucket. You should go to New York or Boston. Or go back west and apply around in Los Angeles."

Sarah just stared at Ava. "You don't listen very well, do you?" Her tone was bitter, and she had a scowl on her beautiful face.

"What did I miss?" Ava asked. She was confused on why Sarah was apparently attacking her for no reason. Again.

"I just said I can't go back to architecture. Not that I don't want to, because I do. I've wanted to for many years. It was what I studied for. It was what I committed my blood, sweat and tears for at KU and Berkeley, getting my Bachelor's and then my Master's degree. But I can't. Get that through your head, Ava."

Ava rolled her eyes. "You just have to get your license back, that's all. I'm sure you can take some refresher classes and retake your exam, but it shouldn't be a problem."

Quinn went over to Ava. "Ava, I think Sarah has a story there about why she can't get her architectural license back. And she doesn't want to tell us. Let it go, Sugar."

Ava opened her mouth and then shut it again. "Okay. I won't pry."

"Thank you," Sarah said. "Anyhow, I know mom informed you I would stay here. I know how our mother is - she tells you something matter-of-factly like it's a done deal, when it's not. So, don't worry, I'm not making assumptions. But I wanted to offer my services to you."

Sarah looked at Ava with such hope in her eyes that Ava melted just a little bit. Ava was starting to remember the love she had always felt for her little sister. Even when she didn't like Sarah very much, and there were many days when that was the case when the two were growing up, Ava always loved Sarah.

"Your services?"

"Yes. As a sommelier. I mean, I'm not certified as one, but I've studied wines around the world for the past 24 years. I've visited wineries in Argentina, France, Australia, Portugal, South Africa, Spain, Italy, Germany, Greece, New Zealand and Chile. I know everything there is to know about wine and how to take into account the tannins, acidity, sweetness, flavor profiles and body when pairing the wine with food. I'm in touch with winery owners around the world, and I've been to enough wineries to know which ones are the best. I know the proper method of storage for all different kinds of wine and the best way to cook with it and-"

"Wait," Ava said. "I need to stop you. Sarah, I would love to hire you on as a sommelier, but I'm tapped out as it is. I have to find the money to renovate this place from stem to stern, not to mention hire somebody to cook for the guests. I just don't think I have the budget for a sommelier."

Ava said that to Sarah, but she knew she would have to ask their mother to be an investor in the place anyhow. Their mother seemed to have a soft spot for Sarah, so if Ava wanted to hire her sister, her mother would certainly give her the money to do so.

Sarah nodded her head. "Ava, you don't have to pay me. Just give me a place to stay. I'll work for free."

"How will that work?" Ava asked. "Even if I let you stay here and I didn't pay you, you're still going to need money. I'll be able to provide you meals, too. But you're going to have expenses you'll have to cover. I'm going to have to pay you if I hired you."

Sarah looked like she was holding her breath. "Ava, I hate coming to you with this," she said. "And, believe me, this is the most humiliating thing I've ever done. But I feel like I really have no choice but to throw myself at your mercy. I don't think I could find a job with anybody as a sommelier. I don't have a certification, so I can't imagine anybody else taking a chance on me. I have no other skills."

Ava blinked. On the one hand, Sarah was her sister, and she loved her. On the other, well, her gorgeous sister made her choices. They were poor choices that brought her to this place - if she was without skills or the proper job experiences that would allow her to get a decent position, that was on her. Ava wasn't responsible for her, and she shouldn't try to guilt Ava into taking responsibility for her, either.

"I'm sorry, Sarah. I just don't have the budget for that. But you can stay here until you get on your feet. I recommend finding a job at one of the restaurants in town, waiting tables or hostessing. Then you can find a rental in town."

Sarah nodded her head. She looked defeated, deflated. "I guess that's fair," she said. "I really thought I could put my knowledge of wines to work, though. I think you would be surprised about how much I could bring to the table if you would just give me a chance."

"Well, maybe you can work your way into being a sommelier for one of the more upscale restaurants in town. Start as a bartender, impress the restaurant owner and see if you can become a sommelier at some point. Work for it. Don't expect it to be handed to you like everything else has ever been during your life."

Sarah breathed in and out, and Ava knew she had struck a nerve. "I'm glad that you think that I've always been handed everything. But you really couldn't be more wrong."

"Oh, okay, I'm sorry. I just thought that the fact that you've been living with a man who has let you sponge off of him for -"

"You know what? I'm sorry I came here," Sarah said. "I knew it was a mistake. I knew you couldn't change. You

The Beachfront Inn

resented me all those years ago, and you apparently still do. I can't seem to catch a break with you. You don't have to let me stay here. I'll find other accommodations."

Ava nodded her head. "I think that might be a good idea."

At that, Sarah got out of her lounger. "Quinn, it was very good to meet you. Hallie, it was great seeing you again. I'll show myself out."

Quinn raised her eyebrows. "You have to at least show her out," she said.

"No," Sarah said. "Don't bother."

At that, she walked through the door that led to the sunroom, which, in turn, led to the stairs. A few minutes later, Ava heard Sarah get into her car.

Ava sighed heavily. "That went well," she joked.

But Quinn and Hallie weren't laughing.

"Ava, do you know how to get in touch with Sarah?" Hallie asked her.

"No," Ava admitted. "I don't have her cell number."

"Don't you think that's a problem?" Hallie asked.

Ava shrugged. "We haven't seen each other all these years, so it's not like I'm going to miss her presence. And it was her choice that we haven't seen each other, by the way, not mine. I've tried many times over the years to get together with her, and she's always been too busy." Ava rolled her eyes. "She always refused to visit me over the holidays or invite me out to see her, so we grew apart. And now, here she is, wanting something from me? That doesn't sit well with me. At all."

"Sugar, that's not the point," Quinn said. "That's your sister. Your flesh and blood. And she needs you."

"Well, it's too late now," Ava said. "She's left without a

word and without leaving a number. I can't help she's so sensitive that she can't accept the truth about her life."

"So, good riddance, is that your attitude?" Quinn asked.

"I don't want to talk about it," Ava said. "I'm sure she'll land on her feet. Somebody will take care of her, just like always."

Quinn and Hallie didn't address the situation anymore that evening. Ava made clear she was in no mood to discuss it, so that was that.

Even so, Ava knew that when she saw her mother, she would have to factor in the salary for a sommelier when she submitted her proposal.

And then she would put Sarah at the top of her list when it came time to hire this sommelier. Because Ava did know that her sister needed her. Sarah was sincere about that. Ava regretted her words to her sister and hoped she could make amends.

If it wasn't too late.

Chapter Twenty-One

Ava

That Monday, Ava made an appointment to see her mother. She felt humiliated because she had to set up the entire visit with her mother's personal assistant, Chloe. Chloe was the one who did everything for her, from setting up tennis matches at the local country club to picking up her mother's dry cleaning. Chloe was the social director of sorts for her mother, too. She ensured that her mother showed up at all the right society functions. Chloe was also the party planner for her mother's own charity balls and functions she'd hold in her massive Victorian-era home.

Ava had never been to this particular home. Her mother had moved to the area several years before, after accepting a First Circuit Court of Appeals position. Colleen was thrilled about getting the promotion to the circuit court in Boston, not just because it was a major step-up, but also because she wanted to be closer to Charlotte and Siobhan, who were living in Boston with Matthew, Charlotte's husband. Ava considered this ironic, considering all the issues she and her mother had over the years. Her mother supported Charlotte and Sarah. Why didn't she ever support her?

Ava felt nervous as she approached the expansive historic home situated in the Beacon Hill area of Boston. It had three levels, a large stone porch, a series of pitched roofs and a turret, and a massive red door that sported a stained-glass bird in the middle. It was a home that was evidently built before 1900 and was listed as historic in the National Register of Historic Places for Boston.

A woman answered the door. She had a short bob, and she was dressed somewhat formally, with a dark blue suit with red piping, pantyhose and pumps.

"You must be Ava," she said, extending her hand. "I'm Chloe. Your mother's personal assistant."

Ava smiled and shook her hand. "Right. I'm Ava. The prodigal daughter returns."

"Come on in," she said. "Colleen is in the library. She's waiting for you."

She led Ava through several rooms, including what looked to be a living room, a den and a formal dining room. At the back of the house was an open space that sported shelves and shelves of books. Historical biographies of famous figures such as Abraham Lincoln, Harry S. Truman, Alexander Hamilton, Lewis and Clark, Mark Twain, Albert Einstein and John F. Kennedy shared space with entire sets of legal tomes. There was also plenty of fiction, many of these by authors she hadn't heard of. Her mother also seemed to have everything Tom Clancy and Stephen King ever wrote.

Ava swallowed hard as she approached her mother, who was sitting in a large wing-backed chair. Her mother was naturally slim and still was ever so, with bony fingers, one of which sported an enormous emerald ring. Considering she was some 78 years old, her face was smooth, with wrinkles around her mouth and eyes that weren't yet deep-set but were still as mild as those seen on women 20 years her junior. Her blue eyes were as clear as they ever were, and Ava imagined that her mind was probably just as sharp.

If anybody wanted to cast an actress to play her mother in a movie, that actress would be Holland Taylor, Ava thought.

Ava always felt encouraged by her mother's aging because she aged gracefully. Ava dearly hoped she'd be as fortunate. If she could look half as good as Colleen Flynn when she was 75, she'd be a happy woman indeed.

Her mother didn't get out of the chair when Ava walked into the room. She gestured to a chair next to her own and raised an eyebrow. Ava sat down in the other chair, which was just as large as her mother's, and was as straight-backed and uncomfortable. Colleen cocked her head as she examined Ava and then nodded slightly.

"Still slouching, I see," she said. "But you aren't as heavy as you used to be, so good for you." Colleen's voice was low, hoarse and brittle as if she'd spent her entire life smoking a pack a day. However, her mother had always been a nonsmoker, so Ava always assumed that her mother just naturally had a voice like Brenda Vaccaro.

Ava realized that her mother was right - she *was* slouching in the straight-backed chair. That was because a straight-backed chair always made Ava physically uncomfortable, so she slumped a bit because that was a much more comfortable position for her.

"Um, good to see you, too?"

Her mother snorted when she said that. "I didn't say that I was happy to see you, did I?" But then she smiled.

"Although I'll have to say that you've piqued my curiosity. I guess you finally ended up flaming out in New York, as I knew you would. But good for you putting that jackass John Wilson in his place." She shook her head. "That piece of work was in a courthouse more times than the bailiff. He knew everyone in the New York federal courthouse by their first name. I'm sorry, but if you know court personnel better than you know your own kids, your life has taken a wrong turn somewhere along the line."

Ava had to smile just a bit. She'd forgotten about her mother's wry sense of humor.

Perhaps this visit wasn't going to be as unpleasant as she'd feared.

"How did you know I would flame out in New York?"

Her mother shrugged. "I was astonished that you lasted as long as you did. You were always so soft. You were the one who never let me kill any bugs in the house. 'Wrap that bug in a tissue and put it outside,' you would tell me. I had to draw the line with the ants that would get in, although you wanted me to march all of them out of the house as well."

Ava didn't remember any of that, so she had to take her mother's word for it.

"I still have a hard time killing bugs," Ava said. "I always feel they have as much of a right to life as I do."

Her mother rolled her eyes at that. "When I found out you went to work for the muckety-muck firm, I thought 'good luck there.' But you lasted longer than I ever thought you would, so kudos to you." She took a deep breath. "Now, tell me why you're here. I know it's not that you missed me so much."

"Yes," Ava began. "I'm starting a business."

"I know. A bed and breakfast in a $7 million home on

Nantucket. Guess you got yourself set up pretty well there," she said with a nod of her head. "You better buy a lottery ticket because somebody up there likes you."

Ava took a deep breath. "Right." Why was she so nervous?

"And what do you need from me?" Colleen asked.

Another deep breath. "I need two things from you. I need your contacts. And I need your investment." She brought out the business plan she had in her leather satchel. The plan showed the vision for the place and the considerable expenses that realizing this vision would cost. "Add to this a $40,000 salary for a sommelier and a $30,000 salary for a cook. You can see my problem."

Her mother shook her head. "Ava, you've been working for that muckety-muck law firm for the past 24 years. Are you telling me that you're tapped out?"

Ava felt like she wanted the floor to swallow her whole. She felt her face flush. She'd have to tell her mother about the horrendous lack of judgment she showed with her second husband, Christopher.

It would be painful.

"Christopher cleaned me out," she said. "He left me without notice, but not before he took out every penny from our joint investment account. He-"

"Oh, good God," her mother said. "You mean that Christopher was as big of a loser as Daniel was, is that what you're telling me?"

Ava felt her hackles rising. "Daniel wasn't a loser. He was a good man."

"Daniel had his head in the clouds," her mother said. "He was taking pictures for a living, trying to sell them after the fact on spec. He would've been lucky to be making $10,000 a year at the rate he was going. He had three babies on the way, and he was content to make his wife both the breadwinner and the changer of all the diapers. He needed to man up and get a job that paid the bills and took care of everybody, instead of thinking that he was the second coming of Richard Avedon."

"Be that as it may, he wasn't a bad guy," Ava said, hearing her voice getting higher and higher in pitch. "I won't be hearing that." She wanted to rise out of her chair and indignantly walk out the door, dramatically, like in the movies, but she didn't. She stayed rooted to her chair because this meeting was just too important.

"Ava, dear, just because a man isn't a bad guy," Colleen said, putting the words "bad guy" in air quotes, "doesn't mean that he's a good guy to marry. Solid men are the ones that you need when you have babies on the way, not tooty-fruity flighty ones. And, wouldn't you know it, he got himself killed because of his stupidity."

"He wasn't driving that night," Ava said.

"No, but he was in the car with a man who was three sheets to the wind, working on a fourth. Any sane person would've taken away the keys from a guy with a .20 blood alcohol level. Obviously, Daniel himself must have been shit-faced, too, if he didn't see how blotto that guy Mick Loose was. As far as I'm concerned, Daniel was just as guilty as Mick was. How hard would it've been for the two of them to call a cab?"

Ava thought back to that night. She was 5 months pregnant, and it was a hot and sultry evening in New York. Their Brooklyn apartment had no air conditioning, so August nights were insufferable. She'd been working on an appellate brief, and she was exhausted, sticky and hot. She'd just settled down to watch a few television shows on Nick at Nite because she wanted to unwind before going to sleep.

The Beachfront Inn

Then came the cops to her door. If she lived to be 100 years old, she'd never forget those two cops. One was short and stout, but he had a handsome face, all green-eyed and olive-skinned. He smelled of Irish Spring soap, and he was chewing Big Red gum. He had a very kindly smile, although he was missing one of his canine teeth. The other was tall and gangly, with a bald head, wide-set brown eyes and a long pointy nose. He smelled of Mexican food, as if he'd just finished eating a taco in the car.

She could never forget what she was watching on T.V. that night. It was an old episode, ironically enough, of *Car 54 Where Are You?* This was an early 60s show that featured two cops - one, Muldoon, who was really tall and thin, the other, Toody, who was really short and fat. When she saw the two cops, her first thought was that they were Officers Toody and Muldoon come to life.

Her second thought, a fleeting moment after the first, was that things were very, very wrong.

Now, some 24 years later, she could remember every detail of the moment when she'd found out that her husband was dead. She could still see the carpet in her tiny living room, with the stain caused by Daniel spilling red wine a few days earlier. Could still feel the stiff springs of the ancient recliner chair that dug into her back as she sat in that chair and listened to the two cops explain how her husband had gotten into a car with an intoxicated friend. The car hit a tree going some 60 miles per hour. Both men were killed instantly. She could still see the red and blue lights swirling outside her thin white curtains that were blowing in the breeze. She could still feel her heart stop while her babies kicked her. Apparently, they, too, were feeling the stress of that moment.

She was brought back to the present moment when her

mother barked, "I asked you a question. Ava, where were you just now?"

"Nowhere," she said. "I was just thinking about that night. What was the question again?"

Her mother shook her head. "Never mind. It was rhetorical. So, let's stop beating around the bush. Why are you here?"

Ava blinked as she tried to focus on her mother's words. She hated it when she was brought back to that night. She'd just get triggered by something - a few words, a smell, the sounds of an old television show - and she'd be right back to that evening. Still, she had a purpose in seeing her mother, and she would have to carry it out.

"As I said, I need an investor," she said. "I would like this B&B to become a destination. I envisioned this place to become like a luxury boutique hotel, complete with jacuzzi tubs in every room, and a cook preparing all the meals. And a sommelier. I need a cash influx."

Her mother's steely blue eyes hardly blinked as Ava humiliated herself in front of her. The last thing Ava wanted to do was ask her mother for this. She wished she could've just taken out a mortgage, but it wasn't an option because the will precluded that.

"A sommelier?" she asked, nodding her head. "You're going to hire your sister, then?"

Ava nodded her head. "Yes. I will. That's why I want the money for a sommelier, so that I can hire Sarah."

"Good," Colleen said. "Your sister needs a hand-up, you know. To tell you the truth, if you didn't include her in this, I would turn you down."

"Which means that you won't turn me down?" Ava anxiously asked.

"I don't know yet," she said. "I'd like some kind of a

guarantee that you're actually going to hire Sarah before I commit to anything with you."

Ava felt her hackles rising, despite herself. "I said I would," she said. "But why do you care so much about Sarah landing on her feet? I mean, if it were me who was on my rear, you wouldn't be nagging at Sarah to give me a hand up." Ava crossed her arms in front of her as she felt tears coming to her eyes.

"Do you want my money or not?" her mother asked.

"I want it, of course, but I really want to know why you've never wanted to help me, but as soon as Sarah needs help, you're right there."

"Are you going to hire your sister?" her mother asked.

"Yes."

"Then count me in," she said. "I want Sarah to have a safe place to land."

Ava just nodded her head. She didn't quite know how to react. She never did with her mother. If it was anybody else, she would have burst into a relieved chorus of "thank you, thank you, thank you," along with a big hug.

However, in this case, she felt that sitting there still as a stone was the better course of action.

But, inside, she was turning cartwheels.

"Now, as you know, I do happen to have a lot of money to invest in this venture," her mother said. "That's because I'm a careful planner, and I didn't marry a half-wit who would clean me out. But if I'm going to be an investor, I want a say. Fair warning. If I think that you're going down the wrong path with this place, I'll speak up. I won't be a silent partner. And I want a stake in the profits. 10%. And I want a note for at least $200,000 of the cash I'm going to give you."

Ava felt her face twitch. She knew that her mother

wasn't just going to give her money without also wanting a say. She even knew that her mother would demand a share of the profits and would want a note. But, somehow, her mother verbalizing her fears stressed her out.

"5%," Ava countered.

"Or what?" Her mother folded her arms. "Don't try to bluff me, Ava. You've already done shown your cards. You need my cash. If you don't get it, you're going to have to set your sights a lot lower for this place. You also need my contacts to make this place a hit. I know every muckety-muck in this area. I have the personal phone number of every billionaire and millionaire in town. If you do this place right, you can attract wedding parties and house socialites in town for fundraisers. You can have a house-warming party that'll be attended by people who have the bucks to make your place a real barn-burner."

As her mother spoke, Ava had to admit she imagined her B&B being a destination boutique hotel right on the beach. She imagined it being filled, night after night, with people who could afford a little luxury and were willing to pay for the extra amenities they couldn't get anyplace else. But her mother was right - without her cash infusion, Ava would have to settle for the place just being average. She barely had enough cash to outfit all the bedrooms with furniture sets, let alone do all the remodeling she'd planned.

And she certainly didn't have the money to pay the estate tax that was due. That was a half-million dollars on its own. But she thought that if she did well with her B&B, she might be able to pay off the estate tax within a couple of years. She didn't ask her mother for money for the tax because that was just too much to ask, in Ava's opinion.

"Okay. 10%," Ava said, feeling humiliated that she

backed down to her mother so quickly. To be fair, her mother was an intimidating woman.

Ava felt sorry for anybody who ended up in her mother's courtroom.

"That's right," her mother said, nodding her head. "Draw up a contract. I'll read it, and if I agree to all the terms in the contract, I'll sign it. But don't try getting cute and put things into the fine print. I'm wise to that."

"Of course," Ava said. "I wouldn't expect you to fall for fine print language. So, don't worry, I won't try to snow you."

"Good. Now, I guess you're going away from this meeting having gotten what you wanted from me. Give me another estimate on how much everything is going to cost, and I'll cut you a check."

Ava felt a sense of relief, along with a sense of foreboding. Her mother would be her partner.

Yet, her mother *still* didn't answer the question that had always nagged at her for all these years. Why did Colleen hate her and love Sarah so much? It had always rankled her that their mother was so much nicer to Sarah than she was to her, and now, here Colleen was, demanding that Ava bail Sarah out. That didn't seem fair to her.

No doubt about it, she and her mother were still at odds, yet they were going to be business partners.

What was she getting herself into?

Chapter Twenty-Two

Ava

With her mother's infusion of cash, things started to really move. Quinn completed her designs for the house. The plans opened up the floor plan for the central part of the house. Her new blueprint also greatly expanded the kitchen so that it was industrial-sized. All the carpeting and hardwood floors were to be replaced with distressed wood. The dining room would be expanded to seat up to 30 people at one time. Everything would be modernized, from the light fixtures, which were mid-century and dated, to the countertops, which would go from tile to granite, to the walls and floors.

And she'd gotten all the necessary permits from the Town of Nantucket, so she was ready to roll on the renovation project.

Ava also had the contractors hired out. They were led by Deacon Cromwell, a tall, built man with a distinct Aussie accent that absolutely slayed Ava. She was a sucker for a man with any kind of accent, but Aussie and British accents were her absolute favorites. He was blonde with a distinctive Eastern European face - broad cheekbones, wide-set green eyes, thin lips and a broad nose. He looked like a taller version of Daniel Craig, who Ava always loved as an actor.

He smiled broadly when he walked through the door and then looked around. "Nice place," he said. "Looks like there are good bones."

Ava nodded. "I hope so. God forbid there's any foundation issues or something like that." She felt her heart pounding just a little as she looked at this guy. She glanced over at Quinn, who was raising her eyebrows at Ava and smiling with a "you go girl" look on her face. Ava recognized that look anywhere.

"Oh, I'm sure that there's nothing wrong like that, mate," he said. "I got your designs, so let me take a look around and see what needs to be done. Next week, I'll be back with a crew to get started on the renovation. Would that be too soon?"

Ava just shook her head. She wasn't usually rendered speechless, but, for some odd reason, this guy had that effect on her.

"No, not too soon. I mean, if it's not too soon for your wife," she blurted out. Then she immediately felt embarrassed. She didn't really just blurt that out, did she? It was the most transparent way in the world to find out if the guy was married. He wasn't wearing a ring, but that didn't necessarily mean anything. Many married men didn't wear rings, especially if they worked with their hands.

He chuckled. "No, no wife to worry about," he said.

"Because she's out of town?" Ava asked. Once again, she suffered from diarrhea of the mouth, and she felt ashamed for pressing him.

"No, because she doesn't exist," Deacon said. "And what about you? Is there a husband around who wants to weigh in on this whole renovation process?"

Ava shook her head, feeling her face flush. "No. I mean, I'm married, but I haven't seen the guy in over a year, plus he stole a lot of money from me, so I doubt that he would show his face around me ever again."

Why was she telling this guy this much? He probably would want to back out of the contract now because he might think that a woman who couldn't handle her finances might not be able to pay. Which meant she had to clear things up.

She was on a roll, so she might as well keep going.

"I mean, he stole a lot of money from me, cleaned out our joint investment account that I worked for 28 years to build up. He had a gambling issue. But my mother is wealthy, and she's an investor, so, don't worry, I'll be able to pay your contract in full." She took a deep breath. "And, I can't believe I just said all that. If you want to back out of our contract, I completely understand."

He smiled and shook his head. "Not on your life. I want to do this project. I've known about this house for several years. I was actually in this house a few years ago. I remember thinking that the place just has so much potential, and if I could just work my magic, I could really make it shine just like a diamond."

"You were in this house?" Ava asked.

"Yeah. I was invited to a party here by the sheila who lived here. Her name is Jessica Bennett. I think she was related to the bloke who owned the house. She told me that his name was James. He was her granddad, or so she said."

He went around the house, looking at all the walls, the ceiling, the floors. "It's not my business, but I thought she told me she would get the house after her granddad died. That's what she told me."

"Well, it *was* a surprise for me to be bequeathed this house. James Bloch was a client at the law firm where I used to work. He became almost like a surrogate father to me. I mean, I never really knew my own father, he died when I was only six, so having an older gentleman to talk to really helped. I guess I have father issues after all."

Deacon smiled and laughed lightly. "That doesn't surprise me if you didn't know your own father. Anyhow, let's take a tour through the house and see what we have here."

Ava followed him around the house, pointing out cracks in the ceiling and peppering him with questions. "I hope that you can do the remodel the way that Quinn and I had envisioned," she said.

He looked at the plans and then went around and examined every wall. "Quinn did a thorough job with the blueprints of the house," Deacon said. "She marked which walls were load-bearing and which ones weren't, and she's on the money with all of it. Good job."

"And the floors?"

"It won't be a problem ripping up the carpets in the upstairs bedrooms," he said. "As for the downstairs, where there are already hardwood floors, which have seen better days, I must add, it also won't be a problem replacing those with some brand-new distressed-wood planks. I understand that you want to go ahead and replace all the windows in the house too. Right?"

"Yes," Ava said. "Would you like to go out on the back deck? We can talk about my plans for that and maybe grab a bite to eat out there. It's my favorite space in the house."

"Sure," he said. "Let's go."

They climbed the stairs to the second floor, got to the sunroom leading to the back deck, and then walked outside. Deacon sat down, and Ava got up and went back into the house for some iced tea and nuts. She brought these things out, and Deacon gratefully took them from her.

"It's beautiful out here," he said, breathing in the salty air. The beach was calm and deserted.

"It is," Ava agreed, sitting down next to Deacon. "I hope I'm not keeping you from any appointments."

"Nah," he said, taking a bite of nuts and drinking his glass of iced tea. "I have other appointments, of course, but not for a few hours." He casually put his long legs on an ottoman and stretched. "I'm a lucky bloke to be living out here, you know."

"I know," Ava said. "I feel the same way. I'm a transplant from New York. And the midwest, which is where I grew up, in Kansas City. And where are you from?"

"Sydney, Australia. I've been in the states for the past fifteen years, though. I moved here when I was 20."

Ava suspected that he was in his mid-thirties. He just confirmed her suspicions. Which made her sad because he was the first guy who had gotten her juices flowing since Christopher left her in the lurch.

Unfortunately, Deacon was just too young.

It was just as well, as she'd gotten very set in her ways, and she really couldn't see herself dating anybody.

"Do you like it here?" she asked him.

He shrugged. "I guess. I got dragged here, kicking and screaming when my sister got sick, and I brought her here to the states to go to the Mayo Clinic in Minnesota. She was a minor, so I had to come with her. Then I fell in love, got married, got divorced and just fell in with carpentry. I guess the rest is history."

"How is your sister?" Ava asked.

"Better. She kicked her cancer, thank God. She's back in Sydney, married with a new rug rat and one on the way."

"Good," Ava said. Then she nodded her head. "You were saying back there that you knew the woman who lived here previously, right?"

"Right."

"And she thought she'd get the house after her granddad died?"

"Yes. She assumed she would. She was talking to me about this place. I looked at it with a carpenter's eye, seeing all the imperfections and seeing how dated everything looked. I told her that if she ever wanted to do a renovation, she should call me."

"And what did she say to that?"

"She said she didn't own the house. Her grandfather owned it. She told me she thought he was sick and would soon pass, and she'd get the house. She'd call me if that ever happened. I was surprised when you called me because I just thought she would've been the one who would've been living here."

Ava cocked her head and took a sip of her iced tea. She had a sinking feeling as Deacon spoke to her about Jessica and her belief she'd get the house after James had died.

She didn't, and Ava did.

Why?

And why did Ava have the feeling that there would be more to the story?

"I wonder why Jessica didn't end up getting the house," she said out loud. "And I did."

Deacon shrugged his shoulders. "Dunno. That's not a problem, though, is it?"

"No. Not unless she ends up challenging the will. Anyhow, was it just her who lived here?"

"Yeah. I thought it was strange, just a single woman living in a huge house like this. It was a waste. I always thought it would be perfect for making it into a little boutique hotel like you plan to do. Either that or I could imagine a large family living here. With it being just her living here, most of the bedrooms were closed up so they weren't cooled by the air conditioning or heated during the wintertime. She lived in a small area of the house, on the top floor. I was happy to find out that the house is going to be used by somebody who really would make the most of it."

"I do plan on making the most of it," she said.

"Good. I know that it sounds strange, and I'm sorry if it does, but I think that houses have certain energies. I feel that the walls absorb energy, too. Negative and positive. I knew that poor Jessica was suffering from some kind of emotional illness while she lived here because the house itself just seemed depressed. It seemed like the house was also sad because most of it was neglected. I know it's weird, but I do feel like that sometimes. So, yes, I was excited that the place was finally going to get its due."

Ava smiled. Deacon might've felt that he was telling her something she'd find strange, but she really didn't. She, too, believed that walls absorb personal energy. She wondered how depressed her old condo in New York felt when living there. After all, she wasn't really living much at all.

She didn't realize it until she moved out to Nantucket, but she now knew she'd been sleepwalking through life before. In New York, she never quite felt like she was living her best life. She'd been unhappy for a while. Her depression and malaise were the reasons why she pretty much let

Christopher clean her out, and she never even fought back.

"Well," Deacon said after he finished his nuts and water. "Now that I've totally freaked you out with my supernatural mumbo-jumbo, what do you say we call it a day and I'll see you next week?"

Ava laughed. "No, you didn't freak me out at all. I've always felt that inanimate objects absorb energy myself. I just wonder what was wrong with Jessica, that's all."

Ava worried that maybe this Jessica was homeless because of her snatching the house right out from under her. Ava always tended to think the worst about situations, and she was doing it here.

She wondered again exactly why did she deserve this house. She wasn't related to James, and, while she had monthly lunches with him for the past 10 years or so, that didn't mean she should've gotten such an extravagant gift, especially when there was a blood relative already living here.

Stop feeling guilty. He gave you this house, and that's that.

Deacon shrugged his shoulders. "I dunno. All I know is that Jessica acted happy, but I could see underneath the mask she was anything but."

Ava nodded her head. "Yes, I know all about masks. I wore one myself for the past, oh, 54 years. But, for the first time, I'm not really wearing a mask. I'm actually happy."

She wondered again why she was telling this guy so much. She didn't really know, but she felt a kinship with him somehow.

Deacon grinned. "Good to know you're happy at last." Then he looked at his watch. "I have another appointment down the road, but I'll see you next week." He stood up and shook her hand. "Bye, now."

"Bye," Ava said.

After he left, Quinn came up to the terrace and mock-fanned herself. "Oh my, you found quite the hunk to fix this place up. Eye candy all the way."

"Now, now, I'm not objectifying him. He comes highly recommended and that's why I'm hiring him. His being extraordinarily pretty has nothing to do with it."

"Uh huh," Quinn said with a grin.

Ava started to laugh. "Oh, what the hell. His being eye candy certainly doesn't hurt, I won't lie."

"No, it doesn't hurt," Quinn said. "It doesn't hurt at all."

Chapter Twenty-Three

Sarah

Sarah slept in her car the night after she left Ava's house, but the very next day, she went into a restaurant to apply for a waitressing job and was hired on the spot. She started that very night and was able to make enough money to get a hotel room at the Brass Lantern Inn, which was a large home with natural wood shingles that housed several rooms that were cute and quaint, with wallpaper and soft lamps, white bedspreads with colorful pillows and hardwood floors. Unfortunately, the place was still $150 a night, which meant she would have to spend all her tip money on the room, assuming she made enough tips each night to pay for the place.

The restaurant, called Chez Toussaint, was French, high-end, and housed in one of the old Greek revival buildings in the historic district owned by whaling captains in the 18th Century. Inside was all modern, however, with hardwood floors and high ceilings. On the tables were white tablecloths and candles. There was also a large outdoor deck that had lights strung overhead. In all, the space was homey yet romantic.

The menu included duck confit, escargot, foie gras, lobster roe, lobster bisque, sweet bread, soft-shell crab, pan-roasted lobster, chicken livers and various kinds of salads and sides such as ratatouille, polenta, spinach, risotto and roasted asparagus. Sarah's mouth watered just reading the menu and wished she could take extra food home. She was no longer in her rebellious junk food mood and was once again looking forward to eating healthy and getting her body back into balance, so the salads and vegetable dishes particularly appealed.

She hated leaving Bella alone in the hotel room, but it couldn't be helped. She was a good puppy, but Sarah felt so badly for the dog because she'd never left her for any period of time before. But it was nice to come home to Bella when she got off her shift because the dog would get super excited and give Sarah lots of puppy kisses.

Of course, Sarah soon found out why she was hired so quickly - her boss started to hit on her almost immediately. Sarah had no intention to get involved with him, though, so she quickly shut it down. Which was too bad because her boss, whose name was Françoise, was a charming Frenchman who was more than impressed by Sarah's speaking fluent French and she could converse about the French countryside and Paris equally well.

"You know the corners of France very well, no?" Françoise asked.

"I've been all over that country," Sarah said. "Definitely some of the most beautiful places are along the Alsace wine route, especially Kaysersberg. I love that town's 16th-century architecture and the castle ruins. And the history of Domme in the Dordogne valley just can't be compared."

"And the fishing villages!" Françoise said excitedly. "The seafood you can get in the Normandy fishing villages are beyond this world."

Sarah had to agree with that. "I love Paris, don't get me wrong, but the French countryside has some of the most picturesque and interesting towns I've ever seen."

"And what brings you to this island?" Françoise asked.

Sarah didn't want to be honest with him because if she were, she would admit she was only going to work at Françoise's restaurant until she had enough money in the bank to move on. She figured that if she were going to make a living waiting tables, she should probably try to move to an area where the cost of living was lower than on Nantucket.

That was what she spent her evenings doing when she wasn't working at the restaurant - she sat on the bed of her hotel room, Bella by her side, looking on her laptop about places she could move and live off a waitressing salary.

"It just looked like a beautiful place to live," Sarah said in response to Françoise's question about why she chose to move to Nantucket.

"It is, it is," Françoise said enthusiastically. "I'm very fortunate to have found a woman as intelligent and cultured and beautiful as you to work for me."

And then he asked her out on a date, and Sarah politely declined. "I'm sorry, Françoise," she said when he suggested the two of them have an intimate dinner for two at his home that weekend. "I make a point not to date my boss."

After that, he wasn't nearly so friendly with her, but she didn't care. She wasn't there to be friendly with her boss - she was there to work. She'd never waited tables before in her life, and she soon realized that it was harder than it looked. And, because it was October, therefore it was the off-season, she was one of only three waitresses, so her station typically consisted of six different tables that were full almost every night. She had to be more organized than she ever thought possible, as she had to juggle the needs and demands of different parties who always seemed to be running out of water and alcoholic drinks, and the kitchen never seemed to get things out on time.

However, she was really enjoying herself because she was able to use her extensive knowledge of wines to recommend just the right rosé to pair with a chicken dish or sparkling wine to pair with the lobster. However, Sarah always preferred to pair more light-bodied wines such as Pinot Gris, Sauvignon Blanc and Grechetto with most of the seafood. For the steaks, the restaurant offered a wide variety of medium-bodied and full-bodied red wines - varietals of Cabernet Sauvignon, Malbecs and Syrahs from around the world. Sarah quickly sized up the wine list at the restaurant, and her pairings always went over spectacularly with the guests.

She was making decent tips at the place, and that was literally all that mattered. She would work a five-hour shift and could bring home $200. Of course, $150 of that would immediately go to her hotel room, and then she had to pay for food, so she realized that getting out of her situation and into her own home in some small affordable town in Anywhere, U.S.A. was a long ways away.

Yet, she was making it on her own, for what it was worth, and she started to feel a sense of pride she hadn't felt in a long, long time. And Françoise had promised her more shifts in the future because she would soon be one of only two waitresses - one of the waitresses, Michelle, had given notice, and Françoise didn't want to hire anybody else until the busy season began after Memorial Day. She imagined herself working double shifts, which would help her get to her dream sooner, but then again, if she worked doubles, she would have to find a sitter for Bella. This might defeat the purpose, she thought.

Then, one day, a few weeks after she was hired, it happened. She saw the woman who had ruined her life.

And she lost it.

Chapter Twenty-Four

Sarah

She was there. Lauren. Sarah's heart started to race as she saw her former friend sitting in the restaurant with some young guy Sarah had never seen before. Tears came to her eyes, and her hands were shaking wildly.

And, of course, she was sitting in Sarah's station. Sarah spotted her and went back to the kitchen to calm down just a little. Tisha, another waitress who worked at the restaurant, put her arm around Sarah when she saw the look on her face.

"Hey," Tisha said. "Are you okay? Your face is so pale right now."

Sarah did what she usually did when she felt stressed - she started to speak in a different language. She was fluent in Italian, French and Spanish, so she decided to pop off in Italian.

"There's a bitch out there who completely destroyed my

life 20 years ago, and I've never wanted to murder somebody before, but I do now," Sarah said in Italian.

Unfortunately, Tisha also seemed to know Italian. "Oh, man, that's rough," she said. "Where is she? Who is she? And what did she do?"

Sarah shook her head. "How did you know what I was saying?"

Tisha shrugged her shoulders. "My mother was an Italian immigrant. But what did she do?"

"Never mind," Sarah said. "I'm a professional. I'm going to take this job seriously. So, I have to go out there and wait on her and her…guy."

Tisha peeked at the parties in Sarah's station and immediately seemed to know who Lauren was. "Fake rack, ridiculous-looking eyelashes, fish lips?" she asked Sarah. "Am I seeing the right person?"

"Yes."

"Oh. Well, she's with the son of a billionaire," she said. "How old is she?"

"I'm guessing she's my age, so around 53. Why?"

"That guy out there is around 30 years old."

"What's his name? Her date?"

"Langdon Prescott," Tisha said. "Isn't that just the perfect name for a billionaire's son?"

Sarah smiled. "I couldn't think of a more perfect name if I tried." She took a deep breath and headed out to the table.

Lauren's eyes got wide when she saw Sarah. "Sarah? Oh my God, it's you! How have you been?" She stood up to give Sarah a hug, but Sarah's arms remained straight by her side, so the hug was unsuccessful.

Sarah tried hard to make her expression as neutral as possible.

Must be professional. Must be professional. Must be professional.

"Are you ready to order?" she asked Lauren nonchalantly. Inside, her stomach was turning over and over, and she felt she would get sick.

"I think that we need some more time," Lauren said, touching Langdon's arm lightly and staring at the man. He had dark hair that flopped over his forehead, blue eyes, strong eyebrows and the smarmy, arrogant expression Sarah knew so well after running with men and women like Lauren and Langdon. "But we would like to order some escargot as an appetizer."

Sarah went back to put the appetizer order in and then took out the wine list to the couple. She was sat another time, so she had to tend to the new table while Lauren and her date looked over the menu. Lauren kept glancing over at Sarah, and Sarah thought that her facial expressions showed zero guilt about what she did.

Lauren was why Sarah would never, ever become an architect again. Lauren was why Sarah was stuck in a relationship that wasn't fulfilling in the least for the last 20 years. There was a definite fork in Sarah's road that happened all those years ago, a fork where, if Sarah had the choice, she would've gotten her life together and left Nolan and gotten back to her first love of designing buildings.

That fork became a straight line, as Sarah no longer had a choice to return to her chosen profession. And that was because of Lauren. And that woman, that spray-tanned, plastic, shallow, stupid woman didn't even feel guilty about it. That much was obvious to Sarah as she watched her former friend giggling with her much-younger man.

The smug look on Lauren's face enraged Sarah so much that she could barely see straight. She wanted nothing more than to take one of the steak knives that was within her reach and stab Lauren right through the heart.

How was Lauren still living her life just the way she was before? How did she have no consequences for what happened? Why did Sarah have to bear every single consequence for that incident?

There was no accountability for that woman. None. And there she was, on Nantucket, with her man-toy and no husband in sight. Sarah didn't know how Lauren managed to stay married to William all these years, but she did know that the two had never divorced.

It wasn't fair that Lauren just glided along without any regard for anybody's feelings. That she could just step on anyone and...

And was she really that much better? She and Ava weren't close, and much of the reason for that was her fault. Ava had tried to make amends over the years - for the first five holidays after their big blow-up fight, Ava had reached out to invite Sarah out to New York and had even offered to fly out West to visit Sarah. Sarah had always refused.

Granted, Sarah usually refused because she was always going out of the country for the holidays - one of her favorite places to visit over Christmas was Prague, as that place was magnificent over the holidays. Prague was always magnificent, but Christmas there was really special - the historic buildings were set aglow, and the place became a winter wonderland. So, she and Nolan went to Prague most Christmases, when they weren't going to Jamaica to get away from the weather or Switzerland to ski. But, still, she should've made the trip to see Ava at least one Christmas, or she should've suggested another time to see her.

But she didn't. She was so hurt by the way Ava looked at her and her life, and, more than that, she knew Ava was right all along, but there wasn't anything she could do to change things. So, she avoided Ava all these years. She avoided her for 20 years and then showed up at her house, having been forced out on her rear-end, and just expected her sister to welcome her with open arms. And then she was just *so* surprised Ava turned her out. Ava was justified in doing that, and Sarah knew she would not only try harder to get in Ava's good graces but to figure out how she could turn it around so she could benefit Ava, not try to suck her dry.

She shook her head. Everybody was the hero of their own story, and, perhaps, Lauren really thought that what she did all those years ago wasn't bad. Maybe she justified it in her head, much like Sarah was justifying her own bad behavior in her own head.

She went back to Lauren's table, feeling much calmer. "If you're ready to order, I'd be happy to take it and make some suggestions from the wine list that would pair perfectly with your meal."

Lauren smiled. "You always were so knowledgeable with the wines," she said. She looked at Langdon. "Sarah was a world traveler and, everywhere she went, she learned about regional wines."

"A world traveler?" Langdon said, looking pointedly at Sarah's uniform of a white shirt, tie and black pants. Then he said in a low voice, but not low enough, as Sarah could still hear it, "how does a waitress travel the world?"

Lauren laughed. "Sarah used to be the paramour of Nolan Shea," she said. "Trust fund baby and son of Joe Shea who founded a large pharmaceutical company. And then Nolan died." Lauren stuck out her lower lip in a mock grimace that struck Sarah as being the most insincere expression of sadness she'd ever seen. It was almost like

The Beachfront Inn

Lauren was mocking Nolan's death with that expression, and, indeed, Sarah thought that this was probably the case.

Sarah stood there, not quite believing that Lauren and Langdon were talking about her like she wasn't even there.

"Yes," Sarah said. "And now I'm actually proud of my life because I'm no longer a slug who contributes nothing to the world. Now, if you're ready to order, I'll take it and give wine suggestions. But, if not, I'll leave you two alone and come back later."

Lauren stood up. "I guess you really are just like your sister, aren't you? Judging me?"

Sarah took a deep breath. "Are we going to do this here? I just got this job, and I can't afford to lose it. So, if you want to do this, let's do this later. For now, I would like to take your order."

"Take it back," Lauren said.

"Take what back?"

"Take back what you just said about me."

"I said nothing about you," Sarah said and then looked nervously over at Françoise, who was looking with interest at the interaction between the women. He obviously was trying to decide if he should come over and intervene.

"You did. You just called me a slug who contributes nothing to the world."

Sarah took a deep breath. "I said that about myself. But if you heard those words about *yourself*, perhaps you should ask yourself why. Now, if you could please let me know if you're ready to order, I would -"

Sarah looked over and saw that Françoise was right next to her. "Hello," he said with his strong accent. "I'm Françoise Toussaint, and I'm the owner of this restaurant. Is there anything I can do for you?" he asked Lauren.

"Yes," Lauren said, pointing at Sarah. "You can make

your waitress here apologize to me for calling me a lazy bitch," she said, glaring at Sarah.

Sarah's heart started to race, and she bowed her head. There was nothing she could say without making a scene.

Françoise nodded his head. "Ms. Flynn, I'm very sorry, but your services are no longer necessary. I will take care of Mr. Prescott and his beautiful paramour since Mr. Prescott and his father are two of my most treasured guests."

Sarah said nothing, but walked away from the table and out the door. Lauren ruined her life 20 years ago, and just when she thought she was getting back on her feet, Lauren came along and ruined that, too.

Sarah got back to the hotel, got out a leash and walked Bella. And then returned back to the hotel room and sat on the bed. With Bella by her side, she let the tears flow for a few minutes.

But, soon enough, the tears were dried up. She'd only worked at the restaurant for a few weeks and had made just over $1,800 total, most of which went to the hotel room, so she had just $200 in cash. That wouldn't be enough to help her get settled in someplace else, but then again, she could sell her car and buy something cheaper, and that would give her enough to land back on her feet.

It was a wonder she'd never thought of that before.

But first, she would go back to Ava's and apologize. Because she saw, maybe for the first time, that her behavior with her sister over the years was truly atrocious.

She would leave the island and find another life with her head held high. But only after she knew she and her sister were truly okay.

Because one thing was for sure - she felt she and Lauren had a lot in common. They both stepped on people and never made amends - just as Lauren stepped on Sarah,

Sarah had stepped on Ava. They both glided through life and expected everybody to hand them everything.

She was like Lauren in some ways, and that made her know she had to change.

Because she didn't want to ever look in the mirror again and think she had anything in common with that horrible witch.

Chapter Twenty-Five

Sarah

Sarah sold her Range Rover for $60,000 to a private party and turned around and bought a used hybrid Ford Escape SUV for $30,000, so she had money in the bank.

She decided to move to Kansas City, where she and Ava grew up. According to the latest data that Sarah could find, the median home price in Kansas City was just under $200,000. This was compared to the median home price on Nantucket, which was currently $2.7 million.

Sarah had recently visited Kansas City and saw that the small midwestern city had become a hidden gem. It had a world-class art museum, which was always the case. It also boasted neighborhood after neighborhood of turn-of-the-century mansions. The architecture of these mansions tended towards the Queen Anne styles, but there were plenty of Neo-Classical, Georgian, Greek-Revival and Tudor-Revival homes. These homes were sturdy and classic, situated in older neighborhoods that were gentrified and filled with well-educated professionals. Sarah was fascinated by all these older neighborhoods and the wide variety of architectural styles they represented.

In addition to the museum and the older historic neighborhoods, the city had a bustling art colony that was located in the Crossroads District, where artists converted warehouses into vibrant studios. On the first Friday of every month, the galleries stayed open late, and thousands of people filled the streets, sipping wine and going from gallery to gallery.

The city also had a new performing arts center that rivaled some of the best in the entire world. The gleaming silver Kauffman Center was a masterpiece of architecture - the exterior consisted of two silver symmetrical half-shells of vertical concentric arches. The interior concert hall was modeled after some of the great European opera houses. The Kauffman Center was downtown. Also downtown was a new arena. Around the arena was a bustling restaurant and bar area known as the Power and Light District.

And, of course, there was the Country Club Plaza. This was a shopping district where the buildings were modeled after the architecture found in Seville, Spain, considered Kansas City's sister city. Over Christmastime, every building on The Plaza was lit up, which always made Sarah feel joyful when she was growing up.

While the cultural attractions of the small city rivaled some of the best in the world, and Sarah would know, Kansas City also boasted one of the best NFL football teams in the league, the Kansas City Chiefs. Sarah wasn't a sports fan, necessarily, but she did follow The Chiefs and was thrilled by that team's turnaround from football laughingstock to the best in the country.

No doubt about it, Kansas City was a place where

Sarah could find herself and could be happy. She could buy a house if she worked hard at waitressing or bartending, and she could work on becoming a certified sommelier. Then she could write her own ticket and get a position with a five-star restaurant in the city. Her research showed that the city had a few fine dining restaurants where she could hopefully apply her extensive wine knowledge.

Sarah was set to leave, but she had to tell Ava her plans. Ever since she had her epiphany that her entitled behavior was why she and Ava didn't get along when she showed up at her sister's door, Sarah knew she would have to apologize and really make amends. She couldn't leave the island with things between her and Ava still so unsettled.

So, she called Ava, talked to her and explained what was going on. Ava invited her over for a glass of wine that evening, and Sarah accepted.

Hopefully, she could get it right this time.

Chapter Twenty-Six

Sarah

Sarah took a deep breath, feeling nervous again. She put the money she received from the sale of her SUV into a new bank account, from which she bought a nice bottle of wine from a local brewery and winery.

She was delighted to find a bottle of Albariño wine, a white wine from the Iberian Peninsula that was not commonly found. The light wine boasted notes of lemon, grapefruit, honeydew melon and nectarine. It also had just a hint of a salty flavor since the Albariño grapes were grown in cool areas close to the Mediterranean Sea. This kind of wine paired exceptionally with fish, which Ava was making for dinner that night.

Sarah rang the bell, and Ava opened the door. She was wearing an apron and a very friendly expression. She opened up her arms, and Sarah fell into them.

"I'm so happy and relieved that you called me," Ava said. "I felt terrible about how you left before, and I realized that I didn't have a way to contact you because I didn't have your phone number."

Sarah knew Ava wasn't entirely telling the truth. Her sister could've asked their mother for her number, and she knew Ava had seen their mother recently.

She decided to let that go.

Ava took the bottle of wine and looked at it with interest. "Martin Codax Albariño," she said, looking at the label. "This is a white wine. Is it a kind of Sauvignon Blanc, Chardonnay, Chablis or Pinot Grigio?"

Sarah smiled. "None of those. It's an Albariño. That's the name of the grape varietal. It's a dry wine, but light and complex with just the right amount of acidity to combine well with fish. It has more acidity than a Chardonnay or a Pinot Grigio but a lighter body. Its profile is pretty close to a Sauvignon Blanc, though, as far as body, acidity and sweetness go. It just has different notes than a Sauvignon Blanc, so it combines better with fish than a Blanc."

Ava looked slightly confused. "I thought that white wines pretty much fit into the Sauvignon Blanc, Chardonnay, Chablis and Pinot Grigio varietals. I didn't know there were other kinds of white wines."

Sarah felt like laughing, but she suppressed it. She knew her sister drank a lot of wine, so she was surprised by how little Ava appeared to know about the subject.

"Those are the popular varietals, but there are so many other varietals out there, both white and red. Most laypeople know only a few varietals of red and white wines - your Cabernets, Merlots, Chardonnays, Pinots, and Zinfandels. That's because those grapes are far and away the most popular, so most wines that you encounter fall into those groups. But there are literally hundreds of varietals from all around the world, and pairing just the right wine with food is an art form."

Ava put her arm around Sarah. "You do seem to know your stuff," she said. "So, you say this Albariño goes well with fish, then?"

"It's excellent with fish. You'll see. The flavor notes, acidity, sweetness and lightness are just perfect for fish."

"I'll take your word for it," Ava said. "Dinner is ready to go, so let's go to the deck. We'll open up your wine, and we'll eat and talk."

"Sounds good."

Sarah followed Ava to the deck and sat down at the elegantly-appointed table. A slight breeze came in from the ocean, which gave the air a briny smell. But, otherwise, it was a very peaceful evening. And, since it was mid-November, and very cool out, Ava had heat lamps going.

"You got some heat lamps," Sarah observed. "Those are new, huh?"

"Yeah," Ava said. "Our mother came through for me with money, so heat lamps were some of the first things I invested in since I love being out here so much, and it gets so darned cold."

"Mom came through," Sarah said, nodding her head. "See, I told you she doesn't hate you."

Ava raised an eyebrow. "I wouldn't say that. She only gave me the money because I promised to hire you as a sommelier. Otherwise, I think she would've turned me down flat. And if she did turn me down, I wouldn't know what to do because God knows I didn't have enough money to renovate this place, let alone hire people to help run it."

Sarah's heart soared when Ava mentioned she might hire her as a sommelier, but she didn't press it. She wanted Ava to make a formal offer before she really got excited.

Ava opened the wine and poured a couple of glasses. Sarah took a sip. "Very good," Sarah said. "This wine will go spectacularly with the fish." Then she took a deep breath. "I hate to ask this, Ava, but what do you mean you didn't have the money to renovate this place and hire staff?"

Sarah knew that her sister was careful with money and that Ava had been making a quarter-million a year at her law firm, so she was more than surprised Ava was broke.

Ava rolled her eyes. "Long story." Then she paused and looked at Sarah for a beat. "My ex-husband had a gambling issue, and he cleaned out our joint investment account. A million dollars gone, just like that." She snapped her fingers.

Sarah put her arm around her sister. "How awful," she said. "I'm so sorry to hear about that."

Ava shrugged. "Well, what can you do? I mean, I'd love to murder him in his sleep, but he was within his rights, legally, to do what he did. It was my stupidity not maintaining a separate account. I mean, I was a lawyer. You would think I wouldn't make dumb mistakes like that."

"You trusted him, obviously," Sarah said. "But how did you not know that he was gambling?"

"I was working all the time," Ava said. "And I mean, all the time. 70-80 hours a week. He apparently lost a lot of it with online gambling, but he also took a lot of business trips to Vegas and Atlantic City," Ava said, putting the term "business trips" in air quotes. "Meaning he would tell me he was going to San Francisco or to Europe, but, really, he was in various gambling meccas, playing high-dollar poker. He even went to Macau, China, a few times a year and lost money with some of the highest rollers in the entire world.

It was all happening under my nose, and I never even caught on."

"How did you finally find out about his gambling?" Sarah asked.

"A friend of his called me to rat him out. Apparently, Chris owed this friend, George, money and had stiffed him, so George called me and told me everything. Man, I was dumb and clueless about all that was happening." Ava shook her head. "I was stupid and blind. Just because I was an attorney doesn't mean that I didn't fall victim to a con man, like a lot of other women would."

Sarah thought Ava's tone was slightly defensive, so she put her hand on Ava's hand and squeezed. "No judgment. I'm just surprised, that's all."

Ava grimaced. "Yeah, me too. I surprised myself that I didn't know what was going on. Anyhow, let me go and get the dinner."

Ava brought out a dinner consisting of broiled grouper, a baked potato, steamed broccoli and a Caprese salad of tomato, basil, mozzarella cheese and olive oil.

"It's a good thing I brought this wine," Sarah said. "If I would've gone with a full-bodied Chardonnay, it wouldn't have gone with this tomato salad at all."

"Oh? Why not?" Ava asked as she took a sip of the wine.

"Because full-bodied white wines don't go with nightshades - tomatoes, eggplant and peppers. For that matter, full-bodied whites don't go that well with finfish, although they go pretty well with shellfish. They also don't go with broccoli and other cruciferous vegetables."

Ava took another sip of wine and nodded her head. "It's good," she said. "I can understand why you brought this wine. I would imagine it'll go well with this grouper."

"It will," Sarah assured her. She took a sip of her own glass and took a bite of the fish, and the flavors combined extremely well together indeed. "Ava, I wanted to let you know that I'm moving back to Kansas City. Where we grew up."

Ava's face fell. "Oh? You just got here. I was hoping -"

Then she shook her head.

"Hoping?" Sarah asked.

"Yes. Well, it's not important now. When will you be moving back?"

"As soon as possible. I'm staying in a hotel right now. I found a job with a French restaurant, and my intention was to work that job for long enough to get some money together to move. But that didn't work out, so I had to sell my Range Rover and buy something much cheaper. So, I have some money now to get settled in Kansas City."

"It didn't work out? Why not?"

Sarah sighed. "It's not what you think."

"What do I think?"

"I'm sure you think I screwed the job up because I don't really want to work. That I was looking for the easy way out, which is why I just sold my car for the quick buck instead of working my way to the life I want. That I'm just waiting around for the next billionaire to take care of me." Then she looked away.

Ava sighed. "Sarah, I want to apologize for being such a jerk to you when you came by before. And, for what it's worth, I didn't assume you lost your waitressing job because you didn't want to work. I don't know why you lost your job, but I will say that I'm very sorry that you did."

"No, *I'm* sorry," Sarah said. "Please don't apologize. You have nothing to apologize for - I'm the one who needs to apologize. I ignored you all these years. I made excuses to not come and see you because I was ashamed of my life. You had my number - you poked me in the place where I was softest, most vulnerable, where I was bruised and battered. You held up a mirror to me, and I despised what I saw. So, I avoided you all these years because I didn't want to see myself reflected in your eyes. And then I show up, all these years later, after turning my back on you, expecting you to help me out. I was acting like a self-centered entitled witch, and I'm sorry."

Ava nodded. "Apology accepted. And I hope you accept mine as well."

"I would, but you don't have anything to apologize for," Sarah said. "You reacted like you should've. You let the door hit me on the way out, and I don't blame you one bit."

"I should've tried to find you after you left," Ava said. "I didn't have your phone number, but I saw our mother a few weeks ago, and I could've asked her for your number."

"But you didn't really want to get in touch with me," Sarah said. "We haven't spoken for these many years, so it's not like your life would be any different without me in it. I understand."

Ava sipped her wine and took a bite of her fish. "This wine pairs perfectly with this meal, by the way. I don't think I could find a more perfect accompaniment."

"Well, that's why you should hire a sommelier," Sarah said. "Not me, necessarily, but a wine expert. You'd be surprised how a talented sommelier can enhance your guests' dining experience. It could set you apart when you're trying to make a name for yourself."

"Yes," Ava agreed. "Now, tell me what happened with the French place. What was the name of the restaurant?"

"Chez Toussaint," Sarah said. "It's in the historic district. And, well, a woman from my past came in and lied about something I said. I told her that I felt a sense of pride because I was no longer a worthless slug. She thought I was talking about her, my boss came over, she made my words out to be much worse than what they were, and I was fired."

Ava's mouth dropped open. "How awful! Who was the friend?"

"Lauren," Sarah said. "You were right about everything you said about her, by the way. And then some. You didn't know the half of it. The quarter of it, really."

"Well, she was always a garbage person," Ava said. "You found that out, better late than never."

"Oh, I found that out many years ago. You see, she's the reason why I can never get an architectural license."

"What do you mean?"

"A long story. How long do you have?"

"As long as you need."

Chapter Twenty-Seven

Sarah

It was going to happen. She was going to tell Ava about her greatest shame. It was difficult to form the words, so she started from the beginning of that evening.

"Lauren was not a good person," Sarah said. "I'm sure that I'm not telling you something you don't know. In fact, I know that you know she was a -"

"Garbage person," Ava said. "Go on."

"Yes. Garbage person. And she was. Selfish, vain, narcissistic, shallow, immoral. And I knew it. I don't know why I was hanging around her, but I was. Until one night…"

---

20 years ago

"Sarah," Lauren said desperately over the phone. "You have to come and get me. I hooked up with these guys from

Lebanon, and they just kicked me out of their place. I can't possibly drive home. Please come and get me."

Sarah sighed. It was 2 AM, early on a Saturday morning, and Sarah had been sleeping soundly. Nolan wasn't around because he was away on a retreat with the rest of the Cal State mathematics department. "Where are you?"

Lauren gave Sarah the address to where she was.

"I'll be there in a half hour."

Sarah got to where Lauren was and saw she was holding onto a streetlight pole for dear life. "Where's your car?" Sarah asked her.

"I don't have a car here," she said. "Jamal picked me up at my house. William was working late, so he didn't know what I was doing."

"K," Sarah said, wincing at the smell of vomit on her friend's breath.

"Please drive carefully," Lauren said, "because I feel like I need to-"

At that, Lauren threw up all over Sarah's shoes.

"Oops," Lauren said, slurring her words. "Sorry."

Sarah put Lauren's left arm around her neck and then loaded her into her car.

"In you go," Sarah said, putting Lauren into the passenger's seat and buckling her in.

Then Sarah took the wheel. As she drove along, Lauren's purse was on the floor of the passenger's seat, and Sarah could see the contents.

"Oh!" Sarah said as she noticed that Lauren had a bag of white powder in her enormous Birkin bag. "What is that?"

But Lauren was snoring. Sarah leaned down to pick up Lauren's purse while she was driving and swerved a little in the lane.

The Beachfront Inn

Her heart started to pound when she noticed the red and blue lights swirling in her rear-view mirror.

Sarah immediately pulled over, her hands shaking wildly on the steering wheel. Within minutes, a female cop was at her driver's side window. Sarah put down the window, her driver's license, proof of insurance, and registration ready in her shaking hand.

She was breathing heavily, and the cop looked at Sarah suspiciously. "Do you know why I pulled you over?" she asked Sarah.

"Yes," Sarah said. Her own voice sounded tinny in her ears. "I swerved."

The cop nodded silently and then went back to her car.

Sarah looked nervously over at Lauren, who seemed to be coming to life just a bit. "What's going on?" Lauren asked, her voice slurred.

"I got pulled over," Sarah said.

Lauren just nodded her head and went back to sleep.

The cop was taking a long time behind her, and Sarah started to get worried. She was completely sober, so she wasn't worried about getting arrested, but she felt more than uncomfortable when she saw a second cop car pull up behind the first one.

Finally, the original cop came back to her driver's side door. "Miss, could you please step out of the car?" she asked Sarah.

Sarah nodded and then got out of the car.

"Please follow the light with your eyes," the cop said, shining a penlight in Sarah's eyes.

Sarah obeyed.

"Please recite the alphabet without singing."

Sarah did so. "A, B, C..." She recited the entire

alphabet and then hoped she wouldn't have to recite it backward. She always had difficulty with that.

"Please walk in a straight line," the cop asked her.

Sarah walked down the street about 20 feet before the cop stopped her.

"Walk back," the cop ordered.

Sarah did so.

"Touch your nose," the cop asked.

Sarah touched her nose.

The cop had Sarah do a few more field sobriety measures before asking Sarah to blow into a breathalyzer. Sarah did as she was told.

The breathalyzer measured 0.0.

Sarah figured she would get a ticket and be sent on her way. She thought she was only asked to do the DWI tests because she was pulled over in the middle of the night after swerving on the street.

She was wrong.

The cop came over to Sarah. Next to her was another cop, a male one. Out of the new cop car, the one that was behind the first one, a man and a dog came out.

"Permission to search your car," the female cop said.

"Why do you need to?" Sarah asked, thinking about Lauren's open purse with the white powder in it.

"When I pulled you over, you seemed extremely nervous," the female cop said. "That was why I asked you to perform the field sobriety test. Since you are not under the influence, I have my suspicions that you might be harboring contraband in your car."

"And if I refuse to let you search the car?" Sarah asked.

"Then I will detain you while I obtain a search warrant," the cop said. "So, you can do this the easy way or the hard way."

Sarah nodded, thinking that Lauren's purse would probably be off-limits in the search. At least, she was hoping for that. "Okay. Please search the car."

The cop searched the car, along with her partner. And, to Sarah's horror, the dog was also in on the search, and the dog signaled the presence of drugs. The dog sniffed around in the car and pawed the floor of the back seat on the passenger's side.

Sarah glanced over at Lauren's bag, which was still on the floor, and no longer saw the bag of white powder. She quickly deduced what had happened - apparently, while Sarah was out in the street and walking the line, Lauren had taken the drugs out of her purse and thrown the bag onto the floor of the backseat.

Lauren was obviously much more coherent than she let on.

Sarah groaned as she saw how big the baggie was. She deduced that Lauren probably got those drugs from her Lebanese "friends," and they were generous, because a bag of drugs that big probably had a street value of around $100,000. There were probably 3 kilos in the bag, Sarah thought as she eyeballed it.

Sarah looked over at Lauren, who was now awake.

Both women were quickly arrested. Sarah's car was left on the side of the road, and a tow truck soon appeared to haul it off. Sarah was taken into the station and questioned, but she was confident that her friend would tell the truth about the drugs. Lauren would admit to the cops that the drugs were hers and that Sarah knew nothing about any of it.

Sarah *knew* that Lauren would clear her. After all, Sarah was the innocent party. Sarah was the one who was roused in the middle of the night and came out for her friend, no questions asked. She was naïve enough to think that the phrase "no good deed goes unpunished" wouldn't apply to her.

She was wrong.

That early morning, Sarah was fingerprinted, mug-shot and put into a jail cell. Lauren was freed.

"Why am I being booked again?" Sarah asked the cop who booked her after her interrogation. His name was Officer Reilly, and he was a short and stout man with a head of curly red hair and a bulbous nose.

"Because your friend informed me that you were the one who possessed the drugs," Officer Reilly said. "And the drugs were found in your car, so, there you go."

Sarah couldn't argue with the basis for the arrest, even if she wanted to murder Lauren. How dare she throw her under the bus like that!

Sarah spent that early morning in jail because she hadn't yet had the opportunity for a phone call. When she finally had a chance to call somebody, at 10 AM, some six hours after she had been put into her cell, she called Lauren, expecting that Lauren would bail her out for sure.

"Lauren," Sarah said to her when she answered the phone.

"Sarah. I can't talk to you. I'm sorry." Lauren's voice was low, as if she was afraid that somebody was listening.

Sarah closed her eyes as she sat on the phone. "Lauren, you have to post my bail. I was arrested because of your drugs."

"I can't talk to you. I'm sorry."

At that, Lauren hung up the phone.

Then she called Rina and Elizabeth. Both women said they couldn't bail her out. They both made some kind of excuse - Rina said she had a hangover and Elizabeth was going shopping with a friend.

Then Sarah was led back to her cell. She was told she wouldn't get the privilege of another phone call for the next six hours.

In the meantime, she was feeling nauseated, and the cell was absolutely freezing. And she got angrier and angrier by the minute. Mainly at Lauren, but also at Rina and Elizabeth, both of whom couldn't be bothered to come out to the jail and help her.

Six hours later, Sarah got the privilege of another phone call. She used that phone call to call a bail bondsman. Three hours after she called the bail bondsman, her $25,000 bond was posted, and she was freed from the jail.

It was 4 AM. Sarah had spent the last 24 hours in jail. For something she didn't do. Her "friend" Lauren had abandoned her and left her to take the blame for her drugs. Rina and Elizabeth wouldn't lift a finger to help her. She could've called her mother or her sister to post the bond, but she didn't want to admit to either of them how right they were about her "friends."

She had to rely on a stranger, a bail bondsman, to get her out of jail. She was humiliated and angry.

And, since Lauren refused to own up that the drugs were hers, and, in fact, told the cops that Sarah had confessed to her that she, Sarah, owned the drugs, and her husband backed her up, Sarah ended up pleading guilty to possession of cocaine with intent to distribute. She was told she would have a felony record if she pled guilty, but no prison time. But if she took the case to trial, she was facing 20 years in prison because the amount of cocaine was enough to convict her of trafficking.

She felt she had no choice but to plead guilty. So she

did, and she lost her architectural license after a hearing. This was devastating to Sarah because she was, more and more, contemplating getting back into designing buildings. She was seriously considering leaving Nolan and rejoining her old architectural firm or maybe getting a job with a firm in San Francisco.

But that was no longer an option.

Sarah told Ava the whole sad story while Ava sat in her lounger silently. "So, that's why I can't be an architect anymore," Sarah told her sister. "That's why I feel so lost right now. Nolan was my lifeline because the only skills I had were architectural, so I never knew what I would do to make a living if anything ever happened between Nolan and me. Now, well, I'm on my own and waitressing. Since I couldn't possibly live on Nantucket on a waitress's salary, I'm going to have to go to an area where I can. Which is why I have to move back to Kansas City."

Ava sat quietly, sipping her glass of wine.

"Sarah, what happened?" Ava asked gently. "Why didn't you get a high-powered lawyer to browbeat those stupid prosecutors until they dropped the charges? I mean, I can understand why you didn't take it to trial because a probation sentence is a great result for a possession with intent to distribute charge, and, it's true, if you took that case to trial, you really would've been rolling the dice. But surely you could've found somebody who would've been able to get the prosecutors to drop the charges completely."

"Didn't you just hear me? Lauren's husband is a huge deal, especially in a smallish community like Monterey. He's a billionaire, he gives a ton of money to charities that

The Beachfront Inn

benefit the police, he's friends with most of the judges on the Monterey County Superior Court, and I still think that he outright bribed the cops that arrested Lauren and me. And, well, Nolan didn't support me at all. So, there you go. You have Lauren, with a hubby who will cajole, bribe or blackmail whoever he can to make sure that Lauren didn't get charged for the drugs and then there was me, who was basically hung out to dry for this. Do the math."

"Wait, Nolan didn't support you? What are you talking about?"

Sarah shrugged her shoulders. "He didn't back me up." She sighed. "I was going to leave him before all this happened, and he knew it. I had headhunters lined up in San Francisco and some really good leads. I'd already gone up there to scout out rentals and found a beautiful one in a historic Victorian home in the Pacific Heights. I dreamt of buying a house there after I was on my feet for a few years. I was all set. Then this happened, and it knocked me back."

"How did Nolan find out that you were about to leave?"

Sarah rolled her eyes. "He got into my emails. I didn't even know that he knew my password. Then again, it was probably a little too easy to guess, if you know me well - it was Olive1973."

Ava smiled. "The name of our first dog and the year we got her," she said. "I didn't know you still thought about her."

"Oh, of course I do. Aside from my beautiful Bella, Olive was the best dog I've ever had. She was so smart, so sweet, so eager to please, and so bonded with us. And I talked about her enough to Nolan that he knew how special she was to me. I'm guessing it didn't take him all that long to figure out my password."

"And he found emails from the headhunters and landlords," Ava surmised.

"Right. So, Nolan figured that my architectural license would be completely at risk if I went down on this drug charge. And, without that license, what would I do in a place like San Francisco, where the rentals, even back then, were astronomical? He wanted me to lose my architectural license, so he refused to pay for a criminal defense attorney." She shrugged her shoulders. "I technically had zero income because I was never married to him, only living with him, so I qualified for the public defender. And that was that."

Ava shook her head. "Bastard. Bastard, bastard, bastard. Controlling bastard at that."

"Right," Sarah said. "And you don't know the half of it. Nolan wrote a letter to the California Architectural Board, and it wasn't a character reference, let me tell you. I got a copy of the letter, and he'd written that I had a drug problem and that he'd caught me giving drugs to minors. All of that was a lie, of course." Sarah shook her head. Just thinking about what Nolan did made her furious again.

"What?" Ava asked. "I mean, what? Why didn't you leave him right then and there?"

"How could I? I had no place to go. No money, no architectural license. I couldn't get a decent apartment with a felony conviction on my record, any place in America. So, I had to take my rage at Nolan and bury it deep. I buried it so deep that I went into denial about how much I really despised him. I had to. It was the only way that I could cope with my life. I couldn't look in the mirror anymore because I hated what I saw."

"Well, you still should've left him," Ava said. "I would've helped you if you just would've reached out."

"Ava, you don't know how powerful denial can be. After

I found out what Nolan did, I raged and tried to plot how to get out of there, to leave him, but, once I figured out that my felony conviction would prevent me from even finding a place to live, I had to give up and stay with him. And thank you for saying that you would've helped me, and I'm sure you would've tried, but what could you do for me? I was a convicted felon. I couldn't just stay with you in your little condo with you and the triplets. I wasn't going to ask that of you, either."

Sarah didn't want to tell Ava that, after what Nolan did to her, she not only stayed with him, but she changed his adult diapers during his final months. And she did all that research, trying to find something promising for Nolan's diagnosis. She did that for him because he took care of her all those years. After she gave up and realized she had to stay with him, she convinced herself she did love him, even though, deep down, she despised him. That was why she took care of him when he was dying.

"Sarah, did you try to get your license back after a few years? I mean, surely the California Architectural Board can't hold that non-violent felony against you forever, can they?"

Sarah sighed and bit her lower lip and then walked over to the deck's railing and looked down. "I never tried to get my license back. I can't exactly explain why except to say that I just had such low self-esteem that I didn't feel that I'd ever get my life back. I had such a powerful need to make everybody, including myself, believe that I was living the life I really loved that I just couldn't admit to the world, let alone myself, how unhappy I was. So, I just didn't rock the boat."

Ava went to the railing and put her arm around her sister. "I wish you would've called me when all this happened. I wasn't licensed to practice law in California, so I couldn't have represented you, but I certainly could've given you advice on how to fight the charges."

Sarah smiled and shook her head sadly. "Oh, Ava, how much I wanted to call you to ask you to help me. But it was my stupid pride. I didn't want to admit that you were right about my friends. And I really didn't want to admit how terrible my relationship with Nolan really was. Because you would've asked me why Nolan wasn't getting me a superstar attorney to fight the charges, and I would've had to admit the truth - my boyfriend was a selfish controlling jerk who was happy to see me fry if it meant he could keep me in line."

"And I would've hounded you to leave him when I found out the truth," Ava said. "You aren't saying as much, but that's what you're thinking, I know. And you'd be right."

Sarah just nodded her head, her hands hanging loosely over the side of the deck railing. "Right. And, as much as I would've wanted to leave him, I was so unsure about everything at that time that I don't think that I could've. Especially after I pled guilty to Lauren's crime. I knew that the word 'felon' would just follow me everywhere I went. You don't know how much of a stigma a felony conviction is, Ava. I just didn't believe that I could make it out in the world with that black mark on my record."

"So, you kept quiet and kept on with your life."

"Such as it was, yes. That's what I did. Nolan was taking care of me, and I didn't feel confident that I could take care of myself without him. Now, here I am. My hand has been forced. And it's been liberating. I can't ever explain how liberating it's been. I mean, yes, I don't have two nickels to rub together. My dream of being a stellar architect has been pulled out from under me, and I still don't know how I'm going to land on my feet. But, for the first time, in a long time, I'm living life on my terms. It's scary as hell, but that's what life is, you know. Scary and exhilarating and beautiful and weird and sad and joyful. I've been sheltered long enough, and it's time to get out there and see what can happen when I apply myself."

Ava squeezed Sarah's shoulder and put her head on that shoulder. Sarah put her head on Ava's head and sighed. All those years, this was what she wanted, more than anything - her sister's head on her shoulder. Her sister's arm around her. She just couldn't reach out because she knew that reaching out to Ava during her lost years would've meant she couldn't possibly keep living her life the way she was. Ava wouldn't have ever given up trying to convince Sarah to leave. And Sarah just wasn't ready to face what Ava would've rightfully demanded.

It was so much easier to just go along and pretend Ava didn't exist, so she could be free to live in her bubble.

"So, what exactly happened to Nolan?" Ava asked. "Why did you guys finally break up?"

"Ava, Nolan died," Sarah said. "ALS. Cut down in his prime." She shook her head. "The sad thing is, I don't grieve him. I thought I would. At his funeral, everybody was treating me with kid gloves, thinking I'd fall apart. Everyone knew that Nolan had never changed his will, so his wife, who he never formally divorced, got everything, even though she never visited him when he was sick and didn't even bother to come to his funeral. There was a lot of whispering about what I would do and where I would go. Poor, poor me, out on the street with nothing, at my age."

Ava squeezed Sarah's shoulder again. "Oh, Sarah, I'm so, so sorry. That must've been awful for you, caring for somebody with such a devastating disease."

"Well, it wasn't a picnic, that's for sure," Sarah said. "But you adjust. This is your life, feeding your previously strong and healthy boyfriend through a straw. Watching him waste away to 90 pounds and having to constantly entertain well-meaning people who drop by to check on him. But you get used to the rhythms of being with a dying person. Your brain can adapt to any situation. You might think, before something like this happens, that it would be the worst thing in the world to handle. But then it does happen, and you're like 'I thought it would be worse.'"

Ava nodded her head. "I know what you're saying. All that's happened to me - my first husband dying, my second husband cleaning out our joint investment account, losing my job, losing you for so long - all of it took some adjustment, but I always was able to make the adjustment. I never felt like crawling into a hole and dying like I thought I might if something tragic happened. So, you're right. Humans are resilient."

"Yes. That's a good word. Resilience. I was much more resilient than I thought I would be, losing everything I'd known for so many years in one fell swoop. Starting over without a clue on what was around the corner."

The two sisters sat silently for a few minutes, Ava's arm around Sarah, Sarah's head on Ava's shoulder.

"Sarah," Ava finally said, looking at the ocean. "When I talked to our mother, I specifically added a sommelier's salary into my proposal. I'd like to extend an offer to join our team here. I'll pay you $40,000 a year to start, plus you can stay here as long as you like. You and Bella, of course."

"You don't have to do that," Sarah said. "I'm fine, really. Kansas City is a great place to live, and I can get by there waiting tables. Thank you, Ava, but I can't put you out like that."

Ava took a breath. "Sarah, I'm not doing you a favor. I've been talking this out with everybody. Everyone agrees that having a good sommelier here will be nothing but an asset. Of course, I'd like for you to become certified by the time this place opens up, but that's easy enough to do - it's a matter of taking a test. There's a written part and a tasting part. I think that you have to take a certification course, but it's online and can be completed in a weekend, I think."

"I know what's required to become certified," Sarah said. "The Court of Master Sommeliers established four levels of tests - introductory, certified, advanced and master. I can take the introductory sommelier test, no problem. I could pass that one now with my hands tied behind my back, although I do have to take a short online course first in order to take the test. I'd like to go to level two as soon as possible - the certified sommelier level. Again, I believe that I can pass that test with flying colors. I'd like to go even beyond those levels, though. After I land somewhere and get 3 years' experience, I can take the three-day advanced sommelier test. My goal is to become a master, of course. There are only 270 or so masters in the entire world."

Sarah smiled as she thought of her goals. She had a game plan and a vision for her future that made her proud. Talking with Ava about her ambitions made her crystallize just how much she wanted to make something out of her life.

Ava grinned as she sipped her wine and looked at the raging ocean. "I'm sorry," she said with a small laugh. "It's just the look in your eyes. It just fills me with joy."

"The look in my eyes?" Sarah asked, feeling curious about what Ava was talking about. "What do you mean?"

"It's just that it occurred to me that you're back. You're my sister again. Your eyes are so different now. When I visited you out in Monterey, I didn't see anything in those eyes of yours. You just seemed to be dead inside if you want to know the truth. But, just now, when you talked about how much you want to become a master sommelier and join less than 300 people in the entire world in getting that certification, you seemed to come alive. I see a passion there, a fire, a drive. None of that was in those eyes before."

Sarah realized that tears were coming to her eyes. She smiled just a little and then looked at her glass of wine and took a sip.

"What's wrong?" Ava asked, seeing the tears in Sarah's eyes.

"Nothing. It's just that I've spent so many years living the life I wasn't supposed to live, when I could've tried to become a sommelier years ago. But I didn't because of inertia and fear. I was comfortable, I was safe, I was having fun traveling the world. But I was secretly suffering from major depression. Now I feel like I can actually grab some true happiness, but look at all the years I've wasted."

"No regrets," Ava said. "You can only move forward, and I feel like you have a solid plan for the rest of your life. I'm proud of you, sis. I really am."

Ava's pride in Sarah puffed Sarah up immensely. "So, I'm not silly and vain anymore, then?"

"Insipid and lazy, and, no, I don't think that at all. I admit, I assumed that you were on this island to snag a billionaire, which you could, by the way. You're still absolutely stunning. But I really should've given you the benefit of the doubt. After all, you're my sister. You'll always be my sister, and I'll always love you."

"I'll always love you, too," Sarah said.

Then it was time to reminisce some more about their childhood. Sarah loved to talk about the old days with Ava,

The Beachfront Inn

because their experiences bonded them together and Sarah often got nostalgic for those innocent days.

Sarah looked at Ava and chuckled. "Do you remember our obsession with The Bay City Rollers?" she asked Ava.

"Oh, God, don't remind me. I think I wanted to marry Leslie, and you wanted to marry Eric, if I can remember rightly."

"You even named one of Goldie's hamster babies after Leslie," Ava said. "Remember?" Goldie was a hamster Ava and Sarah had when they were kids. Unbeknownst to anybody, Goldie was ready to have a litter when she came home with the girls, and she soon popped out 8 tiny bald and blind babies.

"Oh, of course. Leslie was a mean old thing. He bit me all the time. But I kept him because I named him."

The two women started to laugh. "Remember when the Rollers found girlfriends, and we got so mad that we wrote them a hate letter?" Ava asked.

"That we didn't send. We stayed up all night writing all kinds of hate letters to them. And we broke one of their 45 records into little pieces and put the pieces into an envelope."

"And didn't send that, either," Ava said. By now, she was laughing so hard she was crying.

"Oh, but we were going to show them how unhappy we were they were cheating on us."

Ava shook her head, still laughing. "Those were the good ol' days, weren't they? When the worst problem we had was that members of a teeny-bopper group, who didn't know that we were alive, were dating?"

"Don't I know that," Sarah said. "I mean, I love my life, but it has been stressful. When we were kids, we were so carefree."

"We played baseball in the street and walked to school," Ava said. "We stayed out until the sun went down, and nobody cared."

"Mom would tell us to get out of the house and don't come back until dinner," Sarah remembered. "It was so much of a more innocent time back then."

"Yes," Ava said. "Such an innocent time compared to now."

"Oh, if only I had the chance to go back to when we were young and I could choose my life's events differently," Sarah said sadly. "How I would've had a different life."

Ava looked at her sister. "Wow. I was wrong about you all along. I just assumed you had it made. God, I wanted your life, just for a week. To live a life of comfort and luxury and leisure. To have personal chefs make my meals and have a personal trainer put me through my paces. I dreamed about having such a life."

"And I wanted your life," Sarah said. "I wanted a life with children and a profession and respect."

"Oh, you didn't want my life," Ava said. "I think I got a total of 20 hours of sleep the year that the triplets hit their terrible twos. At one point, I really thought I would have to check myself into the mental hospital. I was so sleep-deprived and stressed out, you wouldn't believe."

"Yes, but you were living, and you were contributing. You were making your mark. Now, you can look back on all of that and know you made a difference in the world."

"A bad difference," Ava said. "I was helping billionaires cheat the system. But I get your point. And you'll make a difference, too. When you get your master's sommelier certificate and join the less than 300 people who have attained such an elite status."

Sarah put her hand on Ava's shoulder and squeezed. "I

love you, Ava. I'm so sorry that all these years have gone by with us barely speaking. That was all my fault, too. You wanted to get together, and I blew you off. So many wasted years when we could've been having each other's backs."

"Well, we're here now, tonight. And, Sarah, I really hope that you reconsider moving to Kansas City. I hope that you take my offer."

"I will."

"You will reconsider, or you will take the offer?" Ava asked hopefully.

"I'll take the offer. But Ava, I can't ask you to take me in. You're going to need all the rooms in this house to make money. I'll find a place in town where I can rent."

"Well, I'd like you to stay here at least for the time being," Ava said. "I could use some help around this place, to tell you the truth. And rentals around this place are astronomical, not to mention hard to come by. Besides, the renovation won't be finished for another nine months, so I won't have this place opened until next summer. Choose a bedroom, and I'll get some furniture right away."

"The renovation will take nine months?" Sarah asked. "So, when do you want me to start?"

"Start now," Ava said. "You can start the procurement process now. Get to know the local wineries, scout out different labels around the country, give me some ideas about the wine cellar downstairs. I'd like to have an entire collection of wines in that cellar by the time I open this place next summer, and I'm sure that the process of filling that cellar will take some time."

Sarah nodded her head and felt tears coming to her eyes. "Ava, I just can't tell you how much it means to me that you forgive me for my awful behavior over the years.

I've never felt good about us not speaking all these years. And I've missed you more than you could ever imagine."

"I've missed you too," Ava said. "But I would like to know why you didn't return my calls or take me up on my invitations to get together over the years."

Sarah sighed. "I was living in denial. I knew that I was wasting my life, but I didn't feel like I had a choice. I was so stuck for so many years. I couldn't think my way out of any of it. I don't know. I think that I sunk into a deep depression, and I just felt hopeless. And I knew that if I talked to you, I'd be forced to face my situation. You wouldn't let me get away with lying to the world and lying to myself. And, Ava, I needed to keep lying to myself. I needed the façade. I couldn't face reality, and I knew you'd force me to do just that."

Ava nodded her head. "I think I understand," she said. "You didn't want to have to answer the questions that I would've thrown at you, and I'll admit, I was very judgmental about your choices. And, for that, I'm sorry. I just couldn't understand why my talented and brilliant sister chose to -"

"Become a useless appendage to a rich guy," Sarah finished Ava's statement. "I've asked myself that question every single day for the past 20 odd years."

"Well, that's all behind you now," Ava said. "You're going to get it all together, on your own terms. But what can I do to help you, besides hiring you for the sommelier position?"

"You've helped me more than you could ever imagine," Sarah said. "I can't tell you how excited I am to be able to work with your kitchen staff, find out what kind of dishes are going to be served, and discover just the right wines to go with everything. You can have wine pairings with your food, and your guests will love it. I can help this place succeed, do my part, and just knowing that is enough."

Ava put her arm around Sarah. "Oh, but Sarah, there must be something that we can do to Lauren. I mean, she's on the island, right?"

"Yes, she is," Sarah said. "For how long, I don't know. I have no clue why she's even here in the first place. I mean, she lives in California. Why is she here?"

Ava bit her bottom lip. "Good question. But let's put our heads together and figure out something that we could do to her. She can't just get away with destroying your life and go on her merry way. We have to get her somehow."

Sarah finally smiled. "Yes, let's figure something out. We can be the dynamic duo again. A team." She rubbed her hands together. "This actually might be fun."

Chapter Twenty-Eight

Sarah

Sarah and Ava tried to develop a good idea about getting back at Lauren, but they couldn't think of anything to bring Lauren down.

"We'll have to table that one," Sarah finally said to Ava.

But, as Sarah walked around the island one day, marveling at the architecture of the place, she knew she wanted to find out more about Nantucket. She'd traveled around the world, but she'd never been to a place that was so determined to be preserved in amber, untouched by the ravages of time, and that fascinated her.

She decided to go down to the historical association, which was housed in several federal-style buildings in the downtown area. She walked in to go to the library and study about the buildings around the island and the history behind all of the major houses and other structures. She'd talked to Quinn a little bit about the island's history because Quinn, like herself, had a fascination with historical archi-

The Beachfront Inn

tecture and design. But she wanted to do some independent study on her own.

She was directed to the research library, an unassuming Quaker-style building on Fair Street, built at the turn of the 20th Century. Once she got in there, she felt excited to see the different displays and letters and then went to a light-filled reading room where there were books about the island's history.

Three hours later, after having gotten lost in reading about the lore about the founding families - the Coffins, the Macys, the Swains, and several others who formed a proprietorship to bring English settlement to Nantucket in the mid-1600s - Sarah left the library and started to walk to her car.

A handsome young man was jogging on the street. He had dark hair that flopped over his forehead, piercing blue eyes and strong eyebrows. Sarah furrowed her brows, trying to place the face...

Langdon Prescott! The billionaire who was with Lauren that day at Chez Toussaint. That was who that was.

He stopped when he saw Sarah and pointed at her. "Hello," he said. "I remember you."

Sarah just nodded her head. "Yes. You were with Lauren."

"Yeah," he said. "At Chez Toussaint. Sorry about all that, by the way."

"Not a problem," Sarah said as she headed towards her car.

Langdon followed her to her car. "No, really, I'm sorry about you losing your job like that. Let me make it up to you by buying you a cup of coffee."

Sarah narrowed her eyes at the guy and then suddenly realized she would be a total idiot not to take the guy up on his offer. She cocked her head to the side. "Sure, why not?"

The two of them walked over to the Handlebar Cafe, which was less than a half-mile away from the library and was housed in a small house-like structure with a large bay window. When they walked in, Sarah saw that the floor plan was open and inviting, with tables that looked like picnic tables and a patterned hardwood floor.

Sarah ordered a hot chocolate, Langdon got himself an espresso, and they sat down.

Sarah just watched the man, trying to figure out his angle. He stopped her in the street and apologized. With his smarmy looks and snide remarks about her at the restaurant, he didn't strike Sarah as a particularly sincere guy.

At any rate, Sarah knew she might find out more about Lauren from this guy. Then she could use whatever information she found out to think of how she could finally obtain some justice for what Lauren did to her.

"So," Sarah finally said. "I'm not going to beat around the bush. You were with Lauren Blake. I'd like to ask you some questions about her."

Langdon nodded his head. "I figured you would," he said. "That's why I stopped you on the street. I wanted to talk to you about her."

Sarah cocked her head and took a sip of her hot cocoa. It was rich, creamy and sweet, and it hit the spot on this cold November day. "You were just jogging by and happened to run into me. Right?"

"Right," he said. "But it was really a lucky thing that we ran into each other because I wanted to talk to you anyhow. Lauren told me about what happened between you two."

"Oh, she did, did she? She told you about how she

made me take the fall for her drugs and that I'm a convicted felon now because of her?"

"Yes," Langdon said without missing a beat. "She told me all that."

"Why would she tell you about that?" Sarah asked.

"Because she's proud of it," Langdon said. "She joked about it. She wanted me to know how clever she was she was able to pull that off." He shook his head. "She's a sociopath."

Sarah took a deep breath and tried to calm her heart. Lauren was proud of ruining her life. That didn't surprise Sarah, not in the least, but having it confirmed infuriated her beyond measure.

She closed her eyes. "A sociopath," she repeated. "That's a good word for her." Then she opened her eyes and stared at Langdon. "Why is she here? She lives in California. I mean, how unlucky am I to see her out here? I thought that I got far away from her when I came out here."

"She lives here," Langdon said. "She and her husband have a summer house in Surfside. They've had that house for years."

"And? It's not summer," Sarah said. "It's November."

Langdon shrugged. "I don't know the answer to that question, although I get the feeling that maybe they're separated. So, she's staying in the summer house to get away from William. That's what I think happened."

"And her kids? Where are they?" Sarah asked.

"They both live in Los Angeles," Langdon said. "They're 25 and 27, so I don't think that Lauren keeps up with them all that much."

Sarah nodded her head but wondered what she could do with any of this information. "What do you know about her husband?"

"I know that he'll be in town this weekend," Langdon said.

"He will? Why?" Sarah asked.

"He's trying to sell the house out here," Langdon said. "Which is why I suspect they're going to divorce."

"I see," Sarah said, sipping her hot chocolate. "What's the address to their house?"

Langdon wrote the address down on a napkin. "Here," he said, pushing the napkin over to Sarah. "What are you planning in your head?"

"I don't know yet," Sarah said. "All that I know is that running into you was some kind of kismet. It's almost like the universe just happened to plant you in the same place as me at the same time."

He smiled. "Well, I do happen to believe in fate," he said, staring at her. "Are you hungry? I can buy you dinner. Straight Wharf."

Sarah shook her head. At this point, she had zero interest in men. Even rich men. *Especially* rich men. And she couldn't forget the snide remark he made about how she couldn't have been a world traveler because she was a waitress. It was judgmental, prejudicial and just basically unkind of him to make assumptions like that. It was also really rude of him to make that remark in front of her like she wasn't even there.

Besides, he was out with Lauren. His relationship with her sleazy ex-friend was indeterminate, but just the fact that he was out with her spoke volumes to Sarah about this guy's character.

"No offense, but I'm really not interested," Sarah said. "But thanks for the information about Lauren's husband and about Lauren herself."

Langdon looked crestfallen when Sarah informed him

about her non-interest in him. "I wasn't dating Lauren, in case you were wondering."

Sarah raised an eyebrow. "That's actually none of my business." She got her purse, stood up and then shook his hand. "Again, thanks for caring enough to take me out to coffee and give me those tidbits of information," she said.

"Walk you to your car?" he asked. "I'm sorry, I really don't want you to leave. You're probably the most beautiful woman I've ever seen."

Sarah just shook her head. "Not doing the cougar thing," she said. "And, at this point, I'm not doing the man thing, either. Especially the rich man thing. So, the answer is no." Then she smiled. "But thanks for the info."

As Sarah walked out of the coffee shop, she smiled. She had the chance to take up with another rich guy, and she turned him down flat.

Ava would be so proud.

Chapter Twenty-Nine

Hallie

Hallie was feeling better ever since she got out to the island. She hadn't spoken to Nate since she arrived on Nantucket, and, ever since she got away from that apartment and away from him, she found she was drinking much less. She was still severely depressed. She'd found a doctor on the island who would take her insurance, and she was seeing him about her depression. She was getting frustrated that this doctor kept taking her off of one anti-depressant, only to put her on a different one. And she still had a completely sleepless night at least three times a week.

Yet she felt so much lighter being out on the island. Yes, it was a mirage, she knew. She couldn't possibly move out to Nantucket. That would mean the end of her marriage, and even though she knew that her marriage should end, she wasn't ready to pull the plug. She wasn't ready to say she failed. She felt like she failed at everything else, and she wasn't quite ready to say she was a complete failure in life.

The Beachfront Inn

Besides, what could she do on Nantucket? She'd been around the island, exploring, and, while she loved the vibe and she really loved all the nature preserves - she read that 30% of the island was conservation land, and she loved to explore nature and bird-watch - she saw that there really wasn't a lot of industry on the island, aside from businesses related to tourism.

One day, while she was walking around the historic district, just taking in the architecture and quiet vibe, she stopped in front of a house. She cocked her head as she read the sign out front. Apparently, this house was a business, and it was occupied by one Willow Killeen. She had no idea what this business was, but something was pulling at her to go in and investigate it.

She walked in and immediately smelled burning incense. There were the chimes of little bells as she opened the door. She looked around and saw that there was all manner of books on the shelves. These books were about metaphysical topics - Wicca, Tarot, chakra healing, energy healing, herbal healing and acupuncture. The store also sold crystals, candles, jewelry, teas, herbs, Tarot cards, stones, Tibetan singing bowls, and aromatherapy.

Behind the counter was a young woman who couldn't have been more than 25 years old. She was beautiful in a natural way. Her hair was long and black, and her eyes were piercing green, framed by the longest and thickest eyelashes Hallie had ever seen. She wasn't wearing any makeup, but she didn't need to because her skin was luminous and perfect. She was petite, only around 5'4", and couldn't have weighed more than 115 pounds.

The woman looked at Hallie and raised an eyebrow. "Yep," she said. "You're definitely in the right place." Then she cocked her head. "Dude, I don't want to scare you, but your aura…" She shook her head. "You've got some really nasty energy roiling around. I think you need my help."

Hallie blinked. "I'm sorry?" she asked. "If this is the way you sell stuff-"

"It's not," the woman said. "Trust me, I don't B.S. people just because I want to make a sale. And most of the people who come in here don't give off the dark vibes you're giving off right now. I pretty much just let everybody browse around, buy whatever and go on their way. I don't try to lay it down the way I'm doing with you. But, once in a while, I get somebody walking in here who's like a walking black aura, and I have to get involved. That hasn't happened in years, though."

"I don't understand."

"Let me do a tarot spread," the woman said. "By the way, I'm Willow. I own this joint."

"A tarot spread?" Hallie said. "I don't believe in that."

Willow smiled a little. "Come on back," she said. "If anybody comes in to buy something, the bell will ring. But I really need to figure out what's going on with you."

This was the strangest encounter Hallie had ever experienced. Yet, she was drawn to this beautiful woman. She felt a deep, almost spiritual, connection to her, and she felt it immediately.

Hallie sat down in a back room as Willow got some cards out, shuffled them and asked her to cut them. Hallie did as she was told, and then Willow asked her to pick out ten cards. She picked out the ten cards, and then Willow spread them out on the table in a pattern.

"It's called the Celtic Cross," Willow said after she laid out the cards. There were three cards in a vertical line, with a card covering the middle card. On one side of the three cards was a card and one on the other side. On the edge were four more cards in a vertical row.

Willow studied the cards. "You've got a lot going on," she said. "A bad marriage, you feel lost, and you feel like you're adrift. Nothing is good in your life except your daughter and your friends. But you feel like you're a burden to all of them. You feel like your friends are propping you up, and if they weren't, you would just disappear. And you feel like your daughter doesn't need you and doesn't want you around." She took a deep breath. "Don't go back to New York. There's nothing for you there."

Hallie screwed up her face. "Wait. Did somebody put you up to this?" She looked around. "Ava, Quinn. Come on out. This isn't funny."

Willow just shook her head. "How did you come to my shop?" she asked.

"I was taking a walk and, I don't know, I just thought I would stop in."

"So, you just randomly decided to stop in, then?"

"Yes. That's right."

"Then why do you think that anybody put me up to giving you this reading? It's not like one of your friends dragged you here, kicking and screaming."

"But you couldn't know this much about me," Hallie said. "How did you know all of what you told me?"

"I'm good," she said. "And I can read the tarot like a bad-ass." She pointed at the center card. "This card is you. Queen of Cups reversed. You're depressed, clingy, insecure and this King of Swords crossing you shows that you're in a toxic, toxic relationship with a man."

"What does crossing me mean?"

"It means that it's a block. At least, in this spread, it means that, just because the surrounding cards are so negative. And, see, he shows up again in the spread in the environment slot, but he shows up there as the Emperor reversed. You need to let go, but you can't because you feel like he has a hold on you. He doesn't have a hold on you, by the way. Your chains are all in your head."

"But what about those other things you told me?" Hallie asked. "About how I feel about my friends and my daughter and all that. How does this spread tell you all that?"

"You've got the three of cups in your hopes and fears position. I see three women in this card, you and two other friends. They're your lifelines, but you also are afraid they're only hanging around you because they feel sorry for you and they feel they need to help you. They don't feel that way at all, so stop thinking like that."

Hallie sat back in her chair. Willow was touching on a subconscious fear she had, one she'd never acknowledged, even to herself. And that was that Ava and Quinn were so successful, so accomplished, so smart, why would they be hanging out with her? Yes, she and Ava went way back to freshman year at M.U., but Ava went to Harvard Law, she made six figures at a law firm, and now was running her own B&B. Quinn was a highly sought-after interior decorator. She was extremely successful in New York and was already gaining a reputation on Nantucket.

And then there was her. She'd failed at every job she'd ever tried. Yes, her husband was wealthy, which meant she was, too. But she, herself, was a nobody. A nothing. She couldn't even live vicariously through her successful daughter because her daughter wouldn't let her ride her coattails.

Why would Ava and Quinn want to hang out with her? What did she bring to the table?

"What else did the cards say?" Hallie asked.

"Well, here's your daughter in the past position. Princess of Cups reversed. That card could mean that your daughter has to grow up, but it doesn't mean that here. Considering the position of the other cards, I see this reversed card as symbolic of your relationship with her. You're dependent on her, and she doesn't give you the time of day."

Hallie drew a breath. Man, this reading was hitting everything on the nose.

"And, here you go, you got The Tower in the future position. Everything's going to crumble around you." She nodded her head. "Don't worry, that Tower is totally positive here. See, it's next to you and your husband, and it shows that you're going to leave him."

"You can see that?" Hallie said.

"Yeah. The Tower is pointing to it. And the two of cups reversed as the outcome screams that this will happen. What I'm not getting is why you haven't left him yet."

"I don't know," Hallie admitted. "He's security. He provides a beautiful home."

"Nope," Willow said. "He doesn't provide you a beautiful home. He provides you a beautiful condo, superficially beautiful, anyhow. But that condo isn't home to you because home is where you're loved and accepted and secure. That condo might have gorgeous furniture and paintings and rugs and big-screen T.V.s. When you invite people over to your condo, people love the way you've decorated the place. But that condo has absorbed your depression, your husband's indifference and cruelty and all the toxicity the two of you lay on each other. So, when people come over to your condo, they might see beauty, but they're going to feel like something's really off."

"My husband isn't cruel," Hallie said.

"Oh, but he is. He ignores you, puts you down, and

shows that he doesn't care about you in a million different ways. You've just gotten so used to his attitude towards you that you don't see it for what it is - cruelty."

"I don't understand. If my husband was cruel, I would know it, wouldn't I?"

Willow shook her head. "Why do you feel that you can't leave? He's obviously made you think that you're going to fail if you do leave him. He's hammered that into your head so hard that you don't even recognize it. You just think in your head that you have to stay, and even you don't know why you feel that way. But I'll tell you why you feel that way - he's drilled it into your head with every action and inaction. That's cruel."

Hallie gulped. "I-"

"You have a friend who's an attorney, right?" She pointed at a card called "Justice." "Your attorney friend is one of your biggest influences. That's the position this card is in. Use her. Talk to her, tell her that you're going to leave your husband, and she'll make sure you get the best settlement you can. You can trust her. And you're going to make out like a bandit when you leave him."

And then Willow grinned. "And he knows it. That's why he's not divorcing you. He doesn't want to give you half of everything you guys own. He loves controlling you with the purse strings. He makes the dough, he won't share it with you, and he sure as hell doesn't want to give it to you. If it weren't for that, he would've gotten out a long time ago."

"Is all that in cards, too?" Hallie asked.

"In a sense," Willow said. "But it's more that I'm getting the vibes about him and how he is. And," she said, throwing out three more cards. "Yep. I just threw out three cards that tell me about him, specifically, and, right in the middle, there's the reversed 10 of pentacles. He thinks that you're going to ruin him financially if you guys divorce. He loves the position you're in now. Totally dependent on him, and you don't ask for any of the wealth he's making."

"How much will I get if I divorce him?"

Willow gathered up all the cards, shuffled them and then split them. "Three cards," she said, pointing to the deck.

Hallie chose three cards.

Willow nodded her head. "Oh, yeah. You go toe to toe with him, and it's on like Donkey Kong, baby. 10 of Pentacles, The Sun, The Chariot. All really good cards. 10 of Pentacles is upright here. That's long-lasting wealth. The Sun is the best card in the deck. Success, happiness, abundance, all that good stuff that ain't happening for you right now. The Chariot shows victory, dude. You should be filing for divorce yesterday."

"I don't know," Hallie said. "I'm so scared of doing that."

Willow rolled her eyes. "You need some chakra cleansing," she said. "Come back tomorrow, and I can guarantee that I can clear out all that nasty energy that's trapped in your cells and making you feel like crap about yourself. You need to become a bad-ass. Right now, you're such a little mouse. You know what happens to little mice, don't you? They get caught in traps and die."

Willow said that, and Hallie self-consciously put her hand to her neck, imagining it being snapped in a trap. What a terrible image.

"I'm sorry, I'm just imagining what you said about getting caught in a trap and dying."

Willow nodded her head. "You need to become a lioness, man. Queen of the jungle. You know, everybody always admires that male lion with his magnificent mane and his giant roar. But the lionesses are the real backbones of the pride. They hunt, raise the young, feed the male, and are like regular sister-wives because they all support each other. They're the ultimate in female power. The male lion, all he does is lay around and get served by the females. He sleeps 20 hours a day while his harem is doing all the dirty work."

"A lioness," Hallie repeated.

"Yeah, a lioness. I don't mean the part about servicing the male while he lays around, but the part about how they take control and they support other lionesses. They're the queens. You need to be a queen."

"Uh, what is this about my chakras?" Hallie asked.

"Well, here's the thing. I'm an energy healer. Do you know what that is?"

"No," Hallie admitted. "I don't even know what a chakra is."

"It's just energy centers in your body. Located along the spine. Sometimes energy gets trapped in one of your chakras, and that can cause all kinds of emotional and physical sicknesses."

"I hope I don't offend you when I tell you that that whole thing sounds like a load of hooey," Hallie said.

"Whatever. Listen, the ancient Chinese, the ancient Hindus, and ancient Buddhists all talked about energy flow. Buddhists talked about chakras and the Chinese talked about qi, which was their word for a life force. They both talked about energy flowing freely throughout the body. If that energy is blocked, emotional and physical illnesses happen. These beliefs have been around for thousands of years, way before pharmaceutical companies started bribing doctors to push their poison."

Hallie nodded. "Well, maybe I'll do some research on it before I decide if I want you to work on me."

"Sure, sure. Go ahead. But I'm well-known on the island. I treat energy blockages with crystals, herbal remedies, aromatherapy, sound therapy and acupuncture." At that, Willow gave Hallie a card. "I'll see you tomorrow at, say, 1?"

Hallie looked at Willow's card with shaking hands. *You're a lioness. You just don't know it yet.* "Yes, I'll see you tomorrow."

But, as she walked away from the house, she wondered what the hell she was getting into.

Chapter Thirty

Hallie

That evening after dinner, the ladies did their usual postmeal ritual, now with Sarah joining in - they went up to the terrace, built a fire, drank some wine, and chatted. Bella joined them, and Kona, Quinn's dog, would soon be a part of their group. While the ladies sat on their loungers and drank wine, Bella was quietly laying on Sarah's lap while Sarah petted her and talked to her quietly.

She was such a good dog, Hallie thought.

Hallie was thrilled that Sarah was now a part of their group, for she had always, always, always worried about Ava and Sarah's rift.

Hallie always liked Sarah. She knew her when she and Ava were in college. While she understood that Sarah changed when she went to California and became a paramour to a wealthy man, Hallie thought Ava needed to try harder to mend their relationship. She knew how much Ava loved her sister, and Hallie always thought that it was tragic they weren't seeing one another and they were barely speaking for so many years.

Now, Sarah was part of their fabric, and she was fitting in nicely. Hallie was also happy for Sarah's presence because it gave her one more person to bounce ideas off of.

Hallie sipped her wine, didn't down it and was able to drink socially with her friends. She knew she wasn't an alcoholic but had a drinking problem for many years. She also knew that her drinking issue was a cover-up for her unhappiness. Now, being out on the island, she didn't feel quite so unhappy, so she was able to drink a single glass of wine with her friends and not drink more than that.

"So," Sarah said, smiling at Hallie. "You've been quiet tonight. Did you like the Beef Wellington?" That was the meal Sarah had made for everyone that evening, and it was delicious. Beef in a puff pastry? Yes, please!

"Oh, it was scrumptious," Hallie said. "I'm sorry I've been so quiet, but I've been in my head."

"About what, sugar?" Quinn asked her.

Hallie told the ladies about Willow and the proposed treatment. "I don't know. It all seems kinda weird," Hallie told them. "I mean, crystals? Herbs? Aromatherapy? I'm on board with the acupuncture thing, though, as long as she's licensed."

Sarah was munching on a celery stick and green olives, as she had opted for a Bloody Mary instead of wine. "Hey, don't knock it," she said. "I've been to spas where they offer services from psychics and clairvoyants who also specialize in acupuncture, massage, crystals, you name it. Willow talked to you about energy flow, and she's probably right - you probably do have blocked energy. At any rate, it sounds like she knows her stuff, so if she felt the vibrations from you that told her that your chakras are blocked, you can probably take that to the bank."

Ava nodded her head. "The Four Seasons in New York has those kinds of services. Crystal therapists, hypnotists, past life regression, astrological readings, that kind of stuff. I've always been tempted to book a session myself."

Hallie looked around. "What about you, Quinn? Do you think this whole thing is crazy?"

Quinn put her hand on Hallie's. "Sugar, it can't hurt. Who knows? Maybe it'll help. How much is she charging?"

"Come to think of it, she didn't talk about that. It could be a high-dollar treatment. If that's the case, I won't be able to do it. I have to watch every penny in my bank account at this point."

"Well, find that out," Quinn said. "And if you can swing it, I'd give it a try."

Hallie had to admit she was more than curious about Willow and how much the beautiful young woman would be able to help her. "I've always wanted to try acupuncture," Hallie said. "But I could never convince Nate to give me the money for sessions." She sipped her wine. "Now, well, I guess I'll finally get the chance to try it out."

Then Hallie told the ladies about the tarot spread. "I tell you, I thought that one of you was playing a prank on me," she said. "That's how accurate Willow was and how quickly she figured everything out. She even told me things that I was unaware of but, once she said it, made sense. Like how I feel that I'm a burden on everyone I love who loves me back. Like how I feel like I'm nothing and nobody, especially next to you ladies."

Quinn shook her head. "Sugar, don't ever think that you're a burden. We all have had our share of issues, and you've always been there for us. I mean, I'd just met you when James died, and you stayed all night in my apartment for three nights in a row and made sure I ate. And after my rape and pregnancy from that, and giving up my precious baby for adoption, you were there for me, supporting me all the way."

Hallie nodded, knowing all that was the truth. The death of Quinn's brother, James, was a devastating blow because Quinn and James were so very close. And, around 14 years ago, Quinn was date-raped on one of the few dates she'd gone on. The guy, Charles, put something in her drink and apparently had sex with her while she was passed out. Quinn had no idea she and Charles even had sex. All she knew was she was on a date one moment and in her bed the next. It wasn't until she started getting morning sickness and breast tenderness and missed a period she knew what had happened that night. A positive pregnancy test confirmed her suspicions. She had the baby and put her up for adoption.

Hallie and Ava both went out of their way to help Quinn in any way possible, from staying with her in her apartment, holding her hand when she signed the adoption papers and helping her go to the police about what had happened. And then, when the bastard who raped her got away with it by telling the cops that it was all consensual, and the cops believed him, not Quinn, Hallie and Ava held Quinn while she screamed and cried about it.

"I know I was there through all that," Hallie said. "But it seems like my torment is never-ending, and I just feel like everybody gets tired of hearing about it."

It was Ava's turn to put her hand on Hallie's. "When Daniel died, and I was forced to raise three babies on my own, you took my kids in while I worked," she reminded

Hallie. "And you wouldn't take money for your daycare, either."

"Well, I know, but I was staying home with my daughter, and the more the merrier. Morgan and your kids all loved each other's company, so I felt like you were doing me a favor." Morgan was six years older than Ava's triplets, and she had a ball helping Hallie out with caring for the three babies with the three completely different personalities.

"Regardless, Hallie, you're a good friend to Quinn and me," Ava said. "You've always had our backs. We have yours, too, no matter what. I hope you always remember that."

Hallie took a deep breath as she thought about what would happen when she left the island. Then she closed her eyes and knew she never wanted to leave Nantucket. Never.

But the prospect of staying there on Nantucket and leaving her marriage somehow, someway, continued to fill her with a cold dread. Marriage and vows were forever. Weren't they? They were for her parents. Her parents had their share of problems over the years. When she was young, there were many times when she was afraid that her mom and dad would split up. But they came through all that and, as of that moment, they were madly in love.

Couldn't that happen for her and Nate? They'd find their way back to each other one day and would look back on this period as an obstacle they had to get through. Couldn't that happen?

But Hallie knew, deep down, that that wasn't going to happen. She and Nate were never happy together. If she didn't accidentally get pregnant, the two of them would've never gotten married. Nate would've been a distant memory for her, a man in her past who she would look back on with relief she never went further with him. They never had the same values or beliefs, no common interests. They never had much to talk to each other about.

It wasn't her fault, and it wasn't his, either, that they had a terrible marriage. It was what it was. They were just wrong for each other in every way.

For example, if she ever tried to tell him about Willow and about the treatment processes she would get from her new friend, he would've made fun of her. He also would've brow-beaten her into not going to see Willow again, and she would've backed down because she didn't want to make him angry. And if there was one thing she knew, the prospect of spending money on Willow's services would've made Nate furious.

Hallie opened her mouth and shut it again. She would ask Ava if she would represent her if she filed for divorce from Nate. But, somehow, she couldn't verbalize this request. It would make it real, and that thought scared her.

"Do you want any of us to go with you to see Willow tomorrow?" Ava asked. "To check her out and give you our opinion?"

"No, no, I'm okay," Hallie said. "I'm a big girl. I can do this on my own."

To tell the truth, Hallie *did* want somebody to go with her. But she knew Ava was busy, busy, busy with the renovations of her home, and Quinn was just as busy with all the interior decorating jobs she'd been getting since moving to Nantucket. In fact, Quinn had just begun a project on a 10,000 square foot beach house in the Town Center area that was owned by a prominent billionaire.

Also, Quinn was looking for a home to move into. Sarah was helping her with this, as Sarah had such a background in architecture and design, so she could give Quinn a seasoned second eye on all the houses she was looking at.

Sarah looked at Hallie for a moment. "I've got nothing going on tomorrow. Why don't I come along just for grins? To tell you the truth, I've always been fascinated by alternative healers myself."

Hallie eagerly nodded her head. "Yes, that would be fun. Are you sure, though?"

"Of course," Sarah said. "I've just been hanging around here, annoying Ava, and that will be the case until this place opens. Besides, I have an appointment tomorrow at 3 with the owner of Nantucket Wine and Spirits downtown. I'm going to be working with him to procure some wines for this place."

"Then it'll work out," Hallie said. "We can go and see Willow tomorrow for my treatment and then go on over to Nantucket Wine and Spirits and talk to your guy."

Hallie felt a bit relieved. With Sarah along, she felt less like this whole thing was too weird for words. Sarah somehow would legitimize it all.

There was something about Sarah that made Hallie want her approval. Probably because Sarah was a golden girl in high school and, once a golden girl, always a golden girl. And Hallie was always anxious for the acceptance of the golden girls in her high school and also in college. While Hallie was a GDI in college (goddamned independent), she secretly longed for acceptance by the girls in one of the prestigious houses like Delta Gamma or Tri-Delt. She at least wanted a good friend from one of those "good" houses.

She never did get a good friend from a prestigious sorority house, but now she had Sarah as a friend, which might make up for it.

After all, Sarah was a Delta Gamma at KU.

Sarah smiled and nodded her head. "Oh, it'll be fun. I

wonder if Willow can read my astrological chart. I've always wanted that done."

"I'm sure she can," Hallie said. "Willow seems to be a one-stop-shop for all things metaphysical." Then Hallie smiled. "And she's told me that I should envision myself as a lioness."

"A lioness, sugar?" Quinn said questioningly. "Why would you want to be a lioness? They can't live without the protection of the lion. I think that your spirit animal should be the tigress. She hunts, she raises her young, and she's not hanging out with the male tiger. She's doing it all on her own, and she's doing just fine."

"That's true," Hallie said. "I've never thought about it that way, but you're right. If the male lion weren't around, the lionesses and their cubs might be in danger. I don't want to have to need a man anymore. Not to protect me and not to control me. A tigress as my spirit animal. I like that. I like that a lot."

Later on that night, when Hallie was alone in her room, she got on the computer to do some research on Willow's credentials. She was pleased to discover that Willow was board certified in acupuncture and oriental medicine and she had studied under acupuncture professionals in China. She was also certified in crystal healing, sound therapy and was a certified herbalist.

Well, it couldn't hurt, Hallie thought as she spent hours not only reading Willow's webpage but reading medical journal articles about acupuncture's benefits. The studies were inconclusive on the benefits of acupuncture, but Willow's Yelp reviews were not. She had a 4.8 average on

Yelp with over 600 reviews, which Hallie took as a good sign.

Almost all of her patients gave her five stars, with comments like "I've had back pain all my life, and now, with regular acupuncture sessions with Willow, I've finally found relief." Or "I was suffering from chronic migraines that sent me to the hospital several times. I haven't had a migraine since I've been seeing Willow twice a week." And "I was diagnosed with severe depression, but it's gone into remission ever since I've been seeing Willow on a regular basis."

Maybe clinical studies hadn't established that acupuncture was beneficial, but studies also hadn't established any harm in the practice. And acupuncture was apparently 3,000 years old. People had been sticking needles in their skin for thousands of years, so, Hallie reasoned, if the practice really didn't work, it wouldn't be around for as long as it had been.

Hallie also looked up the concept of spirit animals. When she found out that the tiger represented willpower, personal strength and courage, she knew she'd chosen the right spirit animal.

At the moment, she thought she had no personal strength, willpower or courage. But she dearly hoped she would gain all of those traits soon.

Chapter Thirty-One

Hallie

Hallie and Sarah got to Willow's shop the next day, right at 1. When they walked in, Sarah looked around the shop with fascination. She looked at the books on the shelf, the crystals in the glass case and the candles with interest.

"Ooh," Sarah said as she picked up a deck of tarot cards. "I've always wanted a reading. But maybe not. Maybe I don't want to know the future."

Willow was busy ringing up a couple of women who had bought some crystals and aromatherapy candles, and then she looked at Hallie and Sarah. "Hey," she said to Hallie. "You're right on time." Then she handed Hallie a stack of paperwork to fill out about her medical history. "So you don't sue me," Willow said with a smile.

Hallie groaned. She *hated* paperwork. But she also knew that it was necessary because Willow needed to know something of her medical history. So, on the paperwork, she explained about her chronic insomnia and depression, both of which were getting better on the island but were not quite licked. She also explained, on the sheet, about her menopause symptoms - the mood swings, the night sweats, and the hot flashes.

Sarah smiled at Willow. "I'm Sarah," she said.

Willow nodded her head. "You're the attorney's sister," she said. "Tell your sister she'll be taking Hallie here on as a client sooner rather than later." Then she looked at Hallie. "By the way, what is the name of your attorney friend?"

"Ava," Hallie said.

Sarah cocked her head. "How did you know Ava was my sister?" she asked Willow as Hallie handed Willow her paperwork and Willow looked it over.

Willow shrugged. "I'm good. What can I say? Anyhow, Hallie, come on back. I'll put on some soothing music, and I'll stick you with some needles, and that'll help unblock your chakras and get your energy flowing again. Then I'll send you home with some herbs and some candles and some crystals. Don't worry, I'll give you a specialized book that'll tell you what all the candles, herbs and crystals are for and how to use them."

"And what will all this cost?" Sarah asked Willow.

"$100 for the acupuncture session and $100 for the stuff I'll be sending home with her," Willow said. "I'm giving her a serious discount just because I want her to get better, so I'm not that interested in making a profit off of her pain."

Hallie nodded her head. "That sounds pretty reasonable," she said. "I thought it would be more." Hallie had a good feeling about Willow. She felt that the beautiful young woman was the real deal. The tarot reading convinced her, and she was also convinced because Willow seemed to know who Sarah was right away.

Hallie went to the back room. It was a beautiful room,

with soft green walls and pictures of waterfalls, rainbows and forests. There was an enormous orchid on a table by the far wall, and incense was burning a clean and calming scent. There was a tiny fountain bubbling in the corner.

There was a tiny golden bowl also on the table, and Willow lightly gonged it. It made a melodious ringing sound.

"Tibetan singing bowl," Willow said. "In the key of F, which means that it will help unblock your heart chakra. The singing bowls all correspond with a different chakra, and I chose this one just for you, because your heart chakra is what's blocked."

Hallie lay down on a comfortable table, and Willow put what seemed like hundreds of needles on Hallie's forehead, palms, legs, chest and soles of her feet. Then Hallie closed her eyes and listened to meditative music that featured harps and the sounds of rain beating on a windowpane.

The next thing Hallie knew, Willow was standing next to her and taking out the needles. Hallie looked at the young woman, feeling confused. "I don't understand. I thought that this was a 30-minute session."

Willow chuckled. "It was. You fell asleep like that," she said, snapping her fingers. "I mean, you were like 'who turned out the lights?'"

"Really?" Hallie asked, noting she felt more relaxed than she had in a long, long time. Her legs felt like spaghetti and, according to her FitBit, her heart rate was 59. "Oh, my. I have to find out if my insurance covers this treatment because I definitely want to keep doing it."

"I'll tell you what," Willow said. "Let me take you on as a regular client, three times a week. You just sign a piece of paper that agrees that, when you get your divorce settlement, my fee will be paid from that. Think of it as an advance."

"Really?" Hallie said. "You would do that? I mean, what if I don't get divorced?"

Willow shrugged. "I'm rolling the dice because I really want to help you. Besides, I'm 99% sure that you'll be filing for divorce, and I'm 100% sure that you're good for my fee no matter what happens. And you definitely need regular sessions. You feel completely relaxed right now, but it takes a minimum of three months to relieve severe depression. The last thing I want is for you to not get the benefits of treatment."

"I don't understand. Why do you want to help me so much?" Hallie asked.

"I've a hunch that you're going to be important to me in the future," Willow said. "Professionally. I just had a vision when you walked in that you would be my healing partner. Kismet."

"Your healing partner?" Hallie asked, intrigued. "I don't know anything about acupuncture and crystals or any of that. How can I be your healing partner?"

Willow put her hand on Hallie's shoulder. "You don't know this because you've spent most of your adult life trying to please somebody who'll never be pleased - your husband - instead of listening to yourself, but you're a born healer like me. That's what these treatments are all about. They're about getting your qi flowing freely so that you can focus on you. What you want and what you need. You do that, and everything in your life will fall right into place. Trust me."

Hallie nodded her head. When Willow said "trust me," Hallie knew she did just that. She trusted her.

Hallie walked into the shop from the acupuncture room

The Beachfront Inn

and saw that Sarah was walking around with crystals and candles in her hands, along with a couple of books about tarot and astrology. "Hey," she said and then did a double-take. "You look good. Peaceful."

"I *feel* peaceful," Hallie said, seeing that her heart rate was 62, even though she was on her feet, therefore her heart rate should've been going up. "I'm definitely going to keep doing this."

Hallie paid for the session and for the crystals, candles and aromatherapy bottles that Willow had selected for her. She also picked up a meditation CD that Willow had recommended. And then Hallie made two more appointments for that week.

Sarah paid for her things and put her arm around Hallie as the two ladies walked out the door. "Man, I should do some acupuncture myself."

"Yes, you should," Hallie said. "Everybody should."

Chapter Thirty-Two

Sarah

Ever since Sarah had run into Langdon Prescott on the street and got the address for William and Lauren's summer home, she struggled with what she could do with the information. The universe had put Langdon Prescott into her path for a reason.

Sarah had never really believed in metaphysical things like the universe working on your behalf to guide you along to where you were supposed to be. But she'd picked up several books at Willow's shop and read them, and she was starting to believe that there might be something to the theory that there was a universal spirit that could be tapped into and that the universe really did try to nudge people into different directions. The Hindus believed that there was unity to all beings in the universe and that every living thing was connected.

So, after Sarah read several books she got at Willow's, she decided that Langdon Prescott's presence on the sidewalk was a sign she needed to finally get some kind of closure on what Lauren did to her. She didn't quite know what that closure would consist of, but she knew she had to go to William and Lauren's house on Surfside and confront one or both of them.

She'd never done that - confront them with what they did to her. They both were guilty of railroading her. Without William's corrupt help, Lauren might've admitted that those drugs were hers. But William corruptly helped Lauren, probably bribing the right people to make sure that Lauren would never get into trouble, so, in Sarah's eyes, William was just as guilty as Lauren in the whole mess.

Sarah called her mother, who, as a prominent federal Circuit Court judge, was well-connected with all the wealthy people in Boston, many of whom had summer homes on Nantucket.

"Hey mom," Sarah said.

"Sarah. How the hell are you?" her mother said. "How are things with Ava?"

"Great," Sarah said. "Ava and I are really in a good place."

"Knew you would be. Now, why are you calling?"

"Do you know a billionaire named William Blake?" she asked.

"Lauren's husband, you mean?" her mom asked. "Yeah, I know him. Why?"

"How do you know him?" she asked.

"He's in my courtroom a ton. He has an international business and an office here in Boston, so he ends up in front of me anytime things go south with his Boston branch. Again, why?"

"I'd like to go to his house here on Nantucket," Sarah said. "Unannounced. You know him. I've never met him.

What do you think? Would he call the police on me if I showed up on his doorstep and refused to leave until he talked to me?"

At that, her mother started to laugh. "Oh, sorry," she said after she quit laughing. "The things you get up to. Listen, if you want my opinion, the guy's corrupt as hell. But he's pretty mild-mannered, so if you need to talk to him, give it a shot. If you get arrested, I'll bail you out."

Sarah smiled as she realized that, this time, if she was arrested, she'd have many people who would be eager to bail her out. Ava, Hallie, Quinn and, apparently, her mother - all would bail her out in a heartbeat. As she thought about how nobody would bail her out before, even Lauren, who was responsible for the whole debacle, and now she had people who loved her enough to come out for her in the middle of the night, she felt cheered.

"Thanks mom," Sarah said. "By the way, have you talked to Ava lately?"

"Not lately. Why?"

"Well, I think that you should be nicer to her. Take your own advice to me. You told me to make up with her. I took your advice, and Ava and I have never been better. Maybe you should try the same."

Colleen snorted. "I'm fine with Ava. Let me know how things go when you ambush William."

At that, she hung up.

Chapter Thirty-Three

Sarah

Sarah brainstormed her idea with the girls that evening. "I don't know. I really need some closure on all this," Sarah said. "Lauren laughs about what she did to me. I just can't stand that she not only got away with it, but she's proud of it." As Sarah spoke, she unconsciously stroked Bella, who was lying on her back next to Sarah's lounger. It was comforting for Sarah to pet her dog. Nothing calmed her down faster.

Quinn took Sarah's hand. "Sugar, you do what you need to to put it all behind you. There's really nothing you can do to get your conviction set aside? I'm sure Ava would be thrilled to take your case."

Ava opened her mouth to say something, but Sarah jumped in.

Sarah shook her head. "Unfortunately, no. Once you plead guilty, that's that. No turning back. If I would've taken it to trial and been found guilty, there might've been something I could've done if-"

"If what, sugar?" Quinn asked.

Sarah blinked. "Hey, wait a minute. Wait a minute. Ava can't help me, but my mother might be able to."

Ava nodded her head. "I know what you're thinking," she said. "And it might work. If you could talk to William and get him to admit what he did, it might work."

Hallie was interested. "What? What might work?"

"Our mother is connected," Sarah said. "And she used to be a judge in California. She was a District Court judge out there. She knows the governor of California. The governor has the power to pardon me. But the governor won't do that unless I can give him new evidence. If mom could get involved and write a letter, and I could maybe get William to also write a letter, it might work."

"Sugar, how will you get William to write you a letter?" Quinn asked.

"All I can do is ask," Sarah said.

A week later, Sarah screwed up the courage to go to William's home. She first drove by the palatial mansion a few times to gauge when he was likely to be home. She discovered that he was typically home after 8. During the day, a realtor was showing the home to potential buyers.

She quickly figured out that William would be in town until the house was sold. She also figured out, with her surveillance, that Lauren was nowhere to be seen. Sarah thought that that was by design - Lauren and William probably didn't want to be in the same place at the same time.

Sarah felt like the current situation was ideal. If William

The Beachfront Inn

and Lauren were divorcing, then maybe William would be willing to help her. After all, he threw her under the bus earlier because he was protecting his wife. Maybe he no longer wanted to protect the shady Lauren.

Sarah got to the home, which was protected by an iron gate at the edge of the home grounds. She pressed the call box and waited for somebody to answer.

"Hello?" a voice said.

"Hi," Sarah said to the box. "I'd like to talk to William Blake."

"Who is this?" the voice demanded.

"My name is Sarah Flynn," she said. "I was a friend of Lauren's."

To her surprise, she was buzzed in, and the gates opened. She drove right on through, and, a few seconds later, she was on the doorstep of the palatial home.

She knocked on the door, and a man answered. He was around 70 years old, balding and paunchy, with a ruddy face. He was dressed casually in a golf shirt and a pair of khakis. "Come on in," he said. "I thought you might be along at some point."

Sarah followed him into a living room with a 40-foot ceiling. A fire was burning, and next to one of the chairs was a stack of magazines, including one that was open.

"I'm sorry to bother you," Sarah said as he gestured to a chair next to his.

"It's okay," he said. "Langdon told me that he ran into you."

"You know Langdon?" Sarah asked.

"Sure. Lauren's been messing around with him for a year now."

"And you don't care about that?"

He shrugged. "I don't care what she does. I feel sorry for

him, though. I feel sorry for anybody who gets involved with Lauren. Now, what can I do for you?"

Sarah took a deep breath. "You know why I'm here."

He nodded. "Well, I guess the statute of limitations has run on the crimes I committed against you," he said. "Lying to a government official. Bribery of a government official. What do you need from me?"

"I'd like to apply for a pardon from the governor of California," Sarah said. "I'd like to not be a convicted felon anymore. So, I need an affidavit from you."

He nodded. "Done. I'll get my attorney to draw one up. I'll put in all the details of my involvement in that sorry affair. I guess that's the least I can do for you after what I did."

"Really?" Sarah asked. "What's the catch?"

"No catch," William said. "Listen, I'm not a bad guy. I was just in love with the wrong woman, and I was guilty of doing what I could to protect her. And that's what I was doing - protecting her. Yes, I bribed the cops that night to let Lauren go. I bribed prosecutors not to bring charges against her. And I lied to the cops and told them that the drugs were yours, not Lauren's. I knew better. I knew that the drugs belonged to my wife."

"But did you ever stop to think that there was somebody who was being destroyed?" Sarah asked.

"No," he said. "I'm only being honest. I never even thought twice about you. I only wanted to make sure that Lauren didn't go to prison. She had two young kids at home, and I loved her desperately. I just wanted to protect my own. And, for that, I'm truly sorry."

"And now?"

"Now, well, it's 20 years later, and the bloom is definitely off the rose. We're divorcing. I met somebody else, somebody good. Somebody who would never do the things that Lauren did to you and to me." He shook his head and then prepared to light up a pipe. "Do you mind?"

"No," Sarah said. "I like the smell of a pipe."

"Thanks," he said, lighting the pipe and taking a drag. "I know she was messing around on me from the start, and I didn't care. I just wanted to keep her happy. Emma, my new fiancée, she's great. Sweet, gentle, smart, beautiful. She despises Lauren."

"So," Sarah said. "Did Lauren have a drug problem?"

He laughed. "Of course. Why do you think she was with those Lebanese men that night, anyhow? They were her dealers. She was doing blow daily at that time."

"Does she still have a drug problem?" Sarah asked.

"No. There's no way she could've kept doing so many drugs and still be alive today. She gave it up around ten years ago. She still drinks, though. I've told her that it's a bad idea to drink because once an addict, always an addict, but she doesn't listen to me. Never did."

Sarah closed her eyes. If this worked, if she got a pardon from the governor, she might be able to forgive Lauren. She had to have compassion for her former friend. Addiction was a terrible thing, and Lauren was an addict. Her former friend obviously went through her own pain, a pain which Sarah wouldn't wish on anyone.

"Is it true that Lauren laughs about doing that to me?" Sarah asked.

"Is that what Langdon told you?" William asked. "Lauren's guilty of one thing. Well, she's guilty of many things, but there's one thing that people misunderstand about her. She laughs when she's nervous or frightened. She laughs when she's confessing something she's ashamed of. She probably did laugh when she told Langdon about what happened with the drugs, but if she did, it was because she was truly ashamed of it."

"But was she ashamed of it?"

"Yes. She was. She's talked about it just about every day since it happened, and she was always asking me if there was anything she could do to make things right."

Sarah gripped the side of her chair. "But she got me fired," she said. "By lying to the owner of the restaurant where I worked about something I said to her."

"She told me about that, and she was embarrassed about it. But she really did think that you were insulting her, and maybe you were, even if it was just unconscious on your part. And if there's one thing that sets her off, it's somebody insulting her. Especially if she knows that the insult is true."

"Even so," Sarah said. "That wasn't right."

"No, I agree. None of what she did to you was right. But I can make it right for you, and I will. I'm glad you came here to ask me for this because I've always wanted to do the right thing for you. And here it is, 20 years later, and I finally can do something to set things right."

Two weeks later, Sarah had the affidavit. She'd sent it into the governor, along with the Pardon Application to the governor and filed a Notice of Intent to Apply for Clemency to the Monterey County DA. For good measure, she had her mother write a letter on her behalf, too. It certainly couldn't hurt if the governor knew that her mother was now a prominent Circuit Court judge.

Two months after that, Sarah got a Notice of Pardon Grant. The basis for granting her a pardon was her perfect record post-conviction and "newly discovered evidence that the charges were pursued in error."

So, apparently, William's letter did the trick.

It was official.

Sarah Flynn was no longer a convicted felon.

Chapter Thirty-Four

Ava

February

Months had gone by, and the house's renovation was coming along nicely. Deacon and his contractors came by every single day and knocked out walls, tore up carpets, replaced appliances and expanded the kitchen.

Since Ava didn't anticipate opening up her home as a B&B until May, Sarah had little to do after she spent several months procuring wines around the country, so she was hired back at Chez Toussaint. Apparently, Langdon Prescott had spoken with Françoise, the owner of Chez Toussaint, and explained how Lauren had lied about Sarah. So, Françoise profusely apologized to Sarah and begged her to come back. Sarah reluctantly agreed after Françoise promised to double her hourly salary from $5 per hour to $10 per hour. With tips, Sarah was making around $50 per hour, which was giving her a small nest egg.

Hallie had been going to Willow for treatment three times a week, and Ava was amazed at the changes in her friend. Hallie was soundly sleeping 8 hours a night, she cut down her wine consumption, and her skin was glowing. She was off all anti-depressants and sleep medicine, and she was now going to hot yoga five days a week.

Hallie hadn't spoken to Nate since she'd been on the island, and she'd confided to Ava, Sarah and Quinn she was relieved she wasn't in contact with her husband. "If that's not a sign that I need to file for divorce, I don't know what is."

So, obviously, Hallie stayed on the island much longer than the month she had originally planned. And Ava was starting to think that Hallie might never leave the island, and that thought thrilled her to no end.

Quinn's business continued to thrive as word got around the island about her talent, and she was so in demand she had a waiting list. She was able to buy a home of her own in the 'Sconset Beach neighborhood. It was a rose-covered cottage that was several blocks away from the beach. The Cape Cod home had a large front porch and was surrounded by a white picket fence. It was small, only 3 bedrooms, but was perfect for Quinn's interior decorator eye, with its hardwood floors, pocket doors, cathedral ceilings, fireplace and crown molding throughout.

Hallie and Sarah arranged to stay with Quinn because the renovation was becoming more than an inconvenience, with all the dust, men constantly milling about, and noise. Sarah, for her part, was working on a spreadsheet for her finances because she was focused on saving enough money for a downpayment on her own home on the island.

Unfortunately, since the homes on Nantucket were so expensive, Sarah realized that it would be a while before she would have the money to buy her own home, but Quinn assured her she could stay with her as long as necessary.

The upshot was that Ava went from living with Sarah, Quinn and Hallie to living alone in the huge house.

As for Deacon, he was getting closer to Ava every day. They had become true friends. Ava was helping out with the renovation as much as she could. She was a pretty good painter and was handy with hanging wallpaper, so that was her contribution to the beautification project. So, she worked closely with Deacon, and her heart pounded every time she looked at him.

Butterflies, Ava thought. *When was the last time I've experienced butterflies?* It probably hadn't been since Daniel, because she'd never experienced butterflies with Chris. Which should've told her something, but, as usual, she wasn't listening to her gut with Chris. And she paid the price for that. Dearly.

One Friday evening, Ava had gotten back from the Nantucket Cottage Hospital. Her daughter Charlotte had finally paid a visit, and, while Charlotte was there, Siobhan spiked a fever. It was nothing, just a bad case of the flu, but it was scary, nonetheless.

Ava got back into the house after having been gone for the previous 12 hours and rapidly saw that there wasn't food in the house. Deacon was still working late on a cabinetry project, as he was busily trimming the cabinet doors so they would fit perfectly in with the framing.

Ava just looked around at the dust and mess and immediately felt exhausted. She'd just spent 12 hours in a hard plastic chair as she talked to different doctors about Siobhan's diagnosis and to Charlotte, trying to talk her off the ledge.

Ava shook her head and walked to her happy place, her terrace facing the beach. It was a cold night, and a blanket of snow covered the beach and the dunes leading up to it. She built a fire in the pit, turned on the heat lamp and threw a blanket over her while she watched the ocean waves come in and out. Her mind was a perfect blank because she was stressed about Charlotte and Siobhan and really stressed about the state of the house. As much as she craved coming home to a beautiful environment after spending so many hours in a cramped plastic seat, it just wasn't possible at the moment. Her house was turned upside down and, at the moment, there was nothing she could do about it except silently scream.

I really should call Grubhub Ava thought. She was hungry, starving, actually, because she'd been too stressed to eat at the hospital. She got out her phone, looked for the Grubhub app, and prepared to order something when Deacon appeared on the deck with a pizza.

"I ordered this for you," Deacon said. "But I got it a couple of hours ago because I didn't know when you'd be home. I think it's still hot, though, since I kept the box closed."

Ava's mouth watered as she saw that the pie was a Chicken Bacon Ranch from Foggy Nantucket, Ava's favorite place on the island. Foggy's Chicken Bacon Ranch was her all-time favorite pizza. She'd been living in New York for several decades, so Ava knew her pizza. The pie was full of gooey cheese, smoked chicken, marinara, jalapeño ranch dressing, bacon, red onion and scallions, all on a butter and garlic crust.

He'd also picked up a salad with torn lettuce, radishes,

cucumber, avocado, red onion and pepitas. Ava recognized this salad as coming from a place called Lemon Press, which was an organic restaurant in the historic district. Whenever Ava was craving something completely healthy, she went to that place and picked up a salad, an organic bowl or a smoothie.

"Oh," Ava said when she saw the food. "My hero."

Deacon grinned. "I did good, mate, huh?" he asked.

"Oh, yes. Yes, you did. Here, let me go and get some plates and everything, and we can eat out here." Ava heard her stomach rumbling, and she wondered if she could wait long enough to get a plate for this scrumptious food.

Ava tore downstairs, anxious to get the plates and dying to eat some of that amazing pizza and salad. Then she found a bottle of wine, two wine glasses and a corkscrew and ran back up to the terrace. "Okay," she said. "Here are the plates, and-"

Deacon was over at the table, lighting the candles and, to her surprise, he had situated a bouquet of flowers on the table. "I was hiding these in the sunroom," he said, gesturing to the flowers. They were beautiful, brightly colored wildflowers and sunflowers, all of which weren't in season but were sold by florists who procured the flowers from sunnier climates. "I wanted to surprise you."

Ava's mouth dropped open as she put the plates, silverware and wine glasses on the table. "Well, you did," she said. "Surprise me. These are gorgeous."

Deacon nodded his head. "I knew that you loved wildflowers and sunflowers because you have so many paintings of them," he explained. "And I knew that you probably need some cheer after being at the hospital for so long. How is Siobhan, by the way?"

They both sat down, and Ava poured some wine, put a

The Beachfront Inn

slice of pizza on her plate and his and a scoop of salad on each plate as well.

"Siobhan is fine," Ava said. "Just a bad case of the flu. Horrible timing, though. Charlotte took her back home tonight, because she wanted her baby to sleep in her own bed." Ava took a bite of her pizza and rolled her eyes. "Oh my God," she said. "Do you know that this is my favorite pizza of all time?"

"Yes," Deacon said. "That's why I got it. It is delicious, isn't it?"

Ava cocked her head. "How did you know that it was my favorite pizza?"

"Because I was working on the sunroom one night, and you had the girls over eating this very pizza and a veggie pizza for Quinn. After you took a bite, I overheard you telling them that this was the best pizza you'd ever tasted. I figured that you were a New Yorker, so that's high praise indeed."

Ava smiled and ate some salad, too. "And this salad is divine. I love that Lemon Press place. But you really didn't have to go through all this trouble, you know. Going to different places to pick up dinner and all that."

Deacon smiled. "Well, it was my pleasure. I was going to pick up a salad at the Foggy Nantucket place, but I asked if the salad was organic, and they said no. So, I went to Lemon Press because their salads were organic."

"Oh?" Ava said. "You care about organic too. Good for you. Conventionally-grown lettuce really isn't great, you know."

"So you say," Deacon said. "It really doesn't matter to me either way."

"No?" Ava asked. "But you went out of your way to pick up an organic salad, so it must matter to you a little."

"Nope," Deacon said. "But I knew that it mattered to you, so that's why I went out of my way to get this salad." Then he smiled, and Ava felt her heart melt. The butterflies started anew.

Stop, Ava, stop. Ava wanted to believe that Deacon was going out of his way to please her because he had a romantic interest in her, but she dared not think that way. No, Deacon was just a really, really nice guy, and he would do the same for anyone.

But Ava saw that her hand was shaking as it gripped the stem of her wine glass. She took her hand off the wine glass, so that Deacon couldn't see his effect on her and put both hands on her lap.

"How did you know that I only eat organic lettuce?"

Deacon shrugged. "You had that little chart on your old fridge downstairs," he said. "The fridge that you had before we replaced it with an industrial one. I noticed that you always looked at that chart before going grocery shopping. If the chart said that certain fruits or vegetables needed to be organic, then you bought those fruits and vegetables only from the organic aisle."

That was true. He was referring to a handy chart from *Consumer Reports* that listed various fruits and vegetables and whether or not each individual fruit and vegetable could be bought conventionally or had to be organic. Some vegetables could be conventionally grown - sweet potatoes, broccoli, cabbage, onions, cucumbers, tomatoes and so forth. Other veggies had to be organic - green beans, lettuce, spinach, celery and kale were in this category. Especially spinach - Ava was surprised that all spinach was bad, even the US-grown organic spinach and that only imported organic spinach was good to eat. After Ava got that chart, she stopped eating spinach altogether because it was too difficult to find the imported version of the green.

"Well, you certainly are observant," she said to Deacon. "I'm impressed."

Deacon put his hand on Ava's, and Ava felt a thrill of electricity travel up her spine. "You know, I never told you exactly why I'm in the states," he said. "I think that I can relate to your being overwhelmed, because I can tell that you are."

Ava didn't react. She *was* overwhelmed right at that moment. The home renovation process was stressful, and having a sick grandchild didn't help. She was also quite worried about Charlotte. There was something extremely off with her daughter, although she couldn't pinpoint just what it was. Charlotte insisted she was fine, but Ava's spidey sense was tingling and she had the feeling that Charlotte was on the edge of something bad. She couldn't shake that feeling, and it stressed her out immensely.

"Tell me your story," Ava said. "What brought you here."

"My sister, Ella, she had non-Hodgkins' lymphoma. She was a minor, so I was sent here with her so she could see a specialist at the Mayo Clinic. She had a rare type, and the only specialist who could treat her was there. Her type was very aggressive, and I thought for sure she'd die. It was truly a miracle she lived. It was all thanks to the good doctors there at Mayo."

"Where were your parents?" Ava asked him. She didn't usually like to pry, but she wasn't thinking clearly at that point.

"They died in a boat accident when I was 18," he said. "So I had to look after my little sister, who was only 13 when that happened."

"Oh, I'm so sorry," Ava said. "I'm so sorry that that happened to you."

"Oh, it was 17 years ago, mate," he said. "I had a hard time when it happened. You know, one day you're a surfing carefree teenager hanging out with your mates, and the next, you're a father figure to your little sister. I was spewin' for a long time. Some bloke got pissed in his boat and slammed into my father's boat when they were out for a ride one night. Sank the boat, and my mum and dad both drowned."

Ava thought back to her Daniel. Daniel's friend got drunk and drove that night. What if he'd killed other innocent people? How many more families would've been devastated if Daniel's friend Mick hadn't hit that tree but hit another car? In that, Ava guessed that Mick was lucky. Only he and Daniel had died in that accident, not innocent people.

"I'm so sorry," Ava said again.

"Not a biggie," Deacon said. "I didn't mean to bring you down, Ava. You've got enough to think about with everything that's going on. I just wanted to let you know that sometimes life gets out of hand, but it usually evens out in the long run. I always thought that Ella would die. Always. But she got better, and now she's got a kid and a husband and one on the way. Everything is going great."

Ava smiled and helped herself to more pizza and salad. "That's wonderful to hear," she said. "Miracles really do happen, don't they?"

"They do, and my sister is the proof. By the way, where are the girls?" Deacon asked. "I'm surprised they weren't sitting in those hard chairs in the hospital with you for the past 12 hours."

"Oh, I didn't call them," Ava said. "It wasn't that serious. But I really should call them and tell them what's going on."

Somehow, though, the thought of calling anybody at that moment was overwhelming. Ava knew she was on stress overload, with the Siobhan emergency on top of the months of overseeing the renovation of her house and all the stress that entailed.

Deacon seemed to read her mind. "I'll call Quinn and let her know," he said. "Do you want them to come over?"

Ava shut her eyes. "No," she said. "I need to go over to a lounge chair and just shut my eyes and relax."

Ava woke up in her bed, fully clothed. The sun was shining in through the window, and she looked over and saw that Deacon was sitting in the large recliner in the corner of her room. He appeared to be watching something on his iPad.

"Hey," she said. "What happened?"

Deacon put away the iPad. "You went over to the lounge chair and conked right out," he said. "Like a light. So, I carried you to your bed. I spent the night in the chair because I was worried that you would wake up and not know where you were. You know, you were upstairs on your terrace, and now you're here in your bed, you might've gotten a bit freaked out. So, I slept here. I hope that's not a problem, mate."

Ava smiled. "No, not a problem at all."

Ava got up, padding her bare feet across the cold hardwood floors of her bedroom. "Coffee," she said. "And breakfast. You coming?"

"Sure," he said. "But you might want to think about lunch instead of breakfast. Seeing as it's 2 in the afternoon."

"What?" Ava said. "Oh my God, how long have I been sleeping?"

"Well, let's see. You fell asleep on the lounge chair around 8 last night, and you slept all the way through. So, what is that - I guess you've been sleeping for around 18 hours or so."

"I haven't slept like that since college," Ava said. "One time, I fell asleep at midnight and didn't get up until 5 the next day. That was my previous record. I guess I have a new record now. Go, me."

Ava and Deacon went down to the kitchen, which was the first place in the house that was finished. The kitchen was the size of a regular house kitchen before. Now, it was industrial-sized. Gleaming new appliances lined the walls, and overhead were pots and pans of every size. In the middle was an island with four stainless steel ovens. There was a walk-in freezer and refrigerator and an enormous stainless steel mixing bowl on the floor.

And there was Ava's trusty grind-and-brew coffee pot. Ava preferred to grind her coffee beans each and every day, so she loved her grind-and-brew because it ground the beans for her. Ava always bought organic coffee beans, because she had found out that coffee was one of the dirtiest products in the world, as far as pesticides went.

She went over to the grind-and-brew, put some whole Arabica beans into the grinder, and turned on the pot. In a matter of seconds, after she heard the whirring of the grinder, she soon heard the comforting dripping noise of the coffee being brewed.

"And for lunch, more pizza and salad," she said. "I really need to get to the store."

Deacon just grinned. "Mate, I called Hallie, and she brought over a ton of stuff. Look in your fridge. You'll see."

The Beachfront Inn

Ava went over to the fridge and saw that it was absolutely filled with produce, organic eggs and meat, bread, cheeses and almond milk. Then she went to the pantry and saw dried beans, canned goods, jarred pasta sauce and pasta. "I'm impressed," Ava said. "Hallie knows me well, too. But, of course she does. I've known her since I was 18."

Ava made a note to call Hallie as soon as lunch was over and find out how much she owed her for the groceries. That was a good friend, for you, really. When you need something, they're there, no matter what. No questions asked.

Kind of like Deacon, Ava thought. He was really stepping up to the plate to tend to her needs.

Deacon and Ava drank some fresh-brewed coffee and ate leftover pizza and salad, and chatted about everything under the sun. Ava felt comfortable with him. She felt like she could tell him anything, and he wouldn't judge her.

He appeared to think the same about her.

"Well, mate, thanks for the great food and everything," he said after their lunch. "I guess I should be shoving off, but I'll see you Monday."

Ava felt disappointed. She wanted to invite him to stay and maybe hang out with her and watch movies or something. But she felt she'd be keeping him from something, so she didn't speak up.

"See you Monday," she said. "And thanks for everything. How much do I owe you for the pizza and all that?"

Deacon chuckled and kissed her lightly on the cheek. Ava drew a breath when his lips brushed her skin. "Get me later," he said. "Take care."

And, just like that, he was gone.

And Ava really missed him.

Chapter Thirty-Five

Hallie

Hallie was sitting in her new bedroom at Quinn's house and just thinking about her good fortune. She had a place to land with Quinn's home, a place that seemed permanent to her. And the fact she was feeling, more and more, like Nantucket Island, in general, and Quinn's home, in particular, was permanent was a new feeling for her. New, but entirely welcome.

After Hallie moved in with Quinn, she felt like she was home. It was such a comfort to be with one of her best friends, and Quinn's cottage in the 'Sconset Beach area was cozy and quaint. From the wood-burning fireplace in the living room to the exposed brick in the kitchen to the vaulted ceilings in the bedrooms, Hallie absolutely loved Quinn's home.

Her room wasn't large, but it had newer hardwood floors, wainscoted walls in white, and a bay window with a colorful cushion. The enormous four-poster bed was outfitted in a white quilt and high-quality sheets, also in white. An accent wall right across from the bed had Monet floral wallpaper, with green and white Wisteria set against a smudged purple and white background.

A bookshelf filled with Hallie's favorite books - Quinn took the time to figure out which authors were her favorites - was on one wall, and a large dresser was against another. A vase of brilliant white and pink orchids, her favorite, and a Sand and Fog soy-based candle in lavender-chamomile was on the nightstand next to her bed. On her other nightstand on the other side of the bed was a tiny bubbling fountain.

Everything about the room was geared towards tranquility and relaxation, and Hallie had never felt more at home.

Hallie also promptly fell in love with Quinn's dog, Kona, who came to stay immediately after Quinn bought her house. Kona was a pug-shepherd rescue mutt that Quinn had picked up in a shelter in Manhattan. She had a black face, a fawn-colored body with black fur that ran up her legs and a curly tail. She was around 45 lbs, but she really thought she was a lap dog. She was playful as a puppy, constantly walking around the house with a stuffed animal, a rope or a ball in her mouth, wanting to play outside in the yard. Perhaps most delightfully for Hallie, Kona chose to sleep with her in her bed.

"A pug shepherd mix," Hallie said. "Fascinating. How does something like that happen?"

"I think it involves a ladder and one extremely determined pug," Quinn said with a laugh. "And you don't have to let her sleep with you, but she's a comforting dog. She knows that you're not feeling well, so she'll want to hang around you as much as she can."

"No, I'd love for her to sleep with me in my bed," Hallie said.

Kona and Hallie became fast friends, and, before Hallie knew it, Kona was sharing a pillow next to her in her bed. Every time Hallie was in the bathroom for even a few minutes, Kona waited outside the bathroom door, whining to get in.

Kona and Bella, Sarah's dog, also became fast friends. They met, they sniffed each other's rear ends for a few minutes, and then they started to play and basically never stopped. That was a good thing because, with Sarah staying there at the house with Bella, things could've been dicey if Kona and Bella hated each other.

No doubt about it, this place felt more like home than her beautiful but cold condo in New York ever did. She was so grateful that Quinn found a home so quickly and so close to Ava's own home. Now the girls were able to meet at Quinn's home for their weekly wine nights and twice-weekly Netflix-and-wine nights that had become their ritual. Because the renovation was becoming more and more intense, the girls' gatherings needed to take place away from Ava's home as much as possible.

And Hallie had finally made a decision about her life. She credited Willow for helping her to make this decision. The acupuncture treatments, combined with Willow's crystal therapy, sound therapy, aromatherapy and the use of medicinal herbs, all at Willow's prescription, had really worked to alleviate Hallie's depression, menopause symptoms and insomnia. She was eating better than ever - sugar was a thing of the past, as was junk food, and her diet pretty much consisted of lean protein, fruits and vegetables. She drank wine, but only a single glass and only three times a week when she gathered with her girls. She also ate pizza with the girls, but when she was making meals for herself, she stuck with healthy food.

She went to hot yoga three times a week with Willow and Sarah and loved it. Both Willow and Sarah were old pros when it came to yoga, and, at first, Hallie was very envious when she saw both ladies going through the yoga poses with such ease.

The classes were an hour, and the first time she went, she thought she would die. The room was over 100 degrees, and the yoga poses were incredibly difficult for her to manage. But she kept going, and now she not only got through her hour-long hot yoga class three days a week, but she loved these classes. She loved how she felt after the classes - flexible, supple and strong. And she even loved how she felt during the class itself, even though she never thought she would get to that point.

Hallie thought she was the healthiest she'd ever been. At 54 years old, she was in the best shape of her life. She'd dropped 20 pounds in the last few months, just by eating better, cutting back on the wine and going to hot yoga. She was the size she was in college, 130 lbs and a size 4.

And she was happy. Truly happy.

Time to rip off the band-aid.

She called Ava. "Hey," she said. "I'm ready."

No other words needed to be spoken.

"Be right there."

Chapter Thirty-Six

Hallie

April

"Where is he?" Hallie asked Ava anxiously. They were in a New York City conference room Ava had rented out for the afternoon.

Hallie had filed for divorce from Nate in February, and it was now the middle of April. Discovery had gone back and forth between Ava and Nate's attorney, a high-dollar divorce lawyer named Steve Phillips. Two months of intense negotiations followed, and now, the two parties had reached an agreement. This meeting in the conference room was simply a formality - everybody would look over the paperwork, sign on the dotted line and then Nate and Steve were going to walk everything through on the uncontested divorce docket the next day.

But Nate was late, and Hallie felt paranoid that maybe

he wouldn't show. He seemed fine with all the property division, and Hallie was more than fine with it.

After she signed off on her divorce, she would be an instant millionaire. Even she was shocked when she found out that, all told, the couple's assets totaled around $10 million. Their condo alone was worth $2 million, and there were investment accounts, stocks, bonds, oil paintings that Hallie knew nothing about and even a valuable stamp collection that Nate had kept in a safety deposit box.

Hallie told Ava she didn't want half, even though she was entitled to it. She really only wanted enough to buy her own home on Nantucket and enough to live on while she pursued her new dream, which was to become Willow's partner in healing. And then Ava explained that Hallie probably should take half if she wanted to do all that.

"At least $1.5 million of that will be necessary to buy any home on Nantucket," she said. "Even just a little cottage like Quinn has. And it's going to cost a pretty penny to go into business with Willow, too."

Before she'd met Willow, she'd never really explored the concept of alternative medicine. She always just took pills that her doctors prescribed her, and they never really made her feel better. Especially the Ambien - she had really bad side effects from that drug. Her heart would race, she had horrible nightmares, half the time she walked around in a state of confusion, and she even vomited several times.

The anti-depressants didn't entirely work, either. They'd work for a few weeks, but then they would stop working, and Hallie would end up back at the doctor for a different prescription. She went from Paxil to Prozac to Zoloft to Lexapro and back again. Always something different. The doctors didn't bother to ask her any questions about her lifestyle, though - what she was eating, was she exercising, was she getting enough rest. They just wrote out a new prescription and sent her on her way.

Willow set her straight, and she was beginning to understand the concept of holistic care. It wasn't just the alternative treatments that Willow was giving her - the acupuncture, the crystals, the herbs, the aromatherapy - but she'd also learned about the mind-body connection. She'd learned things like how important it was for her gut to be healthy, for instance, because the gut and the brain were linked together. So, when she cleaned up her diet, she made sure she added probiotic foods that helped her digestion - things like kimchee and sauerkraut. And she'd discovered something called Salty Lemonade, which was a Vietnamese drink made out of brined lemons and was full of probiotics.

Willow also taught her how to meditate, and it was something she did every single day. It was one of the things that had made her stronger mentally, as she spent ten minutes a day focusing on positive thoughts and visualizing herself as a proud tigress, which was her official spirit animal.

She'd also really learned about nutrition, about the vitamins and nutrients and how everything she put into her mouth affected everything else, from her brain on down. And, before she met Willow, she just thought that yoga was like any other exercise. Yes, it made her flexible and strong, but she also found out that yoga was very powerful in connecting the mind and the body together. And Willow explained that yoga was important to keep her qi flowing properly and also to keep her chakras unblocked.

She and Willow had talked, and Hallie knew that, after her divorce settlement, she'd have the money to become Willow's partner. She had to pay Willow back for all the services she'd been given over the past few months, of course, because she'd been getting acupuncture, nutrition counseling, crystal therapy, aromatherapy and herbal therapy for free, with the understanding she would pay Willow when her divorce settlement came through. And after she settled up with Willow, she and the young psychic would find a space to open up a full-service spa that would offer alternative medicine, along with tarot and astrology readings and chakra cleansing.

The plan was for Hallie to pursue an online Masters in Integrative and Functional Nutrition. She'd found a school called Saybrook University which offered this degree, and Hallie would enroll as soon as she had the money to do so. She'd also found an online course on holistic herbalism and certification courses that centered on crystal therapy. While she pursued these certification courses and her Master's in Integrative Nutrition, she would be working with Willow as an assistant.

But first, she had to get through this settlement conference. And Nate might not show.

Hallie looked at her watch. It was 1:30. Nate was supposed to meet them at 1. Where was he?

But she didn't break down. The old Hallie would've been filled with anxiety and would've had travel-sized bottles of tequila in her purse. She would've gone into the bathroom and gotten hammered before the settlement conference, and she would've been right back in the bathroom, tossing back more travel-sized tequila bottles, when she realized that Nate was so late that he might not be coming.

But the new Hallie knew what to do. She closed her eyes and centered her thoughts on positivity. Nate was late, and he might not show. He might've backed out on the whole settlement without telling her, which would mean that the whole mess would end up in a trial. This would, in turn, mean she still would be broke for several more months because a bench trial would be a long ways away. That was the reality.

Hallie mentally said "om" in her head and focused on a healing blue light. She imagined she was in a green forest, with deer leaping about and birds in the trees. Then she imagined herself as a tigress stalking through the brush. A tigress would never let something like a blown settlement conference get her down. A tigress was strong, confident and independent.

When she opened her eyes, Nate was there.

No apologies, of course, for being a half-hour late. No acknowledgment, either. He just sat down, folded his hands and stared at Hallie.

"Okay," Ava said. "Let's get this show on the road."

Two hours later, Hallie and Ava walked out of the high-rise building where Hallie became a millionaire just by signing documents in a conference room. Nate got the $2 million condo and two of the investment accounts totaling $3 million, and Hallie got everything else. The investment accounts she received from the settlement also totaled $3 million. The oil paintings she received were valued at $1.5 million. The stamp collection was valued at around $500,000.

The ladies immediately got an Uber and went to the airport to go back home. "How does it feel?" Ava asked Hallie when the Uber came to pick them up.

"Oh my God," Hallie said. "I'm free. I'm free. I. Am. Free."

"And rich," Ava said. "Don't forget that."

"Yeah," Hallie said. "I mean, that feels great, too, just because I'm really, really, really looking forward to starting my online nutrition degree and my herbalism diploma course. And I'm so looking forward to finding my own house and growing an organic garden. I don't care that much about the money, except what it can do for my future. Become Willow's partner. Have my own home. Help people feel as good as I've felt ever since working with Willow. That feeling is gold."

Hallie hugged herself. "So, yeah, the money is great. But the feeling that I'm free of Nate and my future is all mine… that feeling is platinum."

Chapter Thirty-Seven

Hallie

There was one more area in Hallie's life she really needed to pay attention to, and that was her relationship with Morgan. So, Hallie invited Morgan and her wife, Emma Claire, out to Nantucket to visit with her.

"Oh, mom, so sorry," Morgan said. "But I have so much work here that I just can't get away. Love that you finally divorced dad, though. Was a long time coming."

"That's fine," Hallie said. "How's the gallery coming?"

"Good, good," Morgan said. "One of the spaces I looked at fell through, but I found another space in the Castro District that's perfect. I'm working with five other artists in this gallery, showing all different mediums. We're having a show this Friday, so that's what I'm working on."

The old Hallie would've been hurt by Morgan's not wanting to come out to Nantucket. She would've taken it personally and would've been convinced that Morgan was

The Beachfront Inn

just making an excuse because she really didn't want to see her. The old Hallie would've never accepted Morgan's story about working on a show. She would've cried on the phone and begged her to reconsider.

"I'm so happy for you," Hallie said. "You're doing spectacularly."

A long pause. "Really, mom? I mean, you're not going to try to guilt me into coming out? You're not going to start crying about how you never see me, and you don't ask anything of me but to see you once in a while? Did you get kidnapped by a body snatcher?"

"No," Hallie said. "But I'd love to see the photos from your gallery show. Maybe you can text them to me?"

"I will," Morgan said, her voice sounding skeptical. "But what's the catch, mom? You sound so, what's the word? Healthy, maybe?"

"Dear, you have your life, and I have mine," Hallie said. "I'm living out by a beach, I'm studying for a master's in nutrition, and I'm working with an alternative healer out here. I have a full life. A full, beautiful life. Friends, yoga, wine, but not too much. Just a good life."

"Hmmm....well, next week is free for me," Morgan said. "I could use a vacay. Zendaya won't be here for another month while we're going through the adoption process, so it might be perfect timing to come out for a visit. How would that be?"

"That would be great," Hallie said. "I'll put you guys up at the Nantucket Hotel and Resort. It's still a bit chilly out here, so we can't go to the beach, but I can definitely show you around my beautiful adopted island. See you Monday?"

"Monday," Morgan said. "I can stay a week, but then I have to get back because we have three more shows next month. So, don't start crying when I'm about to leave like you always do."

Hallie started to laugh. "I won't. I'll see you soon, and I can't wait."

Morgan and Emma Claire came out to Nantucket the following Monday, and Hallie had a ball with them. They both marveled about the timeless architecture, the slow pace and the friendliness of the people they met on the street.

But, most of all, Morgan marveled at how her mother had changed. "First of all, you look amazing," Morgan said when she got off the plane and saw Hallie standing by the airport curb, ready to help her daughter and daughter-in-law with their bags. "What happened? Did you get a face-lift?"

Hallie laughed. "No. It's called healthy living and cutting way back on alcohol. You'd be surprised how much being a drunk ages your skin. And stress. That's a huge skin-ager too. But I've been doing yoga and acupuncture and just eating better. More fruits and vegetables, that type of thing."

"And divorcing dad, that probably took about a million years off your skin," Morgan said as she examined Hallie's face. "Well, whatever you did, do more of it."

Emma Claire, for her part, agreed with Morgan. "Hallie, Morgan's right. You look about 20 years younger than the last time I saw you."

Hallie grinned. "What, did I look like I was ready for the rest home before?"

"No, no," Emma Claire said hurriedly. "You looked

your age before. Maybe a bit older than your age. But now, you could pass for 35."

"Well, 54 is the new 30, so they say," Hallie said. "It is for me, at any rate."

A week later, Hallie drove Morgan and Emma Claire back to the airport to get back to their lives in San Francisco. There were no tears, clinging, or caterwauling about how Hallie would miss Morgan and when can she come back to visit again?

"Mom, I had such a good time," Morgan said, as if she couldn't believe it herself. "I love your friends, and this island really agrees with you. And I love you, mom. I'm proud of you, I really am."

"Well, thank you," Hallie said. "Of course, I'm proud of you and Emma Claire. And soon, I'll have a beautiful African granddaughter to be proud of, too. Zendaya is such a beautiful name."

"Zendaya means thankful," Morgan said. "And I can't be more thankful for you being my mom. I'm sorry we haven't been close for these past years."

Hallie shook her head. "Water under the bridge," she said. "Take care."

"You too. And why don't you come out to visit Emma Claire and me when Zendaya gets here? I know you love San Francisco, and you'll love my gallery."

"Just as long as I don't try to control the curating process," Hallie joked. "I'd love to come. Just let me know."

"I will. Bye, mom." At that, Morgan and Emma Claire gave a hug to Hallie and went into the airport.

As Hallie drove back to the home she still shared with Quinn and Sarah, she knew she'd turned a major corner. She was able to love her daughter and let go of her at the same time. Let Morgan live her life and not try to hold on so tightly that her daughter felt suffocated.

And Hallie knew that her relationship with Morgan, Emma Claire and, soon, Zendaya would be a healthy one going forward. And that meant the world to Hallie.

Chapter Thirty-Eight

Ava

Late May

Ava ran around her home like a chicken with its head cut off. The day was finally here!

Ava tried to think back to when she felt this much pressure, and she couldn't. She'd tried many stressful cases in her life when she had wealthy people breathing down her neck, making sure she didn't make a single mistake. She inevitably would make a mistake or two - she was only human, after all - and she'd get a dressing down afterward.

Those days literally made her sick. She used to find herself waking up at 4 in the morning and not getting back to sleep, day after day. She'd toss and turn, thinking about her mistake, whatever it was. She constantly felt like she had a Sword of Damocles hanging over her head. She beat herself up for every little thing, wanting to reverse time so she could correct her past mistake, whatever it was.

But this stress was something entirely different. Her anxiety stemmed from the fear that the entire shindig wouldn't go well and that her new Bed and Breakfast would never take off as she wanted it to.

Her perfectionist tendencies were getting the better of her. She went around the house, making sure that all of her cut flower bouquets were just perfect, the candles that burned in every room were emitting just the right scent, all the pictures on the walls were absolutely straight, and everything was spotless. Not a dust bunny or smudge was to be seen in the house.

She hired Charlotte's chef husband, Matthew, to come in and design the menu for the guests. He did so, and even came in and cooked everything.

She went back into the kitchen to ask Matthew one last time how things were going.

"Great, Ava," Matthew said with a smile. "I've got it all together. The cater waiters will be coming around with deviled eggs with smoked trout, deep-fried lobster bites with garlic butter, mango-avocado bruschetta, escarole chicken dumplings, herbed potato latkes, mascarpone stuffed pears, roast beef canapés, cremini and olives ascolane. There'll also be different puff pastries, eclairs, cakes, tiny pies and chocolate-covered strawberries."

For that evening, he was short-handed, so Charlotte was helping out in the kitchen. She was busily chopping vegetables, a chef's hat on her head and an apron around her waist. Next to her were Robert and Nathan, who were other cooks Ava hired for the evening. They, too, were chopping veggies and throwing potatoes into the enormous floor mixer, which was churning up the potatoes

The Beachfront Inn

with an abundance of sour cream, cream, butter, garlic and herbs.

Ava's mouth watered when she took a look at all the yummy-looking appetizers, especially the olives ascolane, which consisted of enormous deep-fried olives stuffed with a mixture of beef, herbs, and parmesan cheese. Also tempting were the potato latkes, which she always loved.

Colleen was upstairs with Siobhan. She'd volunteered to babysit the little girl that evening when Charlotte called her, panicking about having to help Matthew out that night in the kitchen.

Ava was so happy about how everything was turning out. Everybody she loved was in a good place.

Hallie was doing fantastic. She and Willow had found a beautiful, peaceful home to open up their new spa, and Hallie had enrolled in an online master's course in Integrative Nutrition. She'd also enrolled in courses that would enable her to do crystal healing and herbal therapy. She was doing all these courses in her spare time, such as it was, because she was busy assisting Willow with their new clients. And, once word got around that there was a full-service spa that offered metaphysical services too, and that Willow was a uniquely gifted tarot reader and clairvoyant, the Willow Tree Day Spa, which was what Hallie and Willow came up with for their spa's name, thrived.

And, most importantly to Hallie, things were good between her and her daughter, especially after Morgan's visit to the island. "I've finally been able to relate to Morgan without trying to latch onto her coattails, because I finally have a life of my own and Morgan no longer thinks that I'm trying to smother her," Hallie said. "And we're talking to each other from a position of love and respect, not co-dependency."

As for Sarah, she'd been working hard for Ava. She was integral in getting the wine list together for the guests that evening, and finding just the right pairings for all the hors d'oeuvres. Ava couldn't have gotten the party together without Sarah's help.

And Sarah was still single, even though every rich guy in town, it seemed, was trying to ask her out. She turned them all down. "I really want to focus on me for a while," she told Ava. "Besides, I have to buckle down and make sure that I keep studying for my sommelier exams. I need to make sure that I know as much as possible so that I can be a certified master. That'll help this place thrive more than you can imagine, having a certified master sommelier working here."

Sarah and Ava were closer than ever, which made Ava happier than she'd ever been. Sarah's absence for Ava was a huge hole, but now that that hole was filled, all was right with the world for Ava.

As for Jackson, he got the part that he was auditioning for. It was his very first speaking part, and he couldn't be more excited. Ava couldn't wait for his movie to hit Netflix so she could see her only son on the small screen.

Everyone coming to the party had to find a ride there because the parking was limited. That wasn't a problem for any of them, however. The really wealthy ones were driven by chauffeured limousines. The less wealthy ones hailed Ubers and cabs over to the inn.

7 PM rolled around, and the first guests started to arrive.

It was showtime.

By 9 PM, everything was going fantastic. The guests loved the food, marveled over Ava's view, and admired Deacon and Quinn's handiwork. It was 9 months in the making, the home renovation, but it was all worth it in the end.

Ava had to admit that the place really had become quite a jewel in Deacon and Quinn's capable hands. The floors were all distressed wood, and the foyer/reception room was opened up so that 30 people could gather together in front of the raging fire. Brand-new comfortable leather furniture was strategically placed in this foyer, as were colorful throw rugs. In the corner of the room was a baby grand piano, which was Deacon's idea. Overhead were modern chandeliers that were shaped like enormous white globes.

With the vaulted ceilings, exposed brick and central stone fireplace, the dining room could seat up to 30 people at one time. In the middle of the dining room was a communal table made of solid redwood, with six chairs surrounding the table. That table would be reserved for people who wanted to eat with other guests and get to know one another. But if the guests wanted more privacy, they could sit at any one of the seven other tables in this room.

Out in the sunroom was another eating area. In the center was a table shaped like a slab of redwood with a transparent glaze. The room also sported some outdoor furniture where guests could relax and listen to the surf below. The terrace, Ava's favorite part of the house, had glittering lights overhead that gave this area a festive look. A 10-person hot tub was installed, along with two fire rings surrounded by various wicker sofas, loungers and chairs.

The guest rooms were outfitted with California king-sized beds, with solid cherry wood nightstands, bookshelves and dressers. They all had fireplaces and balconies. The ones that faced the beach had the beautiful view of the vast ocean, and her guests would be treated to one of the most gorgeous sights in the modern world, in Ava's estimation.

Each of the bedrooms also had attached bathrooms with large jacuzzi tubs, enormous showers with stone walls and marble floors, and heated toilets with bidets. Ava never knew that there even was such a thing as a heated toilet seat. When she finally tried one, she wondered how she had ever lived without it.

As Ava walked amongst her esteemed guests, a glass of champagne in her hand, she basked in a job well done. These past few months were stressful, no doubt about it. But, looking around at the diamond that this house had become, she knew that all the stress and hard work was worth it.

Just then, she caught Deacon coming through the door. She hadn't spoken to him for a couple of days, and she realized how much she missed talking to him.

Deacon had become a friend to her, and she knew she would miss him terribly. He'd been a fixture around the house for the past several months, working hard every day with his crew to make sure the place shone. But the job was over, and Deacon wasn't going to be around anymore. That thought made Ava sad.

But she was happy to see him that night. She had to admit, he looked more than handsome in his navy pants and jacket, his blue pin-striped dress shirt open at the collar, his blonde hair cut close to his head.

He smiled big as he came over to her and kissed her lightly on the cheek. "How's everything going?" he asked.

She nodded her head rapidly and took a drink of her champagne. "Great, great," she said.

Deacon just shook his head, a giant grin on his face.

The Beachfront Inn

"Anyhow, mate, I'm not necessarily just here to rub elbows with the rich and famous. I have a surprise for you."

Ava had no idea what he was talking about, but then he went over to the grand piano and started to play. He began with a flawless interpretation of Gershwin's *Rhapsody in Blue*, a very complex piece, and Ava was amazed. She was even more amazed when he turned out some heartbreaking, yet subtle, rendering of Mozart, Rachmaninoff and Tchaikovsky.

As she floated amongst her guests, she wondered about Deacon. From his talented turn at the piano, it was evident that he had some classical chops. She was ashamed to think she never imagined that he'd have it in him to play like that. He was a contractor, after all. With him being in such a manly profession, she could imagine him doing well with shooting targets, playing sports, racing cars. But playing classical piano? That was something that surprised her.

Must stop stereotyping, Ava thought.

Chapter Thirty-Nine

Ava

About midnight, the guests finally dispersed. It was clean-up time. As she looked around her spacious home, now trashed, she despaired. The one thing she didn't think of was to hire a clean-up crew. Quinn, Hallie and Sarah insisted they would stay and clean up, but Ava wouldn't hear of it.

"No, really, I got it."

"Nope," Quinn said. "We're staying."

The four of them fought over that, a battle Ava lost as Quinn, Hallie and Sarah just started to clean up without Ava's consent.

Ava was secretly relieved. The place *was* a mess, and she knew that, with her perfectionist tendencies, she'd never sleep knowing that her house was in such a state. She wasn't going to wait to clean it up until morning. Even if she was up until dawn, she would get the place spic and span before she turned in.

"I'll help too," Charlotte said.

Ava sighed. "My mom is leaving, Charlotte, so you're going to have to tend to your baby. You and Matthew better get her home, anyhow. She's needs her rest."

Charlotte rolled her eyes. "She's fine. She's upstairs in her old room. I'll just bring her down here and put her into a playpen, and it'll be okay."

Ava shook her head. "Matthew's almost done in the kitchen." The kitchen had actually closed two hours prior, so the clean-up was almost finished. "Siobhan doesn't need to be in a playpen. She needs to be in her bed. Now, go."

"Mom-"

"Go. I won't be responsible for Siobhan getting sick again."

Charlotte made a face but then reluctantly went upstairs to gather her baby and then went and got Matthew, who was just getting done with the last part of the kitchen clean-up.

"Bye, mom," Charlotte said after Matthew had gone ahead to the car with Siobhan in tow. "Congrats on tonight. It was a great crowd. I think that you're on your way."

Ava raised an eyebrow. "I hope so," she said with a smile. She secretly agreed with her daughter, though - she felt that maybe she actually was on her way.

Ava faced the mess of her house, feeling discouraged even though Hallie, Quinn and Sarah were already working hard to clean the place up.

She climbed the stairs, intending to begin her part of the clean-up on the deck, which she imagined was trashed beyond belief. She walked out into the cool night air and was surprised to see Deacon on one of the lounge chairs. He was eating a piece of cake, his long legs casually crossed, his body leaning back on the chair.

Ava smiled. "There you went," she said to him. "I was wondering."

He nodded his head. "I made my share in tips tonight, so decided to come out here and celebrate." He grinned. "Just gammin," he said.

"Gammin?"

"Joking, mate. I'd never do something so tacky as to put out a tip jar."

"You should've. You're quite good, you know."

"Well, thank you. I wanted to surprise you with my playing. That was my contribution to tonight."

"Trust me, you contributed much more than you'll ever know."

He patted the lounge chair next to his, and Ava sat down.

"Where did you learn to play?" Ava asked him.

Deacon shrugged his shoulders. "My mum made me take lessons starting when I was four. I hated it, then I loved it. Now, I play whenever I'm bored or anxious. It's an outlet, you might say."

"Do you have a piano at your place?" Ava asked him.

"Yeah. I think it's important, you know. To have a hobby. Other than surfing, of course."

"Well, I was very impressed," Ava said. "Your playing is beautiful and skilled. Not to mention inspired."

Deacon grinned.

And then he did something that shook Ava to her core.

He grabbed her hand.

And then he leaned over and kissed her lips softly.

She lost her breath as the kiss between the two lingered. She had to chase unwelcome thoughts out of her head - *what if he's just drunk? How could he want to get romantic with you? Why would he be attracted to you?*

It was hard for her to get out of her head and just enjoy the moment. But, when she finally managed to banish the negative thoughts, she found herself floating in a cloud of euphoria.

That moment, in the dark, with the sounds of the surf providing a backdrop to what was probably the most romantic moment of her life, she finally lost herself. She started to breathe heavily, wanting this man more than she'd ever wanted anything in her life.

And then, after the kiss, he said something that made her fall head over heels.

"Come on, mate, let's get this place cleaned up."

Next in the Sconset Beach Series

Heartfelt Friendships and New Beginnings
AINSLEY KEATON
The Beachfront Surprises
A SCONSET BEACH NOVEL

vinci-books.com/beachfront-surprises

Out of the frying pan, into the fire...

Quinn struggles to connect with her adopted daughter, Emerson, while an unforeseen opportunity arises that could bring them closer together. Meanwhile, Ava's world is turned upside down when her mother, Colleen, arrives harboring a long-buried secret that threatens to shatter Ava's understanding of her past. As Ava grapples with forgiveness and her own insecurities, she must decide whether to take a second chance on romance in her new life.

Turn the page for a free preview...

The Beachfront Surprises: Chapter One

Ava

The kiss with Deacon was on Ava's mind the entire night. She was nervous and excited and really wanted to see where it would go with the handsome young contractor.

Yet, she was also extremely apprehensive. She had a hard time just going with it. Her head always got in the way. And, it was definitely getting in the way here because he was just too young. Ava always had a hard time getting involved with somebody if she didn't know where it would go. There were too many questions about Deacon in her mind. Did he want children? Was he looking to get involved with her, or was it just going to be a fling? Did he just kiss her because he was drunk?

Worse, she didn't know when she would see him again. He had left early that morning, after the house was completely cleaned up spic-and-span. He didn't indicate when he would be back or even if he would be back. She hated not knowing if she would even see him again.

The Beachfront Inn

But, just when she was going to pick up the phone to call Quinn, or Sarah, or Hallie, her mother appeared.

"Hey, Ava," her mother, Colleen, said. Colleen had been staying in one of Ava's eight rooms while she was in town. She'd only come to town to watch her granddaughter Siobhan while Charlotte, Siobhan's mother, helped out in the kitchen. Charlotte's husband Matthew was the chef for the party. He was shorthanded getting the food ready for Ava's big open-house shindig, which was a rousing success.

Ava just nodded her head. She never got along with her mother, but she never knew why. Her mother was just always very cold with her, right from the start. Yet, with Sarah, Ava's gorgeous sister who Ava always thought had it all but really didn't, Colleen wasn't cold. In fact, Colleen went out of her way to help Sarah move to Nantucket.

And, no matter what, Ava always felt like she was five years old around her mother. Yes, Ava had graduated from Harvard, had worked at a very high-powered law job for many years, and currently was running her very own bed-and-breakfast in the small village of Siaconset on the island of Nantucket.

Yet, whenever Ava was around her mother, she was that little girl who was dying for her mother's positive words. It was almost as if she was holding her breath, waiting for Colleen to say something nice to her.

But those kind words never came.

"Mom," Ava said. "Thanks so much for watching Siobhan. You were a lifesaver."

"Happy to help. Charlotte needed me, so I came. Of course, I would've loved to have been in the crowd, enjoying this gem of a house that came together thanks to me and my money, but it is what it is. I'm just happy last night's party was a real barnburner. That means I'll be making major bank off this place without even lifting a finger. That's my favorite way of making money. Passive income. You're going to be putting in your blood, sweat, and tears. Better you than me."

Ava nodded her head. She had mixed emotions about her mother having to invest in her place. On the one hand, she was extremely grateful that Colleen could give her the money she needed to get the place renovated and ready to go. On the other, well, she didn't want to be so tied up with her mother, for obvious reasons. It put great pressure on her to ensure that the place was super successful. Because, if it wasn't, she would never hear the end of it.

Ava was also apprehensive that Colleen demanded a note for $200,000 of the $500,000 she had given Ava to invest in the place. Ava knew she would adhere to the terms of the note, no problem, but it had an acceleration clause, which meant that Colleen could call in the note whenever she wanted. And that made Ava terrified.

"Well, looks like I'm going to have to make myself scarce. Don't screw this up, Ava. I'm warning you," her mother said with a wag of her finger.

Ava sighed. She had enough therapy over the years to realize that part of why she was such an overachiever was because she never wanted to disappoint Colleen. She strove for straight A's in undergrad, which she got, graduating *magna cum laude* from the University of Missouri with a degree in political science. Then, when she determined she wanted to go to law school, she took her LSAT practice tests so many times that she had all of the analytical games memorized, which was why she got such a high score on the test. After all, the analytical games were what tripped up most students, for good reason - they were damn hard to figure out. She worked her butt off when she got to

The Beachfront Inn

Harvard, writing for the *Law Review*, studying 80 hours a week. Some of the weaker students actually paid her for her outlines because they were legendary. And then, when she got out of law school, she went to work for the prestigious white-shoe firm, where she ended up burning out completely.

She had no idea why Colleen gave her that warning about screwing up. She wasn't a screwup, and she never was.

What was strange was that Colleen was always so kind to her children, especially Samantha, the slacker. Samantha never had her head on straight. She had no ambition to speak of, at least not to Ava's knowledge. Of all her children, Samantha was the one who worried her the most, because Ava just couldn't picture her sweet and free-spirited daughter making anything of herself. Yet, whenever Samantha needed something, she went to Ava or Colleen. Ava usually denied her, but Colleen usually indulged her.

Jackson was higher up on the food chain than Samantha, but only because he did have an ambition in mind, even if his ambition was, in Ava's estimation, pie-in-the-sky. He was trying to break into the dog-eat-dog world of Hollywood. He recently got his first speaking part in a Netflix series set in the 1940s and focused on a detective's life, loves and cases. Jackson's speaking part was minuscule, just a few lines, but he was making his connections like he should. Yet, Colleen only had positive words for Jackson. She never tried to undermine him or tell him he was dreaming. She never tried to give him his odds of making it in that world, let alone staying on top for any period of time, even if he did happen to break through.

As for Charlotte, she was distant from Ava. She lived in Boston, so she was physically the closest to Ava, but she rarely spoke with her mother. Nevertheless, Ava had a bad feeling about Charlotte. There was something off in her marriage, but she just couldn't put a finger on what.

Ava knew that Charlotte had made a big mistake that resulted in her daughter, Siobhan. It was always Ava's understanding that Charlotte and Matthew had decided, before they were married, to not have children. That was one of their iron-clad agreements. But Charlotte was careless and didn't take her birth-control pills correctly. She played Russian Roulette with her pills, month after month because she often forgot to take them. However, she never told Matthew about her mistakes in taking the pill. She managed to not bite the bullet for over a year, and she started to think she was safe, that maybe she couldn't get pregnant at all.

Of course, she never actually asked her doctor about any of this. She just assumed she might be infertile, and she didn't like taking the pill. She gained weight from it, and it gave her migraine headaches. So, she simply stopped taking the pill, again without telling Matthew. As she explained to Samantha, who told all of this to Ava, she really believed she wasn't able to have children.

She was wrong. She got pregnant with Siobhan and then lied to Matthew when he confronted her about whether she was taking the pill as directed. She insisted to him that she'd taken the pill every single day, faithfully, and she apparently was one of the 2% of women who get pregnant while on the pill. Matthew apparently believed her, but Ava got the feeling that all wasn't right with her daughter's marriage.

Again, though, Colleen had a soft spot for Charlotte. Colleen knew about Charlotte's birth control mistake

The Beachfront Inn

because Charlotte told her, and Colleen didn't have any harsh words about that.

Ava should've been happy that Colleen got along with her children so well, not to mention the fact she seemed to just love Sarah, Ava's sister, and she *was* happy. Yet, at the same time, it just astounded her. Oh, what she wouldn't give for the unconditional love and acceptance that Colleen gave everyone around Ava but denied to Ava herself.

"Mom, when have I ever screwed up anything?" Ava asked.

Colleen just shook her head and rolled her eyes. "You really don't see yourself like others see you, do you? Aren't you the one who let your husband clean out your investment account, just rolling over without a word or fight? Aren't you the one who worked for the same law firm for almost 3 decades, never made partner, and never spoke up for herself about it? You may think that you never screw up, but Ava, I'm here to tell you that you're wrong about that."

Ava swallowed hard. On the one hand, Colleen had a point. Ava did allow people to run right over her. The fact that she had become a victim on more than one occasion probably stemmed from her lack of self-esteem and inability to speak up for herself. Both of which were side effects from her mother's coldness over the years.

On the other hand, Ava noted that Colleen just had to dig in the knife. Instead of noting how hard she had always worked throughout her life for everything she had, how conscientious she always was, and how successful she'd been, especially considering she was a single mother of triplets while she was building her career, her mother had to point out her failures. So typical of Colleen's interactions with her.

"Okay, mother," Ava said with gritted teeth. "You made

your point, as you always do. Again, thank you for watching Siobhan on such short notice. I apologize again about your not coming to the party because of it. Now, I'm sure you have someplace to be, so don't let me keep you from whatever it is."

"I get it. I'm going to let the door hit me on the way out. Well, Ava, I'll see you later. Again, if you screw this up, I will kill you in your sleep."

Ava took a deep breath. The sad thing was, she believed that about her mother. Her mother probably would murder her in her sleep if she did something that caused her new business to fail. So, she had to make sure that that didn't happen.

Ever.

Grab your copy…
vinci-books.com/beachfront-surprises

About the Author

Ainsley Keaton lives with her hubby and two fur-babies in Southern California. When she's not binge-watching *Grace and Frankie*, *Succession* and *Downton Abbey*, she's reading historical and women's fiction and scouring the beach for sea glass and sand dollars.